The kitchen was a mess, as always. Jude had to dig through the mountain of dirty dishes to find a saucepan, then wash it up, before he could put some water on to boil.

He washed up a bowl, too, then took his meal of noodles out into the jungle of a backyard, to sit in the cool darkness while he ate.

Mosquitoes buzzed Jude, but he swished them away with his fork between mouthfuls and nodded approvingly to himself at the memory of the afternoon. There was a chance that the band, The Tockleys, were what he'd been waiting for in his life, what he'd been marking time for. He'd been toying with the idea of going back home to Melbourne, to try his luck on the music scene there, or maybe of getting a real job and saving up enough money to go overseas to India or Nepal. If The Tockleys could play music like they had that afternoon, if they could rock out, play their own songs, and get some gigs somewhere, then he'd stay in the city for a little longer, give this place another chance.

In the darkness, with the sea breeze gone and the late summer prevailing easterly wind back, the tangle of jacarandas and vines in the backyard rustled and sighed. Jude lay back on the patchy grass to watch the stars overhead, his empty bowl beside him.

He'd waited a long time to find people he could make music with like Lori and Luk. The three of them together had made some magic, and he couldn't wait to do it again.

The Tockleys
TOP SHELF
An imprint of Torquere Press Publishers
PO Box 2545
Round Rock, TX 78680
Copyright © 2008 by Laney Cairo
Cover illustration by Manic Pixie
Published with permission
ISBN: 978-1-60370-539-4, 1-60370-539-2

www.torquerepress.com

First Torquere Press Printing: November 2008
Printed in the USA

**If you enjoyed The Tockleys,
you might enjoy these Torquere Press titles:**

Bad Case of Loving You by Laney Cairo

Chiaroscuro by Jenna Jones

Living in Fast Forward by BA Tortuga

Sex, Lies and Celluloid by Chris Owen and Jodi Payne

Spiked by Mychael Black, Laney Cairo, Jourdan Lane, and Willa Okati

The Tockleys

The Tockleys
by Laney Cairo

www.torquerepress.com

To Anjela
with love and
gratitude, with many
thanks

love
Laney

The Tockleys

All song lyrics in The Tockleys are used with permission. Copyright remains with the creators.

'Not the Only One,' lyrics by E. A. Pearson
'Fall Back, Retreat,' lyrics by Anjela Conner
'Jackrabbit,' lyrics by Laney Cairo
'Fade Away,' lyrics by E. A. Pearson
'Ascospore,' lyrics by E. A. Pearson
'Possession,' lyrics by Cathy Cupitt
'Holding Back the Sunshine,' by Cathy Cupitt

I'd like to thank the songwriters who have lent me the lyrics I've used in The Tockleys: Anjela, E. and Cathy. Thank you so much!

I'd also like to thank the Strychnine Cowboys for letting me hang around while they made a lot of noise. Thanks Dog, Dave, Meg, and especially Reuben.

Other people have helped out along the way. Thanks to Maia for the interview, to Stephen for the support and heckling, and to Richard and Samira for the assistance.

Manic Pixie, whose art graces the cover, supplied me with music, introduced me to the Strychnine Cowboys, and took me to the Railway Hotel. Everyone needs a Manic Pixie as their very own independent music scene tour guide. Thank you, Pixie!

The Tockleys

Chapter One

Jude spotted the other muso on the train just after City West Station, a guy younger than himself, guitar case over his shoulder and a box that probably held an amp and speaker on an old-lady-type shopping trolley. He helped the kid lift the trolley off the train at Fremantle, sharing a nod of recognition at his own guitar case.

"You going to the audition?" Jude asked. "At Lori's place?"

"Yeah," the kid said. "Do you know where it is?" He pulled a printout from his jeans pocket and unfolded the sheet, holding it out for Jude.

"That's her address," Jude said, glancing at the paper, then pointing away from the Harbor up the hill that overlooked the port. "It's this way. I'm Jude."

"Luk," the kid said, and it took Jude a moment to work out it was his name, not some kind of blessing.

The trolley rumbled noisily over the footpath, and Jude said, "What's the amp?"

"Moody BA-40," Luk said, sounding apologetic, and Jude stared at him in disbelief.

"No way!" he said. "With the original valves?" Jude peered into the box, sighting the worn white vinyl covering and the cracked white leather handle.

"Don't know," Luk said. "I borrowed it from a friend."

"What do you play?" Jude asked. "Are you a friend of Lori's, too?" Luk looked too young to be a hanger-on from Lori's boyfriend's band, Delicate John, so he probably knew Lori through Loud People, the music store she worked at.

"Bass and electric, but I brought a bass along today," Luk said. "And I can sing in a way that doesn't make people complain. I saw the ad at that music store in town. What about you?"

"Electric," Jude said. "And I can sing. Lori's a friend."

Luk clanked faintly as he walked, the chains on his boots and jeans jangling with each step, and as he hitched up his jeans intermittently.

They stopped at East Street to wait for the traffic to clear, and Luk must have caught Jude watching him. "You look kind of normal," Luk said. "To be auditioning for a band, that is."

"Gotta work," Jude said. "Out in the normal world." He knew he sounded hostile, but jumped-up punk kids annoyed him unreasonably, especially when they were kind of cute underneath their chains and attitude and were dragging vintage Moody amps behind them.

Luk patted the bleached fuzz on his scalp and flicked the metal hanging from his ear, shrugging. "I go to uni."

Lori was going to eat this kid for breakfast, unless he could actually play.

Lori lived on the Stirling Highway Bypass, with traffic roaring past her house, a steady roar that kept her rent down and the neighbors from complaining about the music. Jude had been there before, to a launch party for Delicate John when the band had rocked the whole suburb, at least until the police had turned up, and to visit Lori.

The house was easy to identify -- half a dozen rusted-out cars parked on the knee-high lawn, scrounged and rotting lounge furniture on the porch, and steady rolling waves of music, loud over the hum of trucks passing.

"We need to go around the back," Jude said, pointing past the cars and up the driveway.

He led Luk to a double garage out the back, doors propped open, and Lori waved from behind an electronic drum kit, beckoning them in as they fended off the attentions of a pit bull terrier that bounced out of the crumbling house to greet them.

"Close the doors, lock the mutt out," she called out, clambering out from behind the kit to turn the music she'd been practicing to off, so the silence hurt.

Jude propped his guitar case against a speaker stack, and he and Luk managed to drag the two doors almost closed, with the dog on the outside.

Lori hugged Jude briefly, then smiled at Luk. "I'm Lori," she said. "Guess you're Luk."

"Are we it?" Jude asked, looking around the dusty garage, the afternoon sunlight streaking through the louvers and across the assembled musical equipment. The garage held a collection of partially dismantled amps and speakers, tatty barstools and chairs, and Lori's electronic drum kit.

"Looks like it," Lori said. "Let's get set up, and see what we can jam."

A power board dangled from the rafters in the middle of the room, and Lori and Jude both gasped when Luk lifted an ancient but beautiful amp out of the box, then a matching Moody Alnico speaker.

"Fuck," Lori said, and Jude touched the amp housing reverently.

"I can't believe you borrowed this," he said. "This is just perfect. It's got to be the original fit out, valves and all."

"Dunno," Luk said. "Like I said, it's borrowed." He laid down the hard guitar case he'd been carrying and unclipped it, and Jude held his breath. If that was the kind of amp Luk had, what would he play?

He must have made a sound at the first glimpse of red lacquered body and a perfect maple neck, because Luk looked over his shoulder at Jude. "Is that a Fender?" Jude asked, his voice coming out high.

"Yep, it's a Fender Jazz," Luk said, peering into the case, then lifting the perfect, pristine early 70s guitar out of its case and leaning across to plug the cable into the amp.

Jude undid the case he'd had slung across his back and took out his worn fake Strat, the black of its bodywork scratched and stained. It was a cheap imitation that his older brother had bought secondhand years before, and he'd inherited. Its sound was thin and it lost tuning almost immediately, but it was all he had.

When Luk flicked on his borrowed amp, the valves hummed faintly, and his speaker burred as it picked up the output from the guitar.

The partially dismantled amp, already plugged into the board and a speaker stack, was for Jude. It looked like another cheap knock-off, but he was at an audition, not a collectible guitar competition, and he'd have to play his heart out and hope Lori liked the sound enough.

Luk touched his strings, sending a sweet shiver of sound through the garage, and Jude slid the repaired strap of his own guitar over his shoulders and nodded to Lori. "What are we playing?"

"Do you both know 'Not the Only One'?" she asked, flicking her own amp back on and picking up her sticks.

Luk nodded, and Jude grinned. 'Not the Only One' was the song of Lori's that Delicate John had recorded. She'd written a song that was played on the radio, which was pretty damned amazing.

"One, two, three, four," Lori counted, tapping the edge of her snare drum to count them in, then rolling her sticks across her floor tom for the first bar. Luk picked up the bass line on the second beat, and Jude slid into the lead line in the second bar.

It was a little loose, but Lori's drums were steady, and when Jude glanced across at Luk, he had his eyes half-closed in concentration, mouthing what Jude suspected were chord changes to himself.

Jude lifted his eyes, and Lori sang, the lyrics lost against the amps, but she had a delighted look on her face, and she was right. It was a gorgeous afternoon, they were playing a damned fine song, and then Jude was bouncing on the cracked concrete in his sneakers, smearing the oil stains, finding the rhythm.

Jude kept it low key, sticking to the melody line and laying off the tremolo bar. The amp he was using didn't have a stomp box, but by the third chorus, it was all coming good. Luk's bass was sound, and he was singing, too.

They played the last verse just about perfectly and thrashed the last chorus, ending the song on a clatter of snare.

Silence dropped over the garage, apart from the hum of Luk's amp and a spatter of applause from the louvers, where faces peered in.

Lori had a huge grin plastered across her face. She circled the tip of a stick on the snare, making a buzzing noise, and nodded in appreciation.

"Fucking awesome," Luk said. "Can we do that again?"

They sat on the overgrown lawn at the back of Lori's house in the late afternoon sunshine, while the dog blundered around them. Jude's hands hurt, his fingers were so raw that his left-hand fingertips were bloody, and his whole body was still ringing with the music.

Luk looked exhausted, sprawled back across the weeds, face split by a huge smile. Jude let himself look at the smooth skin of Luk's belly, where Luk's ripped T-shirt had ridden up.

The kid was undeniably hot, when he wasn't talking.

And Lori, alternating between packing the bong and shaking her hands to try and get some feeling in them, looked as deliriously happy as any self-respecting goth girl would ever admit to, her eyeliner streaked and her long, dyed-black hair escaping from its plaits.

They'd played for hours, working their way through everything they all knew, then everything two of them knew, with the third person jamming. It hadn't always been perfect, or even listenable, and the other people in the house had wandered off, but it had been the best fun Jude had had in a long time.

The lighter flared and Lori sucked, the pot in the cone crackling faintly. Then she let out a deep sigh as she exhaled.

"Luk, want a bucket?" Lori asked, her voice raspy.

Luk struggled back upright, twigs and dead grass sticking to his shredded T-shirt and his hair, and took the gear.

"Well?" Jude asked.

"What are we going to call ourselves?" Lori asked,

grinning.

"We're in?" Luk asked, looking up from packing the cone. "You want us in the band?"

"After this afternoon?" Lori said. "I'd be crazy not to keep you both."

Luk let out a whoop of joy, and Jude felt so happy that he might explode or something. He wasn't the shouting type, but when he looked down at his hands, studying the raw tips of his fingers, he had to blink rapidly.

"I know I told Jude this already, because he's had to listen to me ramble about having a band for months," Lori said, "but we're not going to play covers, right? All original stuff. If you've written songs, bring them along, and we'll work out arrangements for them. Any ideas for a name?"

"I'm Straight Edge," Jude said suddenly. "Lori knows that already, but Luk should know, too."

Lori nodded, but the look in Luk's eyes was dubious. "You're joking?" he said.

Jude said, "You just gotta respect that I'm not going to bong along with you."

Luk pointed at Jude's sneakers, hole over each big toe. "You're for real? No beer? No pot? No sex?"

Lori patted Jude's knee. "Back off, Luk," she said. "Jude's entitled to his choices, just like you are, including being celibate. So what are we going to call ourselves?"

Jude thought about correcting Lori's assumption that his extended period of being single meant he was actually celibate, but decided that some things were just too complicated to discuss with someone who was wasted. Or with Luk listening.

Luk sucked on the bong, and Jude said instead, "It's really your band, Lori. What kind of name do you want?"

"You know what I'd like?" Lori asked. "The Tockleys

-- just because I couldn't get a gig as a drummer because I haven't got one."

Jude shook his head. "You really want to do that, Lori? Is that a good idea?"

Luk frowned, handing the bong back to Lori. "It's obviously a word for cock, but I've never heard it before. Won't most people be the same? Do we really want to call ourselves The Cocks?"

Lori giggled. "Lighten up, both of you," she said. "The Cocks is a damned fine name for a band, much better than Delicate John, which is just about the wankiest name ever."

"If people have never heard the word, then it doesn't matter. And if they have, then I guess it's just another band name," Luk said. "Let's be The Tockleys."

Jude pulled his knees up and rested his chin on them. "Alright," he said. "As long as you both still think it's a decent name when you're not trashed."

It was dark, with a cool sea breeze blowing in from Fremantle Harbor, when Luk and Jude trudged back to the train station.

Luk was silent, presumably really wasted, which meant that he was managing not to offend Jude for a change.

Jude was happy not to speak. The afternoon was heavy in his mind, a golden memory of musical connection between the three of them. If they could make music like that again, he didn't care about much else.

Chapter Two

Luk dragged the amp, guitar, and speaker up the hill from the bus stop, streetlights painting the lawns and gardens sickly yellow, oncoming cars temporarily blinding him.

He wasn't monged anymore, that had worn off, and his hands hurt like fuck, but he didn't care one bit. He was in a band, a real band. They were going to rehearse, and get gigs, and... His imagination didn't stretch any further than that.

Up ahead, girls clambered out of a car, giggling and talking on mobile phones.

One of them called out, "Lucky! Lucky!" to him, and he lifted a hand in greeting. He vaguely recognized the girl, the sister of someone he'd gone to school with, perhaps, but fortunately, the girls melted indoors and didn't hang around to try and talk to him.

The front lights were on at his house, shining out across the lawn and his parents' cars, but he kept going, turning up the next driveway. He needed to return the borrowed equipment first.

The automatic light came on when Luk reached the top of the drive, and he left the amp and speaker at the base of the steps, carrying the guitar case with him to the door.

He rang the doorbell, and it made him smile, just like it always did. *Boom-chugga-boomboom-tring* echoed through the house, the opening bars of 'Jackrabbit,' one of the most-played Australian classic rock tracks ever.

When he was famous, he was going to use one of his own songs as his doorbell, too.

The front door opened, and Jack, Maddie Hades' partner, peered through the security door. "Hello, Lucien," he said, wiping his hands on his shirt and unlocking the door. "Come on in; I was just serving up dinner. Did you want a bite?"

Jack was tubby and middle-aged, beard down his chest and arms covered in tatts, and he obviously thought Luk was starving.

"No thanks, Jack," Luk said. "I'm just returning the gear I borrowed. Is Maddie around?"

"She's out the back in the sound studio," Jack said. "Just go around the side. Tell her that dinner's ready, too."

Maddie Hades, lead guitarist with Ratatosk, Australia's best known rock band from the 80s, now retired and domesticated, had a free-standing sound studio in her backyard, beside the pool and barbecue area. Luk reached over the back gate and unlatched it.

He could hear the TV, muted by the soundproofing, and a moment later, Maddie opened the studio door.

Maddie was overweight, too, walking with a cane, still with rock-chick blonde hair and over-plucked eyebrows, ample bust stretching the fabric of her black T-shirt. She slapped Luk on the back affectionately, and held the door open.

"How did the audition go?" Maddie asked, taking the guitar case off Luk while Luk dragged the amp and speaker into the studio. "Just let me mute the telly."

One end of the building was still set up as a recording and rehearsal space, with racks of guitars and a bank of mixing boards and tape decks, but the front of the studio housed a huge TV and a couch, bar fridge beside it.

Mad opened the fridge and took out two stubbies of beer. She held one out to Luk, then subsided back onto the couch.

Luk dragged a rehearsal chair over, then popped the top off his beer and took a long drink.

"I got in," he said, grin splitting his face. "It was amazing; we sounded so good, played for the whole afternoon."

"Excellent!" Maddie said, holding her stubbie up in a salute. "Tell me about the band."

"It's Lori's band, she's the drummer," Luk said.

"She must struggle," Maddie said. "It was hard enough playing guitar and having tits."

"And a Straight Edge bloke, called Jude, plays lead guitar. We're gonna be called The Tockleys, and we're not going to play covers, only original stuff."

"Is the drummer hot? Do you fancy her?" Maddie asked, chuckling. "Or is she too butch?"

Luk rested his beer on his knee and considered. "Guess she's cute," he said. "Her boyfriend is in Delicate John, so I haven't really looked at her."

Maddie's gaze was speculative, and Luk changed the subject in a hurry. "Look, thanks for the equipment, it sounded absolutely amazing. The guitar is gorgeous."

"It's a beauty," Maddie said. "Lovely sound to it. You can use it whenever you want to."

Luk grinned. "Are you sure? It's hideously expensive, and I'll never be able to replace it."

Maddie shrugged and rearranged her feet on the coffee table with difficulty, reaching for a pack of cigarettes. "It's not a guitar if it's not played," she said, her voice hoarse from the first lungful of cigarette, clearing as she coughed. "I miss the days. I haven't played anything except acoustic for years, haven't rocked out since I did my knee in."

She slapped the brace on her leg, and Luk nodded. Maddie put down her cigarette and studied him. "Is the band any good?" she asked.

"Dunno," Luk said. "There were a few songs where it was just so unbelievably good..." He shook his head, running out of words, but there was nostalgia in Maddie's smile.

"God, I remember," she said. "Tell you what, get your friends here, let me listen to you. You can practice here, use my amps, and I'll give you some pointers."

Luk grinned at Maddie, and she smiled back indulgently. "Thanks, Maddie," Luk said. "Thanks for everything."

The intercom in the studio buzzed, and Jack's voice said, "Stop fondling your guitars, and get in here before your dinner goes cold."

"Oh, yeah," Luk said. "Jack said to tell you dinner is ready."

Maddie levered herself back up off the couch, hanging onto Luk's arm. "Then I'd better go inside."

Luk let himself out of the side gate and clambered through the garden between the two houses to the side door to his parents' house. His mother was fiddling in the kitchen, the TV on the kitchen table blaring a game show. She looked up when Luk opened the fridge.

"Your dinner..." she said vaguely, waving a hand at the fridge.

Luk took out the plastic container of what looked like stew and potatoes and held it out, and she nodded.

"Thanks," he said, but her eyes were back on the TV.

"Mum?" Luk said, raising his voice.

"Yes, dear?" his mother asked.

"I'm in a band."

"That's nice," she said. "Heat your dinner up."

Luk took a fork out of the cutlery drawer, then carried the container of cold dinner through the house to his bedroom.

Penny's bedroom door was open, and when he glanced in, she tossed a stuffed toy at him, land-line phone against one ear, cell phone in hand. He waved at her, and she held a finger up at him. He liked his adolescent sister, in an ill-defined way.

His father, sitting on a couch in the entertainment room with his back to the hall, must have heard Luk's boots creaking or his chains clanking, because he called out, "Lucien! In here!"

"What?" Luk said when his father craned his head around to glare at Luk over the back of the couch.

"Where have you been?"

"I went to an audition for a band. I got in."

Luk's father pursed his lips disapprovingly. "This can't interfere with uni, understand? Didn't you have classes today?"

"Semester starts next week," Luk said. "You know that. And the band will count as extra toward my music units." It wouldn't, but Luk had no issues with lying to his parents about everything.

"It's a real band?" Luk's father asked. "Not some poofter boy band?"

Luk looked down at his clothes: ripped T-shirt with the Australian flag flying upside down, shredded black jeans, knee-high boots, chains and studs. His hair was buzzed, and his ears and brows were studded with metal. "Do I look like a fucking boy band would want me?"

Luk's father's eyes narrowed. "Language, Lucien,

please."

"It's a rock band," Luk said. "Maddie Hades, next door, is going to listen to us rehearse. You can ask her, after that."

"I don't approve of you associating with Mrs. Hades, either."

Luk shrugged. "Whatever."

Families. Who'd have them?

He slammed his bedroom door shut and balanced the plastic container of dinner on top of the mess on his desk, then threw himself on his bed.

It took some time to undo his boots, loosening the laces, wriggling and pulling until he could drag his feet out. His boots tumbled onto the floor amongst the mess, and he added his socks, glad to wriggle his toes, get some circulation going in his feet.

He leaned across behind his bed and slid his bedroom window open, then pulled his stash out from under his bed. He was in a band, a real band.

Luk lit the joint and sucked the smoke in deep, grinning to himself. Lori was a sweetie, and she played drums like a demon, ripping into the beat. And Jude... Luk took another drag on the joint. Jude could sing, and he played lead adequately, flying with the songs, bouncing around Lori's garage like a mad man in his tight black jeans and sneakers, his braid flying behind him.

Luk didn't get Straight Edge. Why get into the music, go to a gig and really get into the music, and not have a skinful of beer? Why would someone like Jude not want to get laid?

Luk's acoustic guitar was balanced across his bookcase, and he pulled it down. It settled comfortably against him, utterly familiar after at least five years of playing it every day. He dragged the side of his thumb across the strings, then tweaked the tuning. His fingers were too raw from the audition to play -- he needed to let them heal -- but it was still soothing to hold the guitar, just while he finished his joint.

With the buzz back in his system and the afternoon still warm in his head, Luk closed his eyes. He wasn't going to think about how much Jude looked like the hot guy in the porn he'd downloaded that week, because there was no way Luk was up to dealing with the implications of that. Even if Jude did look just like a skinnier, younger version of that guy...

Fuck it, but pot always made Luk horny.

Jude's housemates were out working or socializing when Jude let himself into the house he shared, the quiet unexpected. There was usually someone making a racket somewhere in the old house. He put his guitar in his room, leaning against the wall below his poster of Marc Bolan, and picked up a pack of ramen noodles from the box of food he kept in his room.

The kitchen was a mess, as always. Jude had to dig through the mountain of dirty dishes to find a saucepan, then wash it up, before he could put some water on to boil.

He washed up a bowl, too, then took his meal of noodles out into the jungle of a backyard, to sit in the cool darkness while he ate.

Mosquitoes buzzed Jude, but he swished them away with his fork between mouthfuls and nodded approvingly to himself at the memory of the afternoon. There was a chance that the band, The Tockleys, were what he'd been waiting for in his life, what he'd been marking time for. He'd been toying with the idea of going back home to Melbourne, to try his luck on the music scene there, or maybe of getting a real job and saving up enough money to go overseas to India or Nepal. If The Tockleys could play music like they had that afternoon, if they could rock out, play their own songs, and get some gigs somewhere, then he'd stay in the city for a little longer, give this place another chance.

In the darkness, with the sea breeze gone and the late summer prevailing easterly wind back, the tangle of jacarandas and vines in the backyard rustled and sighed. Jude lay back on the patchy grass to watch the stars overhead, his empty bowl beside him.

He'd waited a long time to find people he could make music with like Lori and Luk. The three of them together had made some magic, and he couldn't wait to do it again.

Chapter Three

That's it," Lori said, pointing at the driveway opposite. "Number twenty."

Jude parked Lori's boyfriend's van in the drive, and the pair of them stared through the streaked windscreen at the neo-tasteless fake Spanish architecture of the house, complete with serried ranks of palm trees.

"Fuck," Lori said. "We're rehearsing in a McMansion?"

Jude shrugged. "It's the address. Do you think Luk lives here?"

"If he does, he's paying for dinner," Lori said, planting one platform boot against the passenger door to force it open.

The driver's door opened more easily, as long as Jude wound the window down and stuck his arm out the window to use the external handle.

Lori had hauled the rear door of the van open, and she handed Jude's guitar case to him. "Want to go check we're really in the right place, before I get to the heavy stuff?" she asked.

Jude climbed the steps, past the concrete statues of lions, to the double-sized front doors with stained glass inserts. He pushed the doorbell, expecting 'Greensleeves,' and got the first few bars of 'Jackrabbit,' the opening guitar riff played by electronic chimes. It was so tacky and unexpected that Jude almost burst out laughing.

The man who opened the front door and peered at Jude was overweight and middle-aged, beard down his barrel chest, beer gut straining at his faded black T-shirt and hanging over his jeans.

"I'm looking for Luk," Jude said. "Is he here?"

The man chuckled, displaying nicotine-stained teeth. "Young Lucien is out the back, in the sound studio. Just go through the garage and the gate."

"Thanks," Jude said. Sound studio? He and Lori had assumed they'd be rehearsing in someone's shed or garage, but Luk had found them a sound studio?

Lori was waiting for him in the driveway, with her electronic drum kit across her back and her amp on a removalist's trolley. Jude pointed up the drive, past the four-wheel drives.

"Hey, kids," a gravelly voice called from the back patio of the house, and a round woman hobbled down the steps, waving her walking stick at them. "I'm Maddie; come on through to the sound studio. I think Lucien is setting up."

She shuffled ahead of Jude, leading the way past a pool that needed cleaning and a rusting barbecue to a substantial brick building at the back of the garden. Behind Jude, Lori whispered, "That's Maddie Hades."

It was, too. The bleached blonde hair was the same, and underneath an additional forty kilograms was the hot chick who'd belted out rock anthems twenty years before, fronting Ratatosk.

And they were walking into her sound studio, in her

backyard.

"Hi, there," Luk said, waving at them from the floor where he was splicing cable using a pair of pliers and some electrical tape. "I think that's fixed, Maddie," he said, shoving jacks into an amp. "Want to flick it on?"

Maddie shuffled across the worn matting on the sound studio floor to the bank of mixers on the far wall, while Lori rested her drum kit on a couch and Jude just stared at the racks of guitars down one side of the room.

Humming filled the room and Maddie nodded. "Thanks, Lucien. Now introduce me to your friends."

Luk bounced to his feet. "This is Lori, she plays drums, and this is her band. And this is Jude, he plays guitar."

"Maddie Hades," Maddie said. "I'm going to sit down here while you all get set up, then you can shake the roof off this studio and scare the spiders in the ceiling."

Jude watched Maddie lower herself onto the couch. "Thank you," he said, because he doubted Lori was going to be coherent any time soon. "For letting us rehearse here."

Maddie smiled indulgently at Jude. "It'll be good for the gear here to get used, for a change. There're amps down the back; Lucien knows where everything is."

Jude nodded and put his guitar case down beside where Luk had set his gear up. Luk grinned at him, looking smug. "Pretty good, huh?"

Jude nodded. "Yeah. So, which amp am I plugging into?"

It took them fifteen minutes, between them, to drag the dusty amps into place and set up Lori's drum kit. The gear was antiquated, all the same vintage as the rig that Luk had brought with him to the audition, but Luk had jacks and adaptors ready to plug them in.

The air was filled with the subtle hum and crackle of valves warming up. Maddie, on the couch, was beaming at them, cigarette in one hand, beer in the other. Lori, perched on a chair, circled the tip of her drumstick on her snare drum, and Jude, sure of the tuning of his guitar, at least for the moment, flicked the switch to take himself live.

"'Not the Only One,'" Lori said.

Jude led, straight into the top run of the melody, Luk right behind him, solid on the beat, chasing the secondary melody line, too, and Lori ripping into the drums.

"Wish I had the courage to do what must be done
I'm just another coward
But I'm not the only one."

Maddie was nodding, keeping time, as they went into the first bridge, when Jude glanced over at her. Then his attention was back on Lori, her mascara already streaking down her cheeks as she sweated, and on Luk, his eyes closed, a blissful smile on his face.

Lori winked at Jude when he glanced back at her, and he let her have the next verse.

"The slump of her shoulders
And the line of his jaw
They're screaming so softly
They're almost unheard."

No bridge, just straight into the chorus, with them all singing. Jude was bouncing up into the air, riding the music high, and it was just about the sweetest feeling he'd ever had, right at that moment.

"We share a frequency
Same bandwidth, same line
I follow their echoes

Because they sound like mine.

"We gather in groupings
Ridiculous, sublime
We know you won't hear us
But it's almost our time."

Maddie was bashing her walking stick against the coffee table her foot rested on, in time with the beat, when Jude grabbed the key change, going into the last verse. He pulled it around, twisting the notes, then all three of them were there.

"Together we're stronger
So you pull us apart
But we've made the connection
Now we're just waiting to start."

The chorus, one last time, and Luk was winding up the back end of the song, chasing them out, so that his beautiful old guitar was the last one standing, lingering on the last bar, counting them down.

In the aftermath, the amps hummed and crackled faintly. Jude's sneakers rustled a little, and Maddie clapped solidly and slowly.

"Damned sweet," she said approvingly. "Better than the idiots that the radio keeps insisting on playing, butchering that song. I'm going to wander off, go watch some TV, but I'll stick my head in again later, see how you're going."

When Maddie had shuffled off, Lori pushed her fringe off her face with the back of her hand and said, "Wow, Luk. She is seriously cool. Is she your mum or something?"

Luk chuckled and shook his head. "I wish. I live next

door. I think Maddie kind of misses the glory days, you know, when she was in the band."

Lori balanced her drumsticks across her kit and leaned over to reach into her case. "I've brought some of my lyrics with me. I thought we might be able to spend some time, work out how to play them, if you two don't mind."

"I've got a song with me, too," Jude said. "Luk?"

"Yeah, me, too. Maddie said to help ourselves to the fridge here, and to the guitars. Let's do some work."

Jude lifted a pretty six string off the rack of guitars, nodding approvingly at the tiny plaque on the back indicating it had been handmade by Scott Wise. Beside him, Luk made a clucking noise at an acoustic bass guitar, and Jude found himself sharing a conspiratorial grin with Luk. The guitars were beautiful, beyond all reason.

Lori, set of bongos in her hands, peered at the mixing board. "Does Maddie record here? Does any of this gear work?"

Luk shrugged, settling himself into a practice chair. "We could ask her."

Lori's eyes were shining when she sat cross-legged on the couch, bongos on her lap, an acoustic guitar leaning against the couch beside her. "We could lay down some tracks, maybe, get some music out there. I guess it would be an analogue recording, the gear is so old, but someone would convert it for us."

Jude, propped in the corner of the couch, touched the strings of the guitar to check the tension. "Perhaps Luk can ask if we can." He strummed his thumb down the strings, the notes resonating true. "Listen to that..."

One song each to be worked on. Lori's song was sad, a torch song that made Jude look at her closely when she was playing the chords, trying to read her face. Luk's song, full of complex chords that Jude couldn't even finger, was more music than trite words, sharp and sweet, and was not what Jude had expected from the punk kid. Luk, fingers sliding across the frets, eyes closed as he followed the music, was turning out to be a classy guitarist, far better than Jude.

When it was Jude's turn, he balanced the scribbled words against the can of lemonade he was drinking from. His nervousness must have shown, because Lori said, "It's okay, Jude. If we're going to play our own songs, it's going to get a little raw at times."

Jude nodded.

"visions of you dance on the water
where my memory laps at me and soaks through my
     skin
I'm tasting the phantoms, choking on the vapor
this feeling was hiding, where has it been?
"wrapped up safe, safe in my promise
promise made gladly, gladly my heart
my heart laughs at me as I look in the mirror
and try to outthink it -- but I'm not that smart

"cursing myself as my heart skips a beat
breathe, now, just breathe... I need to revert
fall back, fall way back, fall way back, retreat
my silence is worth it -- it's only my hurt
It's not right I didn't mean to do that
out of sight you never even knew that
I couldn't stop it, I had to fall
now that you're here will you take it all...?
you were safe, you were distant, you were silent
we knew there was no chance our paths would meet
it must have crept up in the black of your shadow
after you thought you were finally free.

"and I didn't mean to tell you I loved you
let me start over, let me reset
this life isn't perfect, but fuck it, it's mine
this life isn't over, but you aren't gone yet
it's not fair, I didn't mean to say that
I don't care, any way we play that
somebody loses, somebody falls
and no matter who wins, I'll have lost it all."

The chords were simple changes, written to be played on Jude's battered electric guitar. Jude had always figured that was where the song belonged, on an instrument as damaged as his heart had been when he'd written the song, on retreat in the forest, beside a lake.

Lori nodded slowly, then said, "I've heard you play that before."

Lori had been around the year before, when it had all gone bad with Dave, so she wouldn't need an explanation. When Jude glanced at Luk, Luk was running fingering patterns over the neck of his guitar.

"It needs a bridge," Luk said. "Something like this."

He played a four bar pattern, then looked up expectantly.

Jude shrugged mentally. He could write a song like that one, about the worst time in his life, and Luk would critique the chords. He could deal with that.

"Sounds good," Jude said, and when Luk turned around to reach for another beer from the fridge, Lori patted Jude's knee mutely, her eyes sympathetic.

"I'm tired of acoustic," Luk said. "It's all I get to play at home. Can we go electric again? I've got arrangements for my song written out, and I think we can put some together for Lori's, but I don't think Jude's song is ever gonna rock."

Lori put the bongos aside and stood up, holding out

a hand for Jude, pulling him off the couch. Luk was fiddling with the amps, switching everything on, and Lori stretched up so her mouth was close to Jude's ear.

"Don't mind him, he's a prat," Lori whispered.

Jude kissed her cheek quickly, and smiled reassuringly.

"C'mon," Luk called, slipping the strap for the bass electric guitar over his head. "Stop wasting time."

Lori smiled at Jude when she sat down behind her drum kit, and Luk knelt down to plug the kit in again.

Lori was a good person.

They were getting into it again, Luk running wild on the bass guitar through his own song, Lori right behind, Jude driving the melody line by himself, when the door to the sound studio swung open again and Maddie hobbled in.

Luk faltered in the bass line, and Maddie called out, "Keep going, keep right on going."

It took a couple of bars, then Luk was back, charging through his song, jumping on his stomp pedal.

When the music had stopped, and the amps were humming, Maddie said, "You looking for a gig?"

Lori gasped, and Luk nearly dropped an irreplaceable guitar, so it looked like Jude was going to have to be the one talking.

"We'd love a gig," Jude said. "Do you know someone we could audition for?"

Maddie wheezed asthmatically, bending over to get herself a beer out of the fridge. "Mate of mine, name of Alix, owns a café called Monlo's, and he's looking for a group to play some live music for him. I gave him a call, told him you were good, so the gig's yours."

Jude glanced over his shoulder at Lori and Luk, and Lori nodded frantically. Alix would be Alix Monlo, former bass guitarist from Ratatosk.

"Sounds wonderful," Jude said. "When and where?"

"Monlo's Café, Inglewood, at eleven, to set up for the lunchtime crowds. Take your own instruments, and Alix has a basic board and amp arrangement."

Maddie shuffled back toward the door, and Lori said, "Thank you, for everything."

Maddie grinned at Lori. "You're supposed to ask how much the gig pays."

"Um, how much does the gig pay?" Luk asked.

"Fifty, plus your lunches," Maddie said, pushing the door open again. "And Alix will have the set list waiting for you, but you might want to brush up on some Beatles classics, because that's what his customers are going to want."

"No way!" Luk said, as soon as the door closed behind Maddie. "No Beatles covers, ever."

"Hang on," Lori said. "It was very kind of Maddie to get us a gig at all; we can't go refusing it just like that, not when she's lending us rehearsal space, too."

"You said we'd only play our own songs, never any covers," Luk insisted. "Where's your fucking integrity?"

Lori stood up, five foot five only, even in her platform boots. "Don't you dare question my integrity," she snarled.

Luk looked at Jude. "What about you? You're all about the purity of the music, do you think we should play the gig?"

Jude looked from Luk to Lori, who was glaring at him. "Firstly, fifty bucks is a lot of money for me," Jude said. "The band could put the fifty bucks toward buying a website, or blank CDs to burn our music to. Secondly, Lori's right, and we have to respect Maddie, who arranged the gig."

"That's it?" Luk said, peeling the guitar strap over his head and unplugging his amp.

"No," Jude said. "Thirdly, I'm tired of living on ramen and chips, and could do with a free feed. Not all of us live at home still. Lori and I both have crappy minimum wage jobs."

"Fuck you, both of you," Luk said. "What's the point of saying something, if the first time someone offers you fifty lousy dollars, you change your mind?"

He stomped out, slamming the sound studio door behind him, and Jude flinched.

"Arsehole," Lori said.

"Do you want me to go talk to him?" Jude asked.

Lori shook her head, flicking her braids around. "You and I will play the gig, if he won't. You're right, fifty dollars is a lot of money. I'd have to work four hours to earn that much."

"So would I," Jude said.

They packed away the sound gear as best they could, moving the old amps back to the edge of the room, sliding the guitars back onto the racks, and tidying away the soft drink cans and beer bottles.

In the van, Lori leaned back against the passenger seat, looking weary in the streetlights coming through the windscreen. "We made some good music today," she said.

Jude glanced at her and smiled. "Yeah," he agreed.

She touched his arm in the half-light. "That song, about Dave, that was beautiful."

"Thanks," Jude said, and he didn't glance over, not that time.

"Are you alright?" she asked. "Inside yourself?"

"I'm lonely," Jude said, pretending to concentrate on coaxing the old van through its gears. "That's all."

"You'll meet someone," Lori said. "Someone special. Someone who won't fuck you over."

Jude nodded. "What about you? How are things with

Rick?"

Lori sighed. "Sometimes, things are rough; sometimes, they aren't."

"Promise me one thing?" Jude said. "Promise me you won't get jammed on anything."

Lori shook her head. "I'm cautious, you know that, but we're not all cut out to keep Edge."

Jude let the issue slide. He wasn't going to nag Lori, no matter how much what she did worried him. She was a grown up, like him.

And unlike that brat Luk. It was a pity, because he was a brilliant guitarist, but if he was going to throw a temper tantrum and storm out, it was better he did it at the beginning. They could always audition for another guitarist.

Chapter Four

Luk wasn't asleep, but he was pretending to be, when someone knocked on his bedroom door.

"Go away," he called out. It was morning, certainly, with sunlight sneaking around his curtains, but on the last Saturday before uni started, he wasn't getting up for anyone.

Bang, bang, bang.

"Go away! I'm not awake." Luk hated his little sister sometimes.

"Lucien," Luk's mother called. "Mrs. Hades is here, and she wants to talk to you. Something about borrowing a guitar. Have you broken one of her guitars?"

"No, Mum," Luk called, rolling off his bed and reaching for the previous day's jeans amongst the mess on the floor.

He dragged his jeans on, then pulled a T-shirt on, back to front.

Maddie was waiting for him in the kitchen, while his mother hovered anxiously.

"Sleep in?" Maddie asked, smiling at Luk.

"Um, guess so," Luk said.

"Thought I'd better come over, wake you up, make sure you've the guitar you want to borrow ready. You don't want to be late for your first gig," Maddie said.

Shit.

"Um, I'm not playing it," Luk said.

Maddie's smile slipped a little. "Not playing it? Why?"

"Are you ill, Lucien?" Luk's mother asked, but Luk screened her out.

"When Lori started The Tockleys, we all agreed we'd never play covers, only original music. I refused to break that agreement."

Maddie crossed her arms, propping up her bust, and shook her head. "Have I ever told you about the first gig Ratatosk ever played?"

"Um, no," Luk said. "What was it?"

"We did a wedding, someone's sister or aunt or something. Spent the entire time playing John Denver and Bee Gees covers. Go and get showered, and I'll drive you to the gig."

Luk blinked. John Denver? Ratatosk? The band that had recorded the album *Dingo*, the definitive Australian rock album, had played John Denver covers?

"Lucien?" Luk's mother said. "Hurry up, dear. Don't keep Mrs. Hades waiting."

Luk nodded, and took off for the bathroom he shared with his sister.

Maddie was in her driveway, wheezing around a cigarette, when Luk jumped across the garden between their houses four minutes later. He'd showered, slapped on some deodorant, brushed his teeth, and dragged on his cleanest plain black T-shirt, the one he kept for family dinners.

He tossed his boots into the front of Maddie's car to

put on during the drive, and followed her into her yard to the sound studio to grab the gear he'd need.

The bass guitar, the one he'd been borrowing, was propped against the couch in its case. Maddie said, "Do you think that other boy -- what's his name? Jude? -- wants to borrow a guitar, too? His own wasn't holding its tuning the other day."

"I'm sure he does," Luk said, reaching for the Maton solid mahogany guitar Jude had been fondling on the rack at rehearsal.

Maddie, beside him, fiddled with the combination lock on a metal case bolted to the wall. "Let's give a crowd a thrill," she said, swinging the case open.

She lifted out a battered sunburst Byrdland Gibson electric guitar, the low frets worn down to almost nothing, the hardware still showing the last traces of the original factory gold plate.

"Pretty, isn't she?" Maddie said.

Luk nodded mutely. He'd know that Gibson anywhere; it was in every poster of Maddie fronting Ratatosk that was framed and mounted on the studio walls, on every album cover in the glass case above the TV. It was Maddie's own guitar.

"Are you going to play?" Luk asked, awe in his voice, as Maddie laid the Gibson in its case.

Maddie shrugged. "Thought Alix and I might, you know, jam a bit, just for old time's sake. It'll make him happy."

They loaded the three guitars into the back of Maddie's car, and Luk clambered into the passenger seat.

"I'm glad you changed your mind," Maddie said when she eased herself behind the steering wheel.

"So am I," Luk said, reaching down for his boots.

"And, Lucien," Maddie said, and Luk looked up from wrestling with his laces.

"Yes?"

"You're not to tell Jack that I've taken the Gibson out of the house. She's uninsurable, and he'll kill me if he finds out I've done it."

Lori's boyfriend, Rick, was sitting on the front porch of their house when Jude walked across the dead front lawn.

"Hi, Rick," Jude said as he climbed the porch steps. "Lori around?"

Rick glanced up, looking hungover and bleary. "Inside."

Jude opened the screen door, nudging the dog aside gently. Lori was in her bedroom, sitting on the bed amongst rumpled grubby sheets, wearing only underwear.

"Hey," Jude said, pushing the door closed behind himself. "You close to ready to go?"

Lori nodded and held out an eyeliner pencil. "Can you do this?"

Jude propped his guitar against the foot of the bed and sat down in front of Lori. "Lori, hon," Jude said, but Lori looked at him with pleading eyes, and Jude stopped. "Alright. What's the point in having a gay man as a friend if he won't put your makeup on, right?"

Lori closed her eyes. Jude held her chin and cheek to steady her face, and drew lines carefully, thick and bold, around her eyes.

"Smudge?" Jude asked, and Lori handed him a tissue for him to spread the lines out.

Lori opened her eyes. "Do I want to see?" she asked, and Jude shook his head.

"Not if we're going to get to Monlo's on time. Get dressed, hon, and grab your drum kit."

On the front porch, Rick tossed the keys to his van at Jude with so much force that the palm of Jude's hand was bleeding when he unlocked the back of the van for Lori to put her drum kit in.

Jude could put Lori's eyeliner on for her, and drive her to gigs, but there were some things he couldn't fix for her, no matter how much he wanted to.

In the van, Lori laced up her boots and slicked on lipstick, and the closer they got to Monlo's, the happier she seemed.

Alix, who owned Monlo's, was still painfully thin, though his shock of bleached hair from his days as Ratatosk's bass guitarist was gone, leaving only a graying fringe around his bald spot.

He greeted Lori and Jude with delight, dragging the café doors open, chuckling to himself. "I'm so looking forward to this," he said. "Maddie hasn't sent me a new live act for years, so this is something of a treat. Come and set up, work out how you want to arrange things..."

They followed Alix through the unlit café, past the tables with neat linen and tidy chairs to the small raised stage at the back of the main dining area. On the wall behind the stage, in a glass display case, hung Alix's famous custom-built, double-neck Maton left-handed bass with the distinctive customized skull pattern. Lori elbowed Jude as he was putting down his case, and Jude grinned at her. They'd fallen in with rock royalty, even if the rock royalty were balding, arthritic, or overweight.

"No morning trade?" Lori asked, setting the case holding her electronic drum kit down on the tiny stage, when Alix came back from flicking on lights at the front of the café.

"God, no," Alix said. "Then I'd have to get up in the mornings. We're more of a lunchtime and evening café, at least that's what I tell the missus. Sound gear is there, you've got a basic mixing board, lots of inputs. Take your time, do some sound tests. I have to go rev up the nuclear-powered espresso machine, and get the rest of the lights on."

"Thanks," Jude said, sharing another grin with Lori.

"Oh," Alix called out. "When your other player turns up, just let him in. I won't be able to hear him over the exploding coffee machines."

Lori tucked wisps into the unruly bundle of hair on the back of her head and lifted her drum kit up onto its stand. "Exploding nuclear-powered coffee machines?" she whispered.

"Dunno," Jude whispered back, flicking power switches on the mixing board on at random, just to see what happened.

By the time they'd set up, drum kit and guitar in place, belching and hissing sounds were emanating from behind the bar and clouds of steam were bursting out of the espresso machine at random, accompanied by the kind of swearing that made even Lori blink, then burst out laughing.

Alix appeared a moment later from behind the bar, wearing thick padded gloves and a rubber apron. "Apologies, miss," he said.

"Please, no need to apologize," Lori said, still chuckling. "I share a house with a punk band."

Alix shook his head. "I'm so glad my daughter is a studying to be an accountant, not a musician. Are you all set for a sound test?"

Lori sat on the stool behind her kit and picked up her sticks, but before she could count Jude in, someone banged on the closed front doors of the café.

"Maddie!" Alix said, and he loped up the café, rubber apron flapping, to drag the doors open and let in Maddie and Luk.

Jude glanced at Lori, who shrugged back at him, then Luk was carrying an armful of guitar cases between the tables while Alix and Maddie embraced.

"Hi, there," Luk said, putting the guitars down beside the stage. He handed one of the cases to Jude. "I brought you one of Maddie's electrics, to replace yours. She said yours wasn't holding its tune."

"Thanks," Jude said, taking the case.

Luk looked around the café as he cracked open another case. "Nice place," he said. "Is the sound gear any good?"

"We were just about to do a sound test," Lori said. "Plug yourself in, and let's find out."

Luk bounded up onto the stage, and Jude found he was grinning. He didn't know what had happened, or what Maddie had done to make Luk see some sense, but he was glad to see the kid back again.

Jude slipped the frayed strap of his own guitar over his head and rested his guitar against the back wall of the café, replacing it with the beautiful lead guitar from Maddie's sound studio. It only took a moment to check the tuning, then Lori was counting them in to 'Not the Only One.' Maddie sat at one of the front tables, mug of fresh coffee in her hands, while Alix bounced around behind them at the sound panel, adjusting the settings.

At the end of the song, the last of Luk's reverb fading, Maddie nodding in maternal approval, Alix rubbed his hands and nodded.

"Nice sound," he said. "You've got a good balance with the crazy bass and the straight lead, and the drums are solid. Stage-wise, I can't fault you. The girl is sweet, the young guy is just demented, and the lead is very bouncy and bright. It could make a very good stage shtick."

"Um, thanks," Lori said. "For everything."

Alix beamed at Lori. "Now, I'm going to have a chat

with Maddie, then placate my cook. You can all duck out the back for a bong, or whatever, then came back and play nice, ordinary Beatles covers for my old age pensioner customers for a couple of hours."

Alix and Maddie disappeared into the kitchen, and Jude slid the guitar strap over his head. "I'm going for a walk."

He really didn't want to know if Lori and Luk were going to have a joint or a hit before their first-ever gig.

The street outside the café was still morning-quiet, the occasional car whizzing past, and Jude wandered down the paving past antique stores and dress boutiques just opening. Other cafés were open, people sitting at the tables on the pavement in the shade of the awnings. It was warm and getting warmer, in the last gasp of summer. Jude, along with every other resident of the city, couldn't wait for autumn to arrive and the heat to be over.

He walked to the traffic lights, then back again.

The doors to the café stood open, and Jude followed the first customers in. Despite Alix's dire predictions, the customers weren't old age pensioners, they were just the kind of middle-aged, middle-classed people who liked to go out for Saturday lunch and listen to a little inoffensive live music. Jude kind of liked people like that, who wanted real food and music, just nothing too jarring.

Lori didn't meet Jude's gaze, and Luk was just as evasive when the three of them settled themselves on the stage a few minutes later. Alix brought them over a jug of iced water and three glasses, and nodded encouragingly.

Lori tapped her snare drum with her stick, steady count, and said, "'Love Me Do,' two bar lead, on my count."

It wasn't hard work, ambling gently through Beatles covers, the music familiar as Jude's own breath, part of his life forever. Beside him, Luk was staying on track, not wandering off the beat too far, and Lori's drumming was sweet and steady, just what they needed.

The sound gear was kind of minimalist, the volume down low, and the people in the café, more and more of them through the lunch rush, talked and laughed over the music, pausing to clap politely occasionally over plates of fettuccine and glass bowls of mango semi-freddo.

Between sets, the three of them sat out the back in the alley behind the kitchen, listening to kitchen staff swearing and arguing.

Lori rolled a joint carefully and handed it to Luk. "Well?" she said.

"Well, what?" Luk asked, taking the joint.

"How're your corrupted principles going?"

Luk lit the joint, leaning back on the crate he was perched on, so it creaked alarmingly. "You know, this is not too bad," he said. "The customers are just sitting there, stuffing themselves, so it wouldn't make a difference what we played, as long as it sounded like it was something they knew. I guess it doesn't matter that they don't know who we are, or anything."

Lori took the joint off Luk when he'd had a drag. "Yeah. Guess a little insignificance is good for the soul," she said. "What do you think, Jude?"

"Luk?" Jude said, an idea forming. "How do you feel about channeling George Harrison? Reckon you could put together the fingering to open 'Not the Only One' with a huge F with a G on top, like Harrison did to start 'A Hard Day's Night'?"

"You're playing lead," Luk said, pointing at Jude with the joint. "You have to do the opening chord."

"Not a chance," Jude said. "No way can I make my hands do that. You'll have to."

Luk's smile widened, and he leaned forward, elbows on his knees. "And then?"

"And just keep going," Jude said. "I can do the melody flatter, with no pitch changes and some interval jumps. And Lori can keep the beat tight, a simple four with lots of cymbals. I reckon, after three glasses of house white and a big lunch, no one is going to notice it's not a Lennon/McCartney collaboration."

Lori beamed. "For a clean-living pure soul, you're evil, Jude, and I mean that in the nicest way."

"Then let's go mess with some minds," Jude said.

Back on the stage, Alix refilled the jug of water and taped the new set list to the edge of Lori's drum kit. "You're doing well," he murmured. "The punters are happy."

"Thanks, Alix," Lori said, glancing across at Luk and Jude. "Righto, two bar lead, 'Can't Buy Me Love,' on my count."

Three songs later, in the few seconds between songs, Luk said, "Alright, I've got the fingering sorted. Let's do this now, before my hands forget."

Lori nodded, tapped her stick against her snare, and said, "Two bar lead, on my count, for 'Not the Only One.' One, two, three, four. One, two, three, four."

The chord Luk let rip was too deep, on the bass, and the harmonics sounded screwy to Jude, but the audience didn't seem to notice, nodding approvingly over pavlovas and espressos.

A few of the punters blinked and looked surprised when the second bar was the opening melody for 'Not the Only One,' but most of them just kept smiling and rocking in their seats, while Lori sang.

"Wish I had the courage
To do what must be done."

After the first verse, Alix and Maddie appeared in the service doorway to the kitchen, bemused looks on their faces, and Jude caught a glimpse of Maddie whispering to Alix during the bridge, while Jude was trying to look serious and Lennon-like as he ignored the soaring melody line of the song and mooched through the chords.

Alix burst out laughing, loud enough for Jude to hear over Luk's masterful handling of the bass chords, then Maddie and Alix bolted for the kitchen through the swinging service doors.

Busted.

He grinned at Luk and Lori, then concentrated on the melody, trying to think ahead to where the next interval break should go.

At the end of the song, with a sedate smattering of applause and puzzled muttering, Alix and Maddie marched out of the kitchen again, Alix's rubber apron gone.

"Very clever," Alix said. "Very clever indeed. Hope you all know the chords for 'Jackrabbit.'"

Luk said, "Of course. Why?"

"Because something is about to happen that has not happened for many years. Right, Maddie?"

Maddie didn't answer; she was too busy opening the third guitar case that Luk had carried in. Luk was beaming when Jude looked at him.

Alix pushed between them on the stage, and reached up to unlock the glass case holding his double neck guitar. "Good thing I keep her tuned," he muttered to himself.

Maddie slid a faux leopard-skin strap over her head and freed her mane of blonde hair from the strap. "Ladies and gentlemen," she bellowed. "I hope you're not all asleep over your lunches, because today, we've got something special for you. My good friend and your host, Alix, has agreed to come out of retirement, just for one song."

"What are you kids called?" Alix hissed, leaning behind Jude to plug his guitar into the sound board.

"The Tockleys," Jude and Luk said in unison.

Alix made a choking noise and said, "Fucking hell."

A moment later, he and Maddie were in front on the tiny stage as well, Maddie plugged into the sound board too. Alix shouted over the buzz from the café, "Back from the brink, the living half of Ratatosk, backed by the new brats on the block, The Tockleys." He glanced over his shoulder at Lori, and whispered, "Count us into 'Jackrabbit,' Goth Girl."

"Shit," Lori said under her breath. "Two bar lead, on my count, for 'Jackrabbit.' One, two, three, four. One, two, three, four."

It should have been thin, with all of them running through the one sound board and amp, and no one using voice mikes, but the opening chords were solid and deep, Lori's drums right on the beat, the bass drum pad running true. Jude could hear Luk's bass guitar, restrained for a change, marking the first beat soundly, then holding the bar. Jude knew the melody, of course; there wasn't an Australian alive who didn't, but he didn't clutter the melody line, not when Maddie was swinging on her gorgeous old guitar, ripping through the tune. And Alix was grinning, riffing on the bass line, free to fly with Luk doing the background work.

"Longest road in the world
Straight line forever
Between me and you
But distance ain't gonna stop me never."

Maddie's voice, husky and loud, just like it had always been, was on the top of the sound, and Jude couldn't believe it was happening, that he was watching her and

Alix, the last two living members of Ratatosk, perform live.

Alix roared through the bridge, hamming it up for the audience, and that was when it occurred to Jude to look up from Maddie and Alix to the people in the café.

They were on their feet, overweight and worn out like Maddie, arms in the air, rushing forward, camera phones in their hands.

It was suddenly touching that, twenty-five years later, Alix and Maddie's music still meant so much to so many people.

"Gonna drive all night babe
To get to my jackrabbit
Because you're the one
In my veins, like a habit."

Maddie's hair was wet with sweat, the back of her T-shirt stained dark where the guitar strap dug into her, but Jude could see the side of her face, and she was grinning, her face alight with joy, and Alix was beaming back at her.

"Been gone the longest time
Working on the mines
Been drinking dust and beer
Sweating, waiting for the times."

The long bridge in the middle, where Smitho, Ratatosk's other guitarist, had always dueled with Maddie face to face on stage, sometimes for several minutes at a time, was on them. Maddie glanced at Jude, just once, and winked at him, and then she was off.

Jude was not a classy guitarist, not like Luk. He was never going to be able to keep up. So it was a huge relief to hear Luk's borrowed bass guitar wail through the speakers as Luk grabbed the notes Maddie was tossing at Jude, twisting them around and handing them back to her.

Jude stepped back, musically and physically, giving Luk the space he needed to rip the air up with Maddie, the pair of them jamming, Luk right at the bottom of his guitar neck, wringing what he could out of the instrument.

Alix was grinning, providing the backbeat, and Jude picked it up from him. If this was a musical apprenticeship, it didn't get any better.

Maddie came crashing out of the bridge, pulling Luk after her, and she was breathing so hard that Jude wondered briefly if she was having a heart attack or something, but a moment later she was bellowing the next verse, back on top.

"Too many flies and miles
Been lonely for my jackrabbit
Counting off the shifts and hours
In my veins, like a habit.

"Dodging roos in the dark
Long white line forever
Not enough fuel or sleep
Not going back, not ever.

"Gonna be with my man
Gonna have me some jackrabbit
Never leaving you again babe
Cos you're in my veins, like a habit."

They finished, loud and triumphant, Lori banging the bass drum and cymbals just like Tal, Ratatosk's drummer, had in the live recordings. Then the café just went crazy, the crowd screaming and banging on tables, the waiters and kitchen staff in the doorway to the kitchen, yelling and hammering on the doors.

Maddie bowed, twanging her strings, and Jude dove for the sound board beside the stage, killing the sound.

When he turned back, Alix and Maddie were hugging, Luk was wiping sweat from his face, and Lori was pushing sweat-wet hair back off her forehead. Jude was knackered, completely exhausted, perspiration running down his back under his T-shirt. He wanted four liters of cold water, and a shower.

And to play again.

Maddie let go of Alix, holding her hand up to acknowledge the applause, and she and Alix both turned and held their hands out to The Tockleys, handing the applause on.

Lori stood up uncertainly from behind her drum kit, and the three of them, The Tockleys, took their first bow.

Maddie slung her arm around Alix's neck, and shouted over the roar of the crowd, "For fuck's sake, Alix, buy me a drink before you're the last remaining Ratatosk member left alive."

Jude slid his guitar strap over his head and found himself pulled into a three-way hug by Lori, one arm around Lori, the other around Luk's ribs, the three of them laughing.

"We did it," Lori said. "Luk, you were fucking brilliant. Jude, I love you."

Jude, taller than both Lori and Luk, looked across to where Maddie was propped against the café bar, middy of beer in one hand, pen in the other, alternating between downing beer and signing autographs for the crowd gathered around her.

"Crazy first gig," Jude said. "Completely crazy."

"I'm starving," Luk said, disentangling himself from the hug. "When do you think we get to have lunch?"

"Pack up first," Lori said. "Then we can ask."

Alix extricated himself from the crowd at the bar just as they finished packing away all the gear, including Maddie's Gibson.

"Excellent gig," Alix said, holding out his hand to each of them in turn, shaking their hands earnestly, then taking his own left-handed guitar off Luk. "I'll lock the old girl safely back up again. This might just inspire me to take her out more often when other people are around. You kids must be starving."

They followed Alix out to the kitchen, past the bar. The cook was sitting down on a rickety chair at a counter, plate of pasta in front of her, but she sprang to her feet immediately.

"Feed these good folks," Alix said. "Give them anything they want."

"Certainly, Mr. Alix," the cook said. "Come and have a look at the menu, see what takes your fancy."

"What do you all want to drink?" Alix asked.

"Beer?" Lori asked, and Luk nodded enthusiastically.

"Lager it is," Alix said. "What about you, Mr. Lead Guitarist?"

"Just lemonade," Jude said, and Alix's eyebrow's shot up.

"I don't believe it, a clean-living guitar player," he said, disappearing off back to the bar.

Jude couldn't watch anyone eat steak, especially rare steak, so he was carefully not watching either Lori or Luk eat, and therefore had his gaze on the doors.

Maddie pushed the door open while the three of them were perched at a kitchen counter, wolfing down their free lunches.

"I'm off now, Lucien," Maddie said. "If you want to

stay with your friends, I can just take all the guitars home, but I'll need a hand loading them into my car."

Luk chewed and swallowed noisily, so that Jude almost lost his mouthful of asparagus and mushroom fettuccine. "I don't know," Luk said a little uncertainly.

"Hang around," Lori said. "We can all head into the Hyde Park Hotel tonight, listen to some bands, drink some beer. That sound good, Jude?"

"Sure does," Jude said. "Let's go out and celebrate."

Luk grinned, pushing his half-eaten plate of food away. "I'll carry the gear out, Maddie," he said. "Back in a moment; no one eat my steak."

Maddie waved her hand. "Bye," she said. "Thanks for the backup, I had a blast."

"You're very welcome," Lori said, and Jude nodded his agreement. "We're honored to have had the chance to play with you."

Maddie grinned, and slapped Luk. "Remember," she said. "You're not to tell Jack a thing about this. It's our secret."

"Who's Jack?" Lori asked Jude, when the door had swung shut.

"Must be her partner," Jude said, pushing Luk's plate further away so he couldn't smell the meat. "Guess he's the bloke who answered the door when we went there to rehearse."

Jude paused, fork loaded with fettuccine. It had never occurred to him before that 'Jackrabbit' had been written for an actual person, and the idea that Maddie was still with him, all these years later, was sweet.

Chapter Five

The three of them only just fit on the front bench seat of the van, with Lori in the middle, the handbrake handle between her knees.

Jude, at the wheel, craned his neck to look out the filthy back window as he reversed out of the lane behind the café. "Where to?"

"My place?" Lori said. "We can hang around, then head to the Hyde Park Hotel in time for the first gig."

Luk grinned, looking across at the other two. "How come Jude gets to drive? I want to."

"Jude's Straight Edge," Lori said, patting Luk's knee. "He always gets to drive."

Jude, improbably dorky sunglasses sliding down his nose, smiled at Luk. "Everyone loves a Straight Edger with a driver's license."

"Damn right," Lori said. "Consider yourself my designated driver, for the rest of my life."

The afternoon was hot, sun blasting through the windscreen, and Luk tipped his head back against the cracked vinyl headrest and closed his eyes. He was tired, and a little buzzed from beer and smokes. He could do with a swim and some more beer.

"Good idea," Lori said.

"Shit," Luk said, jerking his eyes open. "Didn't mean to say that aloud."

"What do you reckon, Jude? Think we could stop off, have a swim and a beer on the way?" Lori asked.

The van was stopped at a set of traffic lights on Stirling Highway, and Jude looked seriously at Lori. "It's water, Lori," he said. "You'll have to put your make-up back on afterward."

"Wanker," Lori said, giggling. "Shut up and drive."

Jude parked the van up the hill from the beach at Cottesloe, in amongst the family sedans. The three of them ambled toward the Cottesloe Hotel, past the strip of fish and chip shops and cafés where families argued and teenage girls giggled.

Luk, unnerved as always by adolescent girls who weren't actually related to him, looked away and pretended he couldn't see any of the girls in their bikinis. He'd detested high school, and it had been a sweet relief to get to uni, where the intellectual girls wore black sweaters and too much make-up, and talked about Proust all the time.

The Cottesloe Hotel was packed, and they had to elbow their way to the bar through the press of bodies and waves of sweat, beer, and coconut sunbathing oil.

At the bar, Luk pulled out his wallet. "What are you drinking?" he shouted at the others over the background pub roar.

"Lager," Lori shouted back, pointing at the handle on the beer pull.

Jude pointed at the lemonade sign on the wall, and Luk nodded at him.

With the drinks in his hands, and the others clearing his path, Luk managed to get safely out into the beer garden at the back of the pub, where at least the noise levels were lower and the air clearer.

None of the tables were empty, so they sat on a stretch of paving, hopefully where no one would stand on them. Over the sound system, unspeakably bland pop played.

Luk lifted his own plastic cup of beer up in a salute. "To The Tockleys," he said. "We fucking win."

"To us," Lori said, lifting her own plastic cup.

Jude banged his can of lemonade against their cups. "And to Ratatosk."

Around them, bleached-blonde surfer drunks and bikini-clad girls in sarongs milled, arguing, cruising, and drinking, stepping over Jude's outstretched legs in black jeans without comment. Luk leaned back against the brick wall behind him, and found himself grinning.

Lori elbowed him and said, "What?"

Luk opened his eyes and said, "You know? This the first time I've ever been here and it's not been some kind of torture. I've been dragged here a couple of times to hear a band in the front bar, and the place has always given me the creeps. It's just so…"

"Hawaiian print?" Jude suggested. "Cheerful? Sun-tanned?"

"All of those things," Luk said.

"So?" Lori said. "Reckon you're comfortable enough now to take off some of the black and get in the water?"

Luk downed the last of his beer. "Fuck, yeah. Let's go for a swim."

The beach, just across the road from the pub, was crowded. The beach was covered in towels and bags, kids running around screaming, but Lori waded through it all like a princess in platform boots until she found a clear patch.

Luk flopped onto the ground and began the process of unlacing his boots, while Lori lay back on the clean, white sand and lifted a foot into Jude's lap for him to undo her boots. Jude, sensibly, wore the same canvas sneakers as he always seemed to.

When Jude had peeled off Lori's boots, Lori pulled down her fishnet tights and stuffed them into her boots, then undid her shirt. Jude kicked his sneakers off, stuffed his socks into his sneakers, then stood up, towering over Luk and Lori as he peeled his T-shirt over his head, revealing pale, hairless skin, a flat belly, and prominent ribs.

Then Jude pushed his jeans down over long, thin legs, and he was off, running down the beach, wearing just his yellow checked boxers, the little braid of dark hair stark against the white skin of his back.

Lori stood up. Her skirt slipped down her over her knees and she stepped out of it, so she was wearing just a pair of black knickers and a bra. She walked serenely down the beach, head high as she ignored wolf whistles from the crowd.

Luk dumped his jeans and T-shirt, glad he'd worn decent undies that day, and followed Lori, catching up with her at the water's edge. Jude was out in the surf already, bobbing up out of the foam from the breakers.

Lori waded out past some kids on boogie boards, and Luk ran past her into the surf, diving through the waves to surface close to Jude. The water was pleasantly warm after the heat of the afternoon, the kids around them in the ocean only mildly annoying. Lori swam out sedately, her hair loose and trailing behind her, her make-up disappearing rapidly.

"Fuck," she said breathlessly, treading water beside Luk. "I keep falling out of my bra."

Luk didn't look -- it seemed polite not to.

"Do you need me to go get you my T-shirt?" Jude asked.

Lori shook her head. "I just won't throw myself around, that's all. And if I have some kind of nipple crisis, I'm relying on you both to cover for me, right?"

Luk blinked, looking from Jude to Lori, and Jude laughed. "Unfair, Lori," Jude said. "I'm up to the task, but Luk might not feel the same way."

Things were going on that Luk didn't understand. Were Lori and Jude lovers? Lori was supposed to have a boyfriend, the lead guitarist in Delicate John, but after the gig, she'd said she loved Jude. Then there was the way they whispered, and she kissed Jude's cheek. There'd been something about Jude's song, at rehearsal, that Luk hadn't understood...

"I'll help out," Luk said, trying to cover his confusion, hoping he didn't come off too uncool. "But I might not be the right person for the task."

Lori smiled at Luk, and dunked Jude's head underwater in a flurry of splashing arms. Luk swam off, away from the pair of them. He needed to think a little, past the salt water and the beer.

Luk stayed quiet while Jude drove the van to Lori's house, but neither Lori nor Jude mentioned it. They talked, just the two of them, about the recurring gig at Monlo's, about what songs they'd record for their first CD, and about Delicate John's gig that night at the Hyde Park Hotel.

Lori without make-up looked five years younger, her skin freckled and clear. Her shirt was only partly done up, and she had fine sand stuck to her neck and throat.

Jude, driving the van, had left his shirt off in the late afternoon heat, and if Luk leaned forward, sucking his skin off the vinyl van seat, he could see right across to where sand and crystals of salt shone on Jude's chest, caught in the dark blonde hairs that circled Jude's nipples.

Jude parked behind a larger, cleaner removalists'

van outside Lori's house. "That's Rick and the blokes, packing up for the gig," Lori said. "I thought they'd be gone already. Might be better if the two of you stayed here in the van for a few minutes, out of the way of the pre-gig craziness."

Someone shouted inside the house, the front door burst open, and Rick stomped out of the house, wearing only a towel and carrying an amp to the van.

"Lori!" he shouted. "Where the fuck have you been? Where's my black shirt?"

Luk kicked the passenger door open and jumped out, letting Lori scramble out, then he climbed back in while Lori ran to the house, boots in her hands, miniskirt flapping around her thighs.

Jude's face was concerned when Luk glanced at him. "What's wrong?" Luk asked.

Jude looked at Luk, and Luk felt like he was back in school and the school principal was peering over his glasses at him. "Lori," Jude said, as if that explained everything.

Luk dug through his jeans pockets, and found half a joint and a lighter. He didn't offer Jude a drag, just leaned back against the passenger door and made sure he blew the smoke out of the window. Jude's hair, drying rapidly, was escaping from the short plait Jude wore it in, frizzing up with the sun shining behind him, like a halo.

People began to emerge from the house, dragging amps and speakers, wheeling trolleys stacked with sound boards and instruments, adding to the pile on the verge beside the van. Rick appeared again, dressed this time, and unlocked the rear doors of the van.

"Should we offer to help?" Luk asked Jude.

Jude shrugged. "I think that's up to Lori. I don't know the domestic politics of the household or the band well enough to know if we'd make things better or worse for her."

Luk nodded. It made sense. If Rick knew Jude was fucking Lori, he wouldn't want Jude, or anyone from The Tockleys, helping out.

Ten minutes later, when Luk had flicked the roach out onto the road, the mountain of gear had been shifted from the verge into the removalists' van, and seven people had piled out of the house, into either the van or the newest-looking sedan parked outside the house, and driven off into the dusk.

Lori came out of the house and sat on the steps to the front porch. She waved to Jude and Luk, the pitbull terrier that belonged to the house following her out to sit beside her. "It's safe now," she called out.

Jude took the keys out of the ignition and wrenched the van's driver's side door open, but Luk decided he was over forcing the passenger door open and clambered out of the passenger window instead.

Lori stood up, smiling, and led them into the hall of the house. "Sorry 'bout that," she said. "Come on in. You can grab a shower, if you want one, as long as you don't mind there being no towels."

"Just like home," Jude said. "I'd love a shower to get rid of the salt."

"Beer in the fridge," Lori said, touching Luk's shoulder and pointing into the kitchen. "Then you can shower."

"Thanks, Lori," Luk said. The kitchen held a battered table covered in dirty plates, ashtrays, and empty beer and baked bean cans. The kitchen cabinets were cluttered with used saucepans, cases of dog food and boxes of cereal. The two fridges were ancient, and both were full of beer. Luk helped himself to a can and wedged the fridge door shut with a kitchen chair again, like it had been before.

He couldn't find a room that was clearly a living room, everywhere seemed to be bedrooms, so Luk settled for sitting out the back on the verandah with his beer and the pitbull. It was quiet in the house, with just the sound of the hot water system hissing and the shower running, and the dog panting and snuffling at Luk's feet.

The shower thudded and clunked, then started and stopped again by the time Luk got to the end of his beer.

Lori opened the back screen door, wrapped in just a towel, her hair dripping wet. "Shower's empty, if you want to use it," she said.

"Thanks," Luk said, adding his beer can to the pile in the garden beside the verandah, and followed Lori back into the house.

The bathroom matched the kitchen. The showerhead, over an ancient bath, spat hot water at random, and hair was stuck to the cracked tiles around the tub. Luk stripped off quickly and ducked under the water, grabbing soap and shampoo off the windowsill. At least the water was hot, which was possibly more than might be expected for the house.

It only took him a moment to rinse the sand, salt and sweat off, then Luk turned the water off and stepped out of the bath again.

He left his boxers off, since he'd swum in them, and just pulled his jeans and his T-shirt on over his wet skin. He wandered out into the hall, looking into open doors. Lori and Jude were in one room, their backs to the door. Lori was partly dressed, wearing something filmy, and Jude was lacing up her corset, laughing behind her.

Luk froze in the hall, sure they didn't know he was there.

"Tighter?" Jude said, and he sounded breathless.

"Do you think the tits are too much?" Lori asked, short-breathed too.

"Let me have a look," Jude said. "Yeah, that's far too much, definitely jelly on a plate. Want me to tie you off

61

now, then?"

"Please," Lori said. "I'm so glad you're here. Rick is useless for this; he just goes all helpless and feeble."

"I'm not saying anything," Jude said. "There you are, you're all double knotted. You'll need to get someone to undo you at the end of the night; those are good solid knots."

"Thanks, love," Lori said.

Luk stalked off, out into the dusk and the backyard. He was right, Lori and Jude were fucking, and he was seriously pissed with them for hiding it from him. He was in the band, too, and they were blocking him out and lying to him. Fuckers.

The dog followed Luk out, sitting beside him in the darkness. Luk thought about just leaving, but he'd only walked to the train station from Lori's house once, and he'd been monged then, and he was monged again, and he'd just get fucking lost in Fremantle somewhere, then beaten up, or arrested, and fucking hell, he was in a shitty mood.

The backdoor to the house creaked, and the dog woofed happily. Lori squatted beside him, crackling faintly in her corset. "You ready to go?"

"Just drop me at the train station," Luk said. "I'm not in the mood to party."

Lori rummaged around in her cleavage, and Jude was right, it really was like jelly on a plate. "Rick left me a treat," she said, fishing out a tiny baggie from between her tits and waggling it at Luk. "Want an E?"

"Free?" Luk asked, as Lori shoved the baggie back, under folds of flesh.

"Free, to celebrate our gig."

"Alright," he said, standing up. "I could do with going to the Hydey and getting trashed."

Lori stood, hanging onto Luk for support. "Me,

too."

At the van, Luk jerked the passenger door open ahead of Lori, and slid across the bench seat in her place. He could do one thing, at least, to stop the whole coy cuddling-in-the-car thing, by getting in the middle himself.

There wasn't a lot of room, not once Luk had got his knee around the hand brake, like Lori had. More fumbling in the dark, because the interior light of the van didn't work, to get the three sets of seatbelts fastened. Then Luk managed to get himself back around the right way, Jude's hand on his thigh, groping for the hand brake.

Lori was chattering, but Luk wasn't sure what about because he wasn't breathing very well. Fuck it, he was supposed to be past the whole stupidly adolescent thing, supposed to be old enough not to be dealing with being suddenly hard. Jude laughed at something Lori had said, low and sexy, his hand sliding down Luk's thigh and finding the hand brake finally, and Luk just about died, right there and then.

Luk could feel sweat prickling his body, pooling against the vinyl seat, his heart banging inside his chest. Jude's leg pinned against him on one side, Lori's on the other, both of their bodies scorching hot in the lingering heat of the day. Luk felt like he was ripped on E already.

"Fuck, it's hot in here," he said. "Does the fan work at all?"

"Lori?" Jude asked. "Do you know?"

"Hang on," Lori said, leaning forward across Luk's knees and rummaging around with the controls on the dash of the van.

"Careful you don't poke yourself on the stick," Jude said, and Luk almost passed out, until he remembered it was dark, that Jude couldn't possibly know that Luk was rock hard inside his jeans, and that the hand brake stuck up alarmingly right into where Lori's ribs were.

"Got it," Lori said, and something whirred and hissed, spitting dust and grime out of the vents of the dash, making the three of them cough and splutter.

The air out of the vent was as warm as the air coming through the open windows, providing no respite. But Luk didn't dare complain, not while Lori and Jude were singing, Jude's fingers drumming on the steering wheel whenever they stopped at traffic lights, the pair of them sounding so cheerful and in tune.

On Stirling Highway, while Jude was overtaking buses, Lori fiddled with her tits, pulling out the baggie. She took one of the tabs, then handed the other one to Luk. He smiled at her when she glanced at him in the streetlight coming in through the windscreen.

"Thanks," he mouthed, slipping the tab into his mouth. He wasn't sure that an E was actually going to help with the whole raging hard-on thing, though it did seem to have eased to being only half-hard, but he wasn't going to knock back free E.

It was going commando that was the problem. He was an idiot for not thinking of that. The feel of his jeans rubbing against his cock was what was driving him crazy, that and not having wanked that morning. He was going to dance himself stupid, drink a shitload of beer, stagger home and have a wank, and it would all be over.

He felt much better.

The Hyde Park Hotel on a Saturday night was always crowded. Jude parked the van blocks away from the pub, and the three of them walked through the suburban streets toward the distant boomthudboom of the hotel, and whichever band was opening for the night.

The queue at the door straggled down the street, but Lori grabbed hold of Luk and Jude's hands and marched to the head of the queue, where two mountainous bouncers stood guard at the entrance to the huge back barn at the hotel.

"Hi, Lori," one of the bouncers shouted. "You here to see Rick and the boys?"

"I am," Lori shouted back, managing to wriggle so her tits jiggled. "This is Luk and Jude; they're with me."

One bouncer lifted the rope across the entrance, while the other one held out the stamp dipped in ultraviolet ink, ready to stamp their wrists. The people waiting at the head of the queue booed and hissed.

"Hang on, you got ID?" the stamping bouncer shouted at Luk over the pound of music.

Luk took out his wallet and found his driver's license, which the bouncer peered at, then handed back. "You're in, mate."

The barn at the back was packed with thrashing bodies. The band on the stage was ripping the place apart, considering they were the opening act, and it was like a fucking oven in there, stifling hot, reeking of sweat and beer.

Luk made beer motions with his hands and pointed at the bar. Lori nodded and pointed at the stage area, which made sense, since she'd want to go find Rick, maybe score some more off him. Jude was off, diving into the mass of dancing bodies, reappearing a moment later, bounding up high briefly, arms over his head.

Luk shook his head. He didn't get Jude. How could someone sneer at the buzz that was rushing through Luk right then, the tingling and the high, yet get so into thrashing around on the floor?

Luk wasn't ready to do that. He wanted to drink a couple of beers, wait for the E to really get into his system before he started moving. Maybe he'd go lock himself in a cubicle, have a wank, too. That'd feel good, with the E in him.

He shoved his way through to the long bar, bought

two beers, and carried them out to the courtyard, where the air was a little cooler. There was nowhere to sit, so he settled for leaning against a brick wall and downing one beer fast to take the edge off his thirst.

Maybe he wouldn't wank in a cubicle; the privacy at the Hydey was useless, and someone was bound to interrupt him.

Lori found him, beer in her hand, before Luk had finished his second. "Hi, there," she said brightly, and Luk could see she was flying.

He held an arm out for her, and she slipped under his arm into his embrace. He was ripped, too; he could feel it.

"What's wrong?" Lori asked. "Really?"

Luk looked down at Lori. "Really? I'm pissed that you and Jude are fucking, and neither of you are ever going to tell me or anything."

Lori's face twisted, and he realized she was trying not to laugh at him.

"Oh, fuck," Luk said. "Go on, tell me how stupid I am."

"Oh, honey," Lori said. "Jude's my friend, a good friend, that's all. But he's gay. If there's anyone here he wants to fuck, it's you, not me."

"I had no idea."

"I thought everyone knew," Lori said. "It's not like he hides it, really. Does this mean you're not in a bad mood anymore?"

Luk drank the last of his beer, in one long swallow. Jude. Gay. Oh, fuck.

Luk kissed Lori's cheek, and shrugged. "I wasn't in a bad mood," he said. "Wanna go jump around?"

"Delicate John is up next. Let's go mosh."

Luk needed to get really, really trashed.

Jude parked the van on the verge at Lori's house, behind Delicate John's rented truck of gear. Beside him, Lori roused herself enough to say, "We home?"

"We are, Your Highness," he said. "Think you can get yourself inside safely?"

In front of their van, the rear doors of the larger truck swung open and the band members of Delicate John began to appear, lifting down speaker stacks and the drum kit.

Jude opened his door and clambered out, glad to stretch his legs and shoulders. His muscles ached from thrashing around on the dance floor, and he needed yet another shower to get rid of the sweat and grime of the night. Lori slid out of the van on the driver's side, rubbing at her face sleepily.

"I'll get Luk inside," Jude said, but Lori stopped him from moving around to the other side of the van, her hand on his arm.

"Wait," she said, her voice low. "Come and undo my corset first."

Jude followed Lori into the house, between band members bearing electrical gear, and into Lori and Rick's bedroom. Lori closed the door and turned her back to Jude, presenting the laces to him.

"What's up, Countess?" Jude said, finding the ends of the laces where he'd tucked them under the edge of the corset for safety.

"I found out why Luk's been so shitty," Lori said. "He thought you and I were shagging."

Jude blinked, then thought about it while he picked at the double knot securing Lori's corset lacing. "Public declarations of affection," he said. "Kisses. Secrets."

"And you lace up my corset," Lori added.

"You sorted that out?" Jude asked, getting the knot undone and hearing Lori sigh with relief at the pressure easing on her ribs.

"Told him you were gay," Lori said. "Hope that was the right thing to do."

"I've got no problems with that," Jude said, beginning to slip the laces looser, slowly. "It's not like I'm closeted."

"Thing is," Lori said. "Thing is, I think he fancies you."

The laces were undone, the tension off the corset, and Lori began to wriggle it down.

"Luk's not straight?" Jude asked, frowning at the potential complications. Things would be easier for the The Tockleys if everyone knew what was going on, which they obviously didn't.

"I flashed him my tits at the beach, and he didn't even look," Lori said, easing the corset over her hips and stepping out of it. "He was too busy eyeing you off."

Jude rubbed his hands thoughtfully, playing back the afternoon at the beach. He hadn't noticed Lori showing her boobs around, but he wouldn't necessarily. He had taken a good long look at Luk, though, when the kid had stomped off up the beach, sulking. He was hot, in a sleek and adolescent way...

"Jude?" Lori asked, turning around. "Are you going to go all moody on me now?"

Jude smiled in a way he hoped was reassuring and shook his head. "No, I'm just a little, um, surprised, that's all."

"Do you like him?" Lori asked, peeling her chemise off her ribs. "Do you fancy the little brat?"

Jude crossed his arms and shook his head at Lori. "Stop it," he said. "He's a kid, and I'm just not in the right place for anything to happen."

Lori stripped her chemise off, then undid her bra, so she was standing topless. "I can't believe you're still talking about becoming a monk."

"Not a monk, just going on a long retreat, eventually,"

Jude said. "I'm open to the possibility of committing myself to a spiritual path."

The bedroom door opened, and Rick looked around the door. "Stop showing your gay boyfriend your boobs," he said. "Hi, Jude."

"Hi, Rick," Jude said. "I'll get out of your way."

"Thanks," Rick said. "I'm exhausted, and I want my bed and Lori, together."

"Go drag Luk out of the van," Lori said, tossing her chemise at Jude. "Make him sleep on a blanket in the kitchen. You can have the spare mattress in the back room. Unless, of course, you decide to share the mattress with him."

Jude didn't bother trying to sort that one out with Lori, and went to find Luk.

House rules were that the designated driver got the prime sleeping accommodation in the bedroom the equipment was stored in, with a mattress and a pillow. Everyone else who crashed there had to take their chances on the floor, with the dog for company.

Jude deposited Luk, still outrageously drunk or drug-fucked, on the kitchen floor with a blanket over him, and the pitbull, then went to bed himself.

He woke during the night to the sound of someone blundering around the house. He could hear voices, and an acoustic guitar and ukulele playing out on the front porch, so some of the household occupants were still awake. Not a burglary, just someone going to the loo.

The toilet flushed, then water gurgled in the bathroom on the other side of the wall from Jude, and someone gargled and spat. Pale lemon streetlight slanted into the room through uncurtained windows, and the wind outside had picked up, rattling the windows.

The door to the room squeaked open, and when Jude propped himself up on one elbow, Luk was standing in the doorway, blanket around his shoulders.

"Can I sleep in here?" Luk said, and he sounded pathetic. "I think there're rats in the kitchen or something, and the dog was eating one."

Jude hated rats. Really hated them.

"Hop in," Jude said, lifting up his blanket. "As long as you're not going to throw up."

"Promise," Luk said.

He clambered in beside Jude, elbows and knees, loose-limbed like he was still half-asleep or fully-wasted, his clothes smelling of cigarette smoke and beer.

Jude turned onto his side, his back to Luk, his eyes closed resolutely. Lori was going to give him so much shit in the morning for this, if she found out.

Luk's hand touched Jude's back, fingers splayed across the bare skin, making Jude regret stripping down to his boxers to sleep. "Don't," Jude said, his voice low.

"Why not?" Luk asked, and yeah, he was still off his face, his voice warm and indecent in the dark.

The hand slid lower, down Jude's back, and Jude's body was there, ready to go, responding to the feeling, to someone else's warmth, to just being touched.

Jude reached behind himself, grabbed Luk's hand, and rolled over. "Luk..." he whispered.

Damn, Luk was right up against him now, his body scorching hot, legs tangled with the blankets, his mouth just waiting to be kissed.

Jude leaned forward and pressed his mouth against Luk's in the barest of kisses, and it was a stupid, stupid thing to do, but he couldn't help it. Luk kissed him back, his mouth open and eager, then suddenly Luk had control of Jude's hand, and was pushing it down between their bodies, toward Luk's jeans.

Luk's cock was long and hard, full of promise through his jeans, when Jude pressed the palm of his hand against it. Jude lifted his mouth off Luk's, trailing spit, both of them breathing hard.

"Touch me?" Luk whispered, sounding desperate, and Jude jerked his hand away.

"I can't," Jude said, pushing the blankets back and reaching for his own jeans, where he'd left them draped over an amp. "I'm not doing this when you're wasted."

He stood up and dragged his jeans on, yanking the zip done up over his painfully hard cock, then found his shirt where he'd tossed it behind the door, with his sneakers.

He glanced back at Luk, who was blinking at Jude confusedly. "I'm sorry," Jude said, then he closed the door before he could change his mind.

He was an idiot, and it wasn't like Lori hadn't tried to warn him.

The front porch light was on, and the bass guitarist and singer from Delicate John were still out there, talking and smoking. They both nodded to Jude when he paused on the front steps to put his sneakers on.

"Could you let Lori know I've gone to catch the first train?" Jude said, and the singer, a mad man named Robbo, nodded.

"It's only four," Robbo said. "Did you want to take Rick's van home instead?"

Jude shook his head. "No, thanks. I'll walk down to Maccas, grab a muffin first. I need to walk for a while."

Robbo shrugged. "Sure," he said. "We all have nights like that."

Jude walked off into the windy darkness of the night, his guitar slung across his back. He doubted that many people did have nights like he'd just had, whatever Robbo said. Still, if it had happened to Robbo, he'd have written a song about it, and set it to ukulele.

At least Jude didn't play the ukulele.

Chapter Six

Jude slept enough, waking some time in the early afternoon, feeling like he wasn't exhausted. The sheet over him was sweaty, but no more, and he groaned silently in frustration. He'd hoped that falling into bed exhausted and horny would do it, that he'd wake up and his subconscious would have punished him suitably with some twisted dream about fucking a girl, but there he was, naked and rock hard, and responsible for dealing with it himself.

His housemates were up and about; he could hear footsteps in the hallway outside his bedroom, and the shower running at the back of the house.

Jude double-checked that his bedroom door was closed, just in case.

The door didn't move. He was out of excuses, unless he wanted to remain outrageously frustrated.

Jude wrapped both hands around his cock, gripping himself hard, making the nerve endings jump, so he had to grit his teeth to stay quiet. This was going to be quick and dirty.

He let himself remember how Luk had touched his back, and how they'd kissed, and began to rock his hips, pushing his cock into his hands. The feel of Luk's cock through his jeans, the way he'd asked Jude to touch him, and Jude was coming, trying not to think about Luk fucking him, about what might have happened if Jude had stayed.

Ten minutes later, Jude pulled on a pair of jeans and dragged the sheets off his bed. Shower first, then load the washing machine.

Alison, housemate number one, looked up from the living room when Jude walked past, still wet from the shower.

"Late night, hon?" she called out.

Jude paused, part way through pulling his last clean T-shirt over his head. "Yeah," he said, once he'd got his head through. "Came home on the first train. I tried to be quiet."

"I was awake already," Alison said. "No problems there. So, is this a romantic adventure, at long last?"

Jude smiled at Alison and shook his head, but he mustn't have looked convincing enough because Alison appeared in the kitchen a couple of minutes later, while Jude was putting the plug in the sink and turning the taps on.

"You're washing dishes?" Alison said. "Hey, Sammie, you want to see this!"

Sammie, housemate number two, opened the back door a moment later, blinking at the change from the bright daylight to the gloom of the interior. "Dishes?" Sammie asked. "No one washes dishes; it's in the house rules. Why are you doing the dishes?"

Jude found the detergent, buried under the mess, and squeezed it into the water. "Because I stayed somewhere last night that had rats in the kitchen. Alright?"

Alison clattered behind Jude, switching the kettle on. "Tea, Sammie?"

"Too right," Sammie said. "I want to watch this. Something is going on with Jude. He just put his sheets in the washing machine, too."

"It's a love affair," Alison said. "For sure."

Jude turned the taps off and looked over his shoulder at his housemates, who were leaning against the fridge and the counter, watching him. It wasn't easy to be annoyed at them, really.

"I've met someone," Jude said, and Sammie and Alison both whooped with delight, stopping him from going on.

He gave them a moment to calm down. "So, I met someone. I thought I didn't like him, and that he was an immature prat, and straight. Then I liked him anyway."

"Doomed," Alison said, and Sammie nodded.

"You could do something about him being straight, but once a prat, always a prat," Sammie said.

Jude waved a dishcloth at his two housemates, dripping water on the floor. "Do you want to hear this or not?"

"Sorry," Alison said. "Go on."

"Anyway, he's been less prat-like, in general," Jude said. "Almost human. Definitely likeable."

Sammie said, "Now you just have to flip him. He does bathe, doen't he?"

The kettle whistled, and Alison leaned around Jude, opening the empty cupboard where, in theory, clean cups would be kept, if anyone had washed them. "Tea for you, Jude?"

"Please," Jude said. "I'll wash three mugs."

He washed three mugs quickly, propping them on the draining board he'd just scrubbed. The rats in Lori's kitchen were at least part of the reason for the clean up. He hated rats. He hated feeling out of control, too,

74

and he was scrabbling for control when it came to Luk. Sublimation, that would have to do.

"I think he's interested," Jude said, when Alison balanced a mug of peppermint tea on the windowsill in front of Jude.

"Yes!" Sammie squealed, making fist-pumping motions that Jude could see in his peripheral vision.

He turned around to face his two excitable housemates. Sammie was the model of composure, perched on the edge of the table, sipping her tea. "So, if I turn up here with someone, you both will try not to be too hideous, right?"

Sammie shrugged. "No suggestions? No commentary?"

Jude narrowed his eyes, studying Alison and Sammie. He liked the pair of them, and the walls were too thin to ever consider having secrets from them anyway.

"Nothing," Jude said. "No matter how unlikely he is."

Alison's smile widened. "Unlikely? Oohh, what's wrong with him?"

Jude turned back to the dishes. He did not need to work up a list of ways in which Luk was wrong, just to amuse his housemates. One glance at Luk would say it all.

"We're going to the Dhamma talk this afternoon," Sammie said. "Do you want to come along?"

"What's on?" Jude asked. "Because I'm not in the right frame of mind for a talk on the evils of desire and attachment."

Sammie peered at a printout taped to the fridge. "Ajahn M is talking about despair and world peace, then there's a guided meditation, presumably on the same theme. Is that going to tax your hormones too much?"

Jude flicked dishwater at Sammie. "I think I can sit

still and be respectful for a couple of hours, despite the raging storm in my loins."

Alison shuddered. "That's gross, Jude. You can't say that sort of thing while you're washing the dishes."

"You want me to stop?" Jude lifted both hands so detergent bubbles ran down his arms to his elbows.

"We're leaving," Sammie said. "Right now."

When Alison and Sammie had gone back to the living room and the backyard, Jude pulled the plug out of the sink and drained the water out, then refilled the sink. They had a lot of dirty dishes, and he had a lot of sublimation to get sorted out before he'd be able to focus at a talk.

Loud People was empty when Jude pushed the door open late on Monday afternoon. He dumped his pack beside the door, and wandered up to the counter in search of Lori.

Lori was perched behind the counter, nodding her head in time to the classic Stones playing over the speakers and tapping at the PC keyboard in front of her, but she glanced up at Jude and grinned at him.

"Hi, hon," she said. "Want some tea?"

"Tea would be good," Jude said, leaning against the counter and handing over a chamomile tea bag he'd brought in with him.

Lori lifted a delicate eyebrow at him in mute query, but didn't say anything, just disappeared behind the faded curtain behind her. A moment later, a kettle began to hum.

Guess he looked as morose as he felt, then.

The kettle whistled, and a fridge door squeaked open and shut, then Lori was back, carrying two mugs of tea.

"There you go," Lori said, sliding a mug across the

counter toward Jude. "Tea and sympathy. Tell Countess Lori all about it."

The shop door chimed, and Luk called out, "Hi, there," which saved Jude from having to answer.

He turned to look at Luk over his shoulder, but Luk looked exactly the same as ever: kind of ditzy and adolescent and self-absorbed.

Self-absorbed? Jude pointed a great big metaphorical finger at himself.

"Hey," Lori said. "All over your hangover?"

"All gone," Luk said. He hitched himself up onto the counter beside Jude, whacking Jude randomly with his boot. "Thanks, mate, for giving me your bed on Saturday night. I can just about remember crawling in there, complaining about that fucking dog chewing on rats. That was mighty noble of you to go home so I could sleep in comfort."

"Not a problem," Jude said. "You were pretty out of it, and it was nearly time for the first train anyway. I got home at about six, went to bed and slept until the afternoon, all in blissful comfort."

Blissful, solitary comfort.

"Jude was moping when you came in," Lori said. "I was just about to force him to open up. Want to gang up on him? You start in while I go make you a cuppa."

"Wassup?" Luk asked.

Jude patted Luk's shoulder. "I was being all angsty at Lori, but it was no big deal. I've just had a shitty day at work. How was the first day of semester?"

Luk grimaced. "They're crazy. I have to go to classes and shit like that. I dunno if this degree thing is worth it."

"I've heard you play, and if that's what you're learning, then I don't think you can complain," Jude said.

Luk colored, managing to look embarrassed, and Jude

wondered if he really had blacked out everything that had happened in Lori's spare room, or if he was a damned fine actor as well as musician.

Lori sloshed a cup of tea across the counter to Luk and leaned forward, elbows on the counter, chin on her hands. Her shirt gaped open, displaying a considerable amount of cleavage and black lace, and that time Jude remembered to check if Luk had noticed.

Luk was still recovering from blushing, fiddling with the notebook scribbled with musical notation he'd retrieved from his pack, flicking through ink-smeared pages nervously.

When Jude caught Lori's eye, she was perched on her work chair, cup of tea in her hands, looking smug.

"So," Lori said. "The idea is to make some plans, work on our arrangements here, where we can't be distracted by jamming. Then, later in the week, we'll do a full rehearsal, either at my place, or at Maddie's if Luk can arrange it, to put it all together."

"I've made some notes," Luk said, pushing his workbook forward. "For Lori's song, and mine, based on the arrangements we worked on last time. And I've worked up a full arrangement for Jude's song from memory, so I might not have got it quite right. Sorry, mate."

"You can remember a song you've heard once? Words and chords?" Jude asked.

Luk shrugged. "Yeah, well, it's just a knack. Other people obsess about cars and things." He looked up, and the ditzy adolescent was gone, for a moment. "What about you two? What do you both obsess about?"

Lori shrugged. "Getting through each day," she said. "Don't get me wrong, I love drumming and wouldn't want to give it up for anything, but sometimes I just want life to calm down."

Luk's gaze was on Jude's face, and Jude was only

distantly aware of Lori, and 'Angie' playing over the shop sound system.

"I obsess about living an honorable life," Jude said. "I like to play music, it brings me joy, but I couldn't do it if it was hurting someone, or if it wasn't honest."

"Oh," Luk said, and Jude was damned sure they both knew what he was talking about.

Lori tapped Luk's notebook with her dark purple fingernails. "If Jude can put his Buddhism away for a moment, can we do some work?"

After they'd finished, Jude waited outside Loud People while Lori locked the shop up, and Luk hung around, peering through the shop windows between the tour posters, scuffling his feet, pack over one shoulder, guitar case over the other.

"You did good work," Jude said. "On the arrangements."

Luk bounced back to the shop door, where Jude leaned against the frame. "Thanks. Are you for real about being a Buddhist? Is that why you're Straight Edge?"

Jude nodded. "Yeah. It's really important to me; it's part of everything I do, including music. Does it make a difference to you? Is this an issue for The Tockleys?"

The light in the doorway was dim, coming sideways down the flight of steps from the street, and the steps smelled faintly of urine. Luk hopped up a step, so he was the same height as Jude. "I wish I'd known," Luk said quietly.

He was close to Jude, right beside him, and Jude brushed his fingertips against Luk's hand. "We can talk," Jude said. "About what happened. About anything."

Luk's skin was warm and dry against Jude's fingers, and his eyes went wide, but he didn't run. He stayed there on the step, while buses rattled past on the street up above, and Jude's fingertips found the twisted veins on the back of his hands.

"I'm not..." Luk said. "I didn't..."

The door behind Jude rattled, squeaking open, and Lori called out, "Hey, you both waited for me!"

Jude drew his hand back, and Luk bolted up the steps and was gone.

Lori slammed the door, holding it shut while she locked it, then said, "Where's Luk? He was here a moment ago."

"Had to run to catch a bus, I think," Jude said. "He waited as long as he could."

Lori smiled at Jude. "Good afternoon?"

"That was a good session; we got a lot of work done."

Lori slid her hand into Jude's elbow, steadying herself on her heels. "It was. Walk me to my bus stop?"

"That was why I waited for you."

"Lucien?" Luk's mother called, when Luk tried to slide past the kitchen unnoticed. "Is that you?"

"Yes," Luk said, pausing in the hallway, but not bothering to put down his guitar or backpack. "At least, I think it is."

His mother appeared in the doorway, small and fretful, tea towel in one hand. "I'm just about to serve up dinner. Are you going to eat with us? I'd like to hear about your classes, and maybe that band you're in."

Sitting down to dinner with his parents was torture, something Luk avoided as much as he could, but his bedroom and his guitar didn't seem like much of a refuge, not right then.

"Alright, Mum," Luk said.

At the table, Luk's sister Penny stared at him, and his

father sniffed disapprovingly when Luk sat down.

"Did you wash your hands?" Luk's father asked.

"Yes," Luk lied, hiding his inky hands in his lap. He'd spent the bus ride home staring at the back of his hand where Jude had touched him, trying to work out what it had all meant.

We can talk. About what happened. About anything.

Luk's mother set a plate of food in front of him, something with chicken and rice in it, and Luk remembered Lori's kitchen all over again.

"Tell me about your classes," Luk's mother said, and Luk looked up at her from his plate of food. He could do that much, and get through the meal at least.

Once Luk's father had pushed his chair back from the table and gone grumbling off to watch the news on the TV, Luk reached for Penny's plate. "I'll clear," he said to her.

Penny sneered at him and whispered, "Suck," but she didn't stop him, just disappeared off to her room, leaving Luk to follow his mother into the kitchen, carrying used plates.

"Mum," Luk said, keeping his voice low, one hand on her arm while she fiddled with the dirty plates. "Mum, can I ask you something?"

Luk's mother stood up, wiping her hands on a tea towel. "What is it?" she asked. "Are you in trouble? Is it drugs?"

"No," Luk said. "Nothing like that."

His mother waited expectantly, and Luk stared at her, trying to work out where to start, when he didn't even know what was going on himself.

"It doesn't matter," he said.

She nodded, looking relieved. "Go and do your study, dear. I'll clean up in here."

In his bedroom, his door secured against surprise

sibling raids, Luk threw himself on his bed, burying his face in his pillow.

He was fucked.

About what happened.

He'd persuaded himself, right up until the moment that Jude had said that, that he'd dreamed touching Jude. It had been a beer-and-E fueled wet dream, he'd been so sure of that, even when Jude had started talking about honest music.

But, fuck, it hadn't been a dream, and Luk had really thrown himself at Jude, and Jude had kissed him. And Luk had asked Jude to touch him.

Luk groaned, into his pillow.

He was not dealing with this.

Luk was late for rehearsal, dragging himself up the long hill from the Fremantle train station through the sticky heat. He hadn't slept, had skipped classes and stayed home, and he really didn't want to be at Lori's place, walking into a rehearsal in her garage on a sweltering Wednesday afternoon. But, unless he rang Lori at Loud People during the day, there was no other way to contact her. People were supposed to have mobile phones and internet connections.

Lori, wearing only a bikini top and a sarong in the scorching heat, pinned an escaping braid to the top of her head and looked up from hot-wiring the sound board in the garage, waving a pair of pliers at Luk.

"Hi, hon," Lori said. "Can you flick the power on at the power board?"

"Sure," Luk said, reaching up and switching on the power board that dangled from the rafters. "Where's Jude?"

"Gone to buy circuit breakers for the house," Lori said. "We fused the place, trying to power up the rig. Still no juice in the sound board. Let's get out of this sauna, at least until Jude gets back."

Lori sat on the steps to the back verandah, picking at loose nails with the pliers, and Luk squatted on the dead grass in front of her.

"Lori," Luk said. "There's something--"

The door to the house squeaked open, and Jude waved a paper bag from a hardware store at Lori and Luk. "Hi, Luk," he said.

Luk swallowed, not able to get his throat to work.

Lori stood up and took the paper bag out of Jude's hands. "Let's put these babies in place, get some power out the back."

When Lori turned around to follow Jude back through the house, Jude's T-shirt was stuck to his skin with sweat, and Luk was back inside the memory of reaching out and touching Jude's back, the feel of his skin stretched thin over his spine, the pound of his heart against his ribs.

"I'm quitting," Luk said, standing up and wiping the grit from his hands onto his T-shirt.

Lori turned and looked at Luk, and Jude reappeared in the doorway to the house.

"Quitting The Tockleys?" Lori asked, frowning.

Luk nodded. "Yeah."

Lori pursed her lips, so they blanched white in the creases. She looked thoroughly pissed off. Jude, behind Lori, looked bewildered, rather than angry.

"Is it because of him?" Lori asked, jabbing a finger over her shoulder at Jude.

Luk felt himself flush with embarrassment.

"Right," Lori said. She turned around and hissed at Jude, "Idiot. Sort it out."

When she turned back to Luk, she shrugged. "Let's

be clear about one thing. If the two of you can't resolve whatever drama is going on, then it's Jude that's out the band, not you, Luk. I'm going to go have yet another cold shower, and a beer. When I come back, this had better be settled, one way or another."

She shoved past Jude and slammed the back door of the house hard enough to rattle the window beside it.

"Damn," Jude said.

Luk stood there, late afternoon sun blasting against the back of his neck, incinerating his skin, and he couldn't remember feeling quite so embarrassed before, at least not since the beginning of high school.

Jude dropped down the steps from the verandah, grubby feet in worn sandals. "Come on," he said. "Let's at least go for a walk, somewhere there's not quite so many people watching."

Watching?

Luk glanced at the kitchen window, where it seemed that half of the independent music scene in the city was lined up, faces pressed to the glass.

"Just when I thought it couldn't get any worse," Luk muttered, shoving his hands in his jeans and ducking his head.

He followed Jude down the side of the house and out past the wrecked cars to the street. Rush hour traffic roared past, and the heat rolling off the street made the air painful to breathe. "Where are we going?" Luk asked.

Jude pointed, to the traffic lights at the next intersection. "There's a football oval there; it's got to be cooler, and have fewer observers."

The grass on the oval was dry, crackling underfoot, but the wilting trees around the perimeter provided some shade. Luk threw himself on the dead grass under the first tree. "Was Lori serious? About firing you?"

"I believe so," Jude said, sitting down beside Luk. "I

guess she weighed your guitar playing against my sober driving, and opted for music over transport, which is, of course, the right choice. She can always find someone else to play indifferent guitar and sing a bit. She might even find someone who owns a car or a van. But she's not going to be able to replace your playing."

Luk nodded.

"Or," Jude said. "We could resolve this."

Some stupid kids were playing on the oval, running around with a dog in the heat, and Luk watched them for a moment.

"So I really hit on you?" Luk asked. "I'm not imagining that?"

Jude was fiddling with gumnuts when Luk glanced at him, and it was the first indication Luk had seen that Jude was not completely comfortable talking. "Yes, you hit on me. And I kissed you. Then I left, before things got even more confused."

Jude glanced up from the gumnuts, and he looked like Luk had kicked him or something.

"If I hadn't kissed you, I think we might have been able to call this whole thing Luk Behaves Badly, and it would all have gone away," Jude continued. "But I made things a whole lot more complicated, and I'm sorry for that. I wasn't really ready to admit even to myself that I liked you, and now it's become a band issue."

Luk looked back at the kids on the oval, the seagulls swooping above them and the dog jumping up at the seagulls. The kids must have food, to be attracting the gulls.

"This is hideously embarrassing," Luk said, and when he glanced at Jude, Jude was smiling wryly.

"I had noticed. What do you want to do? Do you want me to leave The Tockleys?"

"That doesn't seem fair," Luk said. "I'm an idiot, and

you have to leave."

"I think the theory is, at least from Lori's point of view, that I didn't handle it well, which makes it all my fault," Jude said. "Are you going to be comfortable knowing that I like you? How are you going to feel, since I'm guessing something is going on for you, in terms of identity?"

Luk went bright red; he could feel his cheeks and ears burning. He didn't want to talk to anyone, ever, about that, didn't want to even begin to think about it. He'd been doing everything he could, ever since he'd known for sure he'd touched Jude, to not think about what it might mean, and how turned on he'd been.

Jude was still studying Luk, his gaze steady and accepting, when Luk glanced back at him an eternity later. "I'm gay," Jude said gently. "Do you really think I don't know how difficult it is to make that first step?"

"My family..." Luk said, trailing off at the thought of his father.

Jude nodded. "They'll either accept you, or not. There are only two options. Do you want to live your life in your parents' shadows? Do you always want to define who you are by their limitations? Whether you're gay, or queer, or just trying stuff out before settling down with some girl named Brianna who rides a moped and breeds ferrets, this has to be about you, and only you."

"I've never really got into sex," Luk said. "Fucked a few girls, but it was kind of sad and strange, and I couldn't see what the fuss was. So I figured the girls were the wrong girls, that when I got to uni, it would be different, that I'd feel different about them..."

"But?" Jude asked, and his voice was low and kind.

Luk shook his head. "I thought everyone else was just lying about fucking, that it was hugely overrated with an extravagant advertising budget and some classy publicists. What if it's me? How could I not notice?"

"We're living in a straight world," Jude said. "The dominant cultural, religious, legal and social structures want you to believe you're straight, too. It's called hetero-centrist."

"Oh, for fuck's sake," Luk said. "I'm nineteen. How could I not know what my dick likes?"

Jude burst out laughing, and when Luk looked back at him, Jude was sprawled back on the brown grass, one arm over his face, his T-shirt riding up over his shaking belly.

"What's so fucking funny?" Luk demanded, but playing back the conversation, he could see why Jude was laughing, and began to laugh, too.

Jude sat up again, shuffling forward so he was beside Luk, and Luk found himself returning Jude's smile, still laughing.

"Can we forget I said that?" Luk said.

Jude's eyes, warm and brown, held Luk's gaze. "Are we good?" Jude asked.

Luk nodded. "Yeah, we're good."

Jude smiled, creasing the skin around his mouth. "Good."

Luk jumped up, and Jude stood beside him, gumnuts stuck to his T-shirt and in his hair. "We should head back," Jude said. "Reassure Lori that I'm not an idiot, and that you're still gonna play guitar for her."

"Wait," Luk said, grabbing hold of Jude's arm. "You've got..."

He was going to pick some of the gumnuts out of Jude's hair, at least, except now he was standing right in front of Jude, hanging onto him, trying to work out what the fuck to do.

"Luk," Jude said, his voice sounding strained, though his eyes were still laughing. "Firstly, I only have a finite amount of patience. And secondly, if you're not wasted,

I'm going to assume you mean any advances you make."

Luk pulled a gumnut out of Jude's hair, extracting it carefully from the strands that were held back in Jude's braid, and Jude's hands settled on Luk's ribs, pressing his sweat-damp shirt against his skin gently.

"Is this what you want?" Jude asked.

Luk let both hands rest on Jude, trying out the feel of Jude's body heat through his worn T-shirt. Luk could feel Jude's bicep moving a little as one hand slid down Luk's back, pulling Luk in closer. The other hand moved up to Luk's neck, touching the bare skin there, and Luk closed his eyes and tilted his head up.

Jude exhaled, sharp and sudden, sounding exasperated, then his mouth was moving down Luk's jaw. "I'm not a monk," Jude muttered, his lips on Luk's skin. "Whatever Lori might say."

The tension inside Luk, waiting for the feel of Jude's mouth against his own, was just about enough to make him faint, but when he opened his eyes, Jude was hovering above him, pupils huge, tongue dragging across bottom lip.

Jude was serious about making Luk ask for this. Right at that moment, with Jude's fingers circling gently on the back of Luk's neck, so that ripples of fire spread out through Luk's body, Luk could do that.

"Yeah," Luk said. "I wanna try this."

Jude's lips were gentle, like they'd been the night of craziness, but Luk gripped Jude's arms tightly, pressing his mouth urgently against Jude's, wanting more, wanting everything, right then.

When Jude pulled back, lifting his mouth slowly, Luk was breathing fast, and he didn't want it to end.

Luk should be embarrassed, snogging another man in daylight in a park while cars whizzed past and kids squealed nearby, but maybe he was all out of embarrassment, used up by the earlier humiliation, or maybe it was all overridden by the need roaring through his body, leaving him hard and trembling.

"More?" Jude asked.

Fuck, if he needed to ask, then Luk wasn't standing close enough.

"Yeah, more."

"Then we need to sit down, because my knees aren't going to survive this," Jude said.

Luk wanted to ask what 'this' was, but it might slow Jude down, and that would be a bad thing. Jude led Luk over to the nearest tree, sitting down underneath it and pulling Luk down with him, so Luk straddled him.

The ground was rough under Luk's knees, gumnuts and rubble digging into his knees through his jeans, and the gum tree Jude was leaning against was coarse when Luk braced one hand against it.

Kneeling over Jude, Luk could lean into kissing instead of looking up, and it was even hotter, being able to click his teeth against Jude's and kiss thoroughly.

Jude kissed back, one hand under Luk's shirt at the back, sliding up his sweat-slick back, slipping across his skin, until Jude's hand got enough of a grip to pull Luk farther forward.

If Luk had any doubts about Jude, there was all the proof he needed right there, and somehow Luk hadn't thought of that, of what it'd be like to have another man's cock rubbing up against his groin, through his jeans. It was fucking hot.

Luk gasped against Jude's mouth, and Jude leaned his head back against the tree. "Think we might need to slow down a little," he said.

Luk nodded. He glanced down at their crotches. His own cock was straining at his jeans, held back by a layer of denim and cotton underneath, so hard it hurt.

Jude had obviously dressed for the heat in loose cotton drawstring shorts, which were doing nothing in the way of containment, his cock standing up thick and fat and hard under the thin material.

"Fuck," Luk whispered. This was real; he was making out with another bloke, there was no way he could avoid admitting that.

"In case you hadn't noticed, you're driving me crazy," Jude said, his hand gliding down Luk's back, brushing down across the top of Luk's jeans.

Luk wiped his hand on his shirt, then reached down tentatively, pressing his fingertips against the shape of Jude's cock through the cotton. Jude moaned, and Luk kissed him again. He didn't care if kids were screaming, and traffic was beeping horns. He didn't care if it was swelteringly hot, and ants were crawling up his jeans. He didn't care about anyone else's rules, or about what might happen next.

Jude's hand closed over Luk's, squeezing his fingers around the thickness of Jude's cock, then lifting his hand away. Luk went to protest, but the feel of Jude's fingers rubbing through his jeans stopped him.

"See?" Jude said. "You really want to walk back into Lori's place having creamed yourself?"

Luk shook his head.

"Neither do I, and that's what's about to happen."

When Luk glanced down, dampness was spreading through the cotton of Jude's shorts where the fabric was pulled tight. Something about the sight, about what it meant, was almost more than he could bear.

"Hey," Jude said, touching Luk's face, lifting his chin so Luk couldn't avoid his gaze. "Don't go tying yourself up in knots about this."

"It's not that," Luk said. "Take me home, after rehearsal."

"You want to come back to my house?" Jude said.

Luk nodded.

Jude grinned. "Does this mean you've decided it's not all just advertising?"

Luk leaned his head forward. "I dunno, but I'm so hard it hurts."

"Get off me," Jude said. "Because I'm about to come here."

"Fuck," Luk said, scrambling off Jude.

They walked back to Lori's house through the dusk, after Jude had stalked around the now empty oval alone, trying to persuade his cock to calm down enough for him to be able to go back. The garage was lit up, so the new circuit breakers worked, and when Luk pushed the garage door open, Lori was sitting at her drum kit, headphones on, practicing.

She looked up and pushed the headphones off, wiping the sweat from her face. "Well?" she asked.

"We've sorted it out," Jude said. "We're both staying."

Lori lifted her eyebrows, and Luk studied the cracked concrete floor. "Very interesting," she said. "Not what I'd expected, though definitely the best option for the band. Get set up, and let's get going."

Luk's gear was where he'd left it on the trolley, so he undid the amp case and lifted the amp out. When he looked up from plugging his amp and speaker into the power board, Lori was sitting behind her drum kit still, arms crossed, studying him smugly.

And when Lori was counting them into 'Not the Only One,' Jude caught his eye, and they shared a smile. That was when it occurred to Luk what was about to happen. He was going home with Jude. He wasn't exactly a virgin, under the circumstances, but it was another threshold he was crossing.

Jude bounced around the garage, swinging his ancient lead guitar around, Lori thrashed the drums, while Luk drove the bass line right through the song, all of them soaked with sweat in the stinking heat, and it seemed to Luk it was the best rehearsal they'd had so far.

Chapter Seven

T he walk downhill to the train station was still unpleasantly warm, even though the sun had set a couple of hours before. The sea breeze, blowing in cool every summer afternoon, locally called the Fremantle Doctor because of its ability to soothe all ills, had failed completely that day, leaving the city baking in residual heat radiating from pavements and roadways.

Luk handed Jude the bottle of water he'd filled in Lori's kitchen, and switched the hand he was using to pull the trolley holding his amp and speaker. His guitar case strap dug into his shoulder through his shirt, and sweat trickled down his back.

Jude drank deeply and handed the empty bottle back.

The train was air-conditioned, and Luk sank onto one of the long benches gratefully, dragging his guitar case strap over his head and propping the case on the seat beside him. The carriage was almost empty, halfway through the evening, so there was room for Jude to sprawl beside Luk, his guitar and pack on the other side of him.

"Changed your mind?" Jude asked, ignoring the glares

of the transit guard who was glowering at the pair of them from the end of the carriage. "You can always just get off the train in the city and catch your usual bus home."

Luk shook his head. "Nah, I've not changed my mind."

The hum from the rehearsal, always good, had wrapped itself around the tightness in Luk's belly, so that every time he'd glanced at Jude during the rehearsal, his cock had leapt at the memory of them kissing.

Fuck, Luk had never been into kissing before. It had always been a bit messy and yuck, somehow distasteful, like all of sex had been, but now...

"I can tell what you're thinking about," Jude said, and he moved his arm from where it was draped across the back of the seat, so his fingers rested against Luk's neck, just where Luk's hair started.

"Fuck, can you?" Luk said, before he realized Jude was teasing him. At least he hadn't looked down at his own crotch, to make sure he wasn't showing too much.

Jude grinned, sliding closer on the seat, so he was right beside Luk. Luk could look at Jude's crotch, that would be fine.

Except, now, Luk couldn't breathe.

"Having trouble believing you're doing this?" Jude asked.

Jude's fingers were inside the back of Luk's shirt, rubbing each side of his spine, and when Luk turned his head to look at Jude, Jude was leaning forward.

"You can't--" Luk said, but obviously Jude could, because his mouth covered Luk's, his lips moving slowly.

As a kiss, it was a world away from what had happened at the oval, brief and gentle, but it still did things to Luk, made him all twisty inside, so he hurt.

When Jude pulled away, the transit guard was standing in front of them.

"Tickets, please," the guard said.

Luk swallowed hard, rummaging through his pockets to find his travel pass, which the transit guard scanned with a look of distaste and handed back.

When the guard had checked Jude's pass, too, he moved back to the end of the carriage, where he'd been standing before.

"What the fuck was his problem?" Luk muttered, slouching back on the bench, out of sight of the guard who was still staring at them. "Why's the fucking transit guard watching us like that?"

"He probably has opinions about people making out on his train. I'm well acquainted with the local legislation covering public decency," Jude said. "So far, we're on solid ground."

Luk looked at Jude, who was leaning back on the bench too, turned sideways to face Luk. "You've been arrested?"

"Not for making out on the train," Jude said. "Got busted at a Big Day Out gig, getting heavy with my ex."

Luk nodded. Big Day Out was a huge music festival, twelve hours of beer, heat, dust and noise. A lot of people got arrested, for a lot of things.

"What happened?" Luk asked.

"Community service order," Jude said. "Long gone now, since this was a couple of years ago."

"I thought Straight Edgers never got into trouble," Luk said. "You're all so damned well-behaved."

"You've never seen any of the Headbangers for Christ get angry, have you?" Jude asked. "At least, if I'm messing around, you know I mean it."

They were back to the room at Lori's place, when Luk had touched Jude. "I'm not trashed now," Luk said.

Jude moved his hand so it rested on Luk's thigh, like it had in the van. "Yeah, I'd noticed. We wouldn't even be talking about doing this otherwise."

Transit Guard Man appeared in the aisle, over Jude's shoulder, but Luk didn't fucking care. "What's 'this'? What are we going to do?" Luk asked.

"Do you remember what you asked me to do, that night?" Jude asked.

Luk nodded. Jude's hand on his thigh inched a little higher, and Luk didn't give a damn that that there was some bastard with a two way radio and a night stick only a couple of meters away, he was so close to just losing it.

"We'll do that."

"You two, cool it," the transit guard said.

Jude lifted his hand off Luk's leg, acting innocent, and Luk tipped his head back against the cold plastic of the carriage wall, and half-closed his eyes.

"Oh, fuck," he said weakly.

Jude slid his arm out from around Luk's shoulders and sprawled back in the seat. Luk was glad of the space, of the chance to get back in control of his pulse and his libido.

He was not going to let himself even begin to think about what it would be like to finally be alone with Jude.

A quick change of trains in the city, and Luk found himself dragging his trolley of sound gear off the train at Carlisle station, five stops out of the city.

The air temperature was finally dropping, down to merely unpleasantly warm, as they walked through the suburb, past people drinking beer on their balconies and watering their dead gardens in the still evening.

The suburb was an even mix of old, run-down houses and brand new housing developments, and Jude pushed the gate open at one of the old houses. The house lacked the squalor of Lori's place, with no rusting car bodies on the verge, but the front steps still creaked alarmingly when Luk lifted his trolley of gear up them.

The front screen door was locked, the house in darkness, but a female voice called out, "Hey, there," when the screen door banged closed after them.

Jude pushed open one of the doors off the hall and said, "Want to put your gear in there? Loo is out the back, if you need it."

The room was almost empty, just a mattress on the floor, an old bookshelf that held two shelves of books and three of folded clothes, and a crate of food, all on a bare floor. The walls were bare, too, apart from a couple of classic rock posters.

Luk pushed his gear into the room and slipped his guitar off his back, resting it against the wall, beside where Jude had propped his own.

He needed to piss. A light was on at the back of the house, in a laundry, and Luk pushed the back screen door open. Two women were sitting on paving, Jude squatting beside them, talking to them, but Luk turned his head and ignored them, going straight to the outdoor loo.

Jude was waiting by the back door when Luk had finished.

"C'mon," Jude said, flicking the laundry light off and leading Luk back through the house to his room.

The door closed, and the room was in darkness. Luk could hear his own breathing, loud and harsh, then Jude's hands touched his shoulders. "Do you need a light on?" Jude asked.

"I can't take my boots off in the dark," Luk said. "Which may or may not be an issue."

Jude laughed, and Luk felt some of his tension ease. "Give me a moment, then."

When Jude came back, he fumbled around at the bookcase, then a match flared and he lit two candles. "I'm going to hear about this from Alison," he said. "I took the candles off her altar."

"Altar?" Luk said. "Isn't that, um, sacrilegious or something?"

"Or something," Jude said, standing in front of Luk again. "I'll deal with that tomorrow." He touched Luk's shoulders, his hands sliding down to curl over the tops of Luk's arms, pulling him closer. "Ready?"

He didn't wait for Luk to answer, just kissed him, and kept kissing him, until Luk couldn't breathe, could barely stand.

When Luk opened his eyes, Jude was still hanging onto him, face only centimeters from his, glowing in the heat and golden light from the candles. "Want to take your boots off now?"

Luk sat down on the mattress, trying not to think about it being a man's bed -- Jude's bed -- and began to unlace his boots. Jude kicked off his sandals, then peeled his T-shirt off and tossed it across the room.

When Luk had dragged his boots off, then his socks, he hesitated for a moment, then lifted his T-shirt over his head, too.

Jude lay back on the mattress, his hand on Luk's arm, pulling Luk down beside him.

"Point of no return?" Jude asked, his hand settling on Luk's chest, near his shoulder.

Luk shook his head. "That was earlier." At the oval, or on the steps of Loud People, or in Lori's spare room, or at the beach, or, just maybe, at the very first audition.

The room smelled of candle wax and hot day. Luk could smell himself, sweat and skin and a little fear, over the sweet smell of Jude's skin and sheets. Was he supposed to have showered?

Jude propped himself up on one elbow. "I want to touch all of you..." Jude's hand slid lower on Luk's chest, fingertips dragging over his ribs, down across his nipple.

Jude leaned forward and licked at Luk's throat, at the hollow at the base, tongue hot and slippery.

Luk touched Jude hesitantly, hands on his back, feeling bands of muscles moving under his skin, the ridge of his spine, and this time Jude lifted his head and kept his gaze on Luk's face.

It was real.

Jude's hand drifted down Luk's belly, making the muscles jump, then his fingers found the top button of Luk's fly.

Luk's breath caught, just for a moment, while Jude thumbed the button undone. The sound of the zip sliding undone was loud, rasping in the room.

Jude leaned forward, his mouth against Luk's, open and moist, and he slid his hand into the top of Luk's boxers, pushing under the material.

Both of them were breathing hard, and Luk's fingers were digging into Jude's back, then Jude's fingertips found the shaft of Luk's cock.

"Your jeans," Jude said against Luk's mouth, and fuck, he was right, Luk's jeans were in the way.

It took a moment, that was all, and Jude was off Luk, and Luk was shoving his jeans and boxers down and kicking them off, so he was naked, his cock lying up his belly. His first instinct was to cover himself up, to clasp his hands over his cock and balls, but that would have been stupid, given what they'd been doing a moment before.

Jude kissed Luk, hard and deep, pushing him back down on the mattress, and Jude's hand touched Luk's thigh, then belly, before, finally, one finger trailed from the base of Luk's cock up to the head.

Then fingers curled around Luk's cock, strong and steady, right at the base. Luk yelled, tipping his head back and arching his back, because something was happening inside him, something was uncoiling deep in his groin, burning and aching.

Jude bit at Luk's neck, groaning, and the sting of his teeth mixed in with the feel of his hand on Luk's cock, squeezing and sliding.

"Can you touch me?" Jude asked, his voice rough against Luk's ear. "Please?"

The way Luk felt, right at that moment, from what Jude was doing to him, Luk would have done anything, just to make it keep happening.

Luk's hand was clumsy, clutching at Jude's shorts, but he pulled them loose and shoved them down.

Luk touched Jude, hand on his cock, dragging chord-playing calluses over the delicate skin, and Jude moaned, rolling his hips, pushing his thick cock harder into Luk's hand.

"Gonna come," Jude said, his hand tightening around Luk's cock, and Luk was too, any moment, because it was all so fucking perfect.

Jude's cock jumped in Luk's hand, and Jude made the best sound, deep and needy, as he shot over Luk's belly, so freaking hot and slippery.

It should have been gross, except Jude let go of Luk's cock for a moment to grab a wet handful, then he was jerking at Luk hard, wiping his come over Luk's cock, and Luk was shouting and coming, feet planted on the bed, hips up, riding the fire.

Luk flopped on the bed, legs like jelly, his body shaking, Jude half-sprawled across him, a dead weight.

"Fuck," Luk said, and even his voice sounded wrecked.

"I think we broke things," Jude said. "Like the space-time continuum. It's a damned good thing I don't have a bed."

Jude sounded just like Luk felt: shattered.

Luk wiped his cheek experimentally, and tried to work

out if he was embarrassed that he had his own come on his face.

No, there was a time and place for embarrassment, and this was not one of them.

Better to smile, certain that Jude wouldn't see, since Jude's head was buried against Luk's neck.

Luk stroked Jude's back with a hand that felt numb, and found the short plait of Jude's hair. Tufts and strands were escaping, and the band holding the end was loose, so Luk tugged the band off, then pulled the braid undone.

Jude's hair was fine to the touch, wispy and kinked from the braid, and he settled deeper into Luk's shoulder and neck as Luk pulled the hair smooth.

"Feels good," Jude said, his voice muffled.

It did feel good to be lying on Jude's bed, too fragmented to move, touching him.

"You alright?" Jude asked.

Luk ran his hand down Jude's back and thought about how he felt. Sweaty. Thirsty. So relaxed he couldn't move.

"Yeah, I think I am."

Jude moved, just enough to lift his leg over Luk's, so his thigh rested across Luk's groin, and his cock pressed against Luk's hip.

"I need a couple of liters of cold water," Jude said. "As soon as I can manage to crawl to the kitchen."

Luk lifted his free leg experimentally. "Think I could manage it," he said.

"Honey, you can't walk out there," Jude said. "At the moment, you're a glowing advertisement for male virility, covered in come. The girls will steal you and throw me out of the house. Better not to risk it. I'll go."

Jude levered himself up off Luk onto all fours, and crawled over Luk and off the mattress, clumsy with his shorts bunched around his knees.

When he stood and pulled his shorts up, tucking his still half-hard cock away, his smile for Luk was complicit. "Back in a moment."

When Luk was alone, he lay back on the mattress, wiping at the come on his face with the back of his hand. He could hear voices, Jude and his housemates, through the door. Yeah, both he and Jude had been making a lot of noise, yelling and carrying on. Luk was usually good at being quiet; he had to be to wank at home, but this time...

This time had completely blown his mind.

The door opened again, letting in a sliver of electric light, then closed behind Jude.

Jude sat on the edge of the mattress and held out a two-liter bottle of water, beaded with condensation, to Luk. "Your housemates?" Luk asked, taking the bottle of water gratefully.

"My housemates are nosy," Jude said. "That's all. I've been celibate a long time, and apparently that makes my sex life a matter for public consumption."

"My housemates are my family," Luk said, when he'd drained a quarter of the bottle. "Everything I do, say, or think is considered their business."

Jude took the bottle and drank deeply, then handed it back with a burp. "Let's hope my housemates never meet your family."

Luk stood the mostly empty bottle on the floor, beside the mattress, and watched Jude drop his shorts on the floor.

Luk slid over on the mattress to make room. "How long have you been celibate?"

Jude propped himself on his side, one hand stroking Luk's hip where the skin was smoothest He leaned close to Luk, so his nose brushed against Luk's face. "About two weeks longer than I wanted."

Luk laughed, but the laugh didn't finish because Jude's hand had moved between Luk's thighs to cup Luk's balls.

"It's been over a year," Jude said, his fingers doing something wicked that made Luk twist on the mattress. "Do you like that?"

"Yeah," Luk said, because with Jude lying half across him, so their bodies were stuck together with sweat, there wasn't any point in pretending that he wasn't getting off on what Jude was doing to him. "Do you... you know?"

"Do I what?" Jude asked, his breath loud.

He was breathing Luk, right against his face and neck, breathing in the smell of the come dried on Luk's skin, and it should have been creepy, but it wasn't. Just like what Jude was doing to Luk's balls, it was all good.

Oh, fuck, he was supposed to be answering Jude's question, not getting off again.

"Do it all."

"Anal sex?" Jude said. "Yeah, I have, before. If you're panicking about that, then don't. It's not something that's going to happen suddenly, and if it ever does, it's probably going to be you doing it to me."

Luk blinked at Jude, who grinned at him. "You like that?"

"Having someone inside me?" Jude asked. "As close as they possibly can be? Yeah, under the right circumstances, it can be the best feeling. Reckon I can dig the tube of lube out from under my mattress now without it making you want to run away?"

"We're not doing anything with it?" Luk said.

Jude's hand squeezed Luk's balls, then moved up to Luk's cock. "Just a long, wet jerk off."'

Luk had doubts about how long he'd last, with the way his body was humming again, but he nodded. "Yeah, that'd feel good."

Jude kissed him, letting go of Luk's cock and reaching across him to rummage under the edge of the mattress. The humming was building, turning into heat, and the feel of Jude's hard cock pressing against Luk's hip made him burn just a little more.

Luk pushed a hand between their bodies, and when he touched Jude's cock, he could hear the catch in Jude's breathing where their mouths were joined. It felt good, knowing he could do that to someone, that he could touch someone and know for sure they liked it, and liked him.

"Stop thinking," Jude said, lifting himself up, holding a tube of lube in his hand. "I can almost hear you."

Luk squeezed Jude's cock, just a little, to watch Jude's face tighten. "You want me to not think?"

"Yeah, house rules," Jude said. "At least, mattress rules, since I have no idea if Sammie and Alison would agree, and I'm not going to go ask them. Once the lube comes out, it's time to lapse into double-digit IQ territory."

"No Proust?" Luk asked hopefully.

"Fuck, no," Jude said. "I'd hope there'd be no literature, in any European language, here at all. You could, if you felt the need, quote Metallica lyrics."

Luk burst out laughing, he couldn't help it. Jude could act all superior and intellectual, but he didn't take himself too seriously, not all the time.

The feel of cool lube, slippery and slick, on Luk's cock made him stop laughing, almost made him stop breathing for a moment, when Jude curled his hand around Luk's cock and smoothed the lube across his skin.

Jude tossed the lube onto the sheets beside Luk with his free hand, and settled beside Luk, on his side. Yeah, Luk could take a hint.

Luk popped the lid off the tube with his teeth and squeezed some lube into his hand, dropping the tube in an attempt to stop the gel from disappearing between his fingers. It'd be easier if Jude was cooperating just a little, by stopping what he was doing or by not laughing.

First touch of Luk's lubed hand on Jude's cock and Jude jumped, then Luk's hand was sliding in time with Jude's, slipping skin over the hard flesh below.

Somewhere in there, in the feel of Jude sucking on the skin of his neck, and the heat in his belly, Luk realized they were in 7/4 time, a complex time signature that was a fucking nightmare to play, except in 'All You Need is Love,' where the history and familiarity of the song carried the whole damned thing.

It was musical theory, not literature, but still not something to mention, not right then.

Better to close his eyes and listen to the sound of flesh and lube, breathing, heartbeat and Jude's gasps.

Jude's groans rose steadily in volume, matching the building tightness in Luk, until the lube was warm and thick, and Jude's face was buried in the pillow, his body arched over Luk's as he thrust his cock into Luk's clasped hands, over and over, while he came with a shout.

Jude collapsed down onto Luk, and Luk grabbed his own cock, working his hand over it desperately, and seconds later, he was yelling and coming in a tangle with Jude.

Chapter Eight

Luk had to wedge the door to Loud People open to get his trolley inside. It hadn't been his first choice, but if he'd dragged it all the way home, by train and bus, then turned around and gone to class, he'd have missed half the day.

Leaving the speaker, amp and guitar with Lori would save him two hours on a bus, and his neck.

Lori and some bloke in a suit were hunched over the counter, paperwork spread in front of them, so Luk closed the door again and pretended to browse the rack of UK vinyl imports.

The man in the suit left, canvas banking bag in his hand, and Lori said, "Hi, Luk. Sorry, couldn't say anything, that was the boss."

"S'alright," Luk said, nodding at Lori. "Can I leave my rig out the back here while I go to uni?"

Lori stood in the aisle, arms crossed, and Luk tried not to flinch under her inspection. "Still got your amp and speaker from rehearsal?" she said. "Same clothes, too? Isn't that interesting?"

It wasn't interesting, it was embarrassing. Luk had hidden in Jude's bedroom, pretending he was asleep, until he'd been sure the house was empty, just to avoid having to talk to anyone about it.

"Can I leave the speaker here at least?" Luk asked.

"You know, it's all fun and games until someone loses an eye," Lori said, scowling disapprovingly. "Trust me on that one."

Luk remembered how Jude's cock had felt, jabbing into his hand, hard as stone, and colored deeply.

"Oh, God," Lori groaned. "I did not need that mental image, thank you very much." Her hand flickered out, and her nails brushed Luk's neck, just for a second.

"Lori!" Luk said, jerking his head away.

He knew he had a huge love bite there, he'd seen it in Jude's bathroom mirror. He didn't need anyone reminding him.

"I can't believe the two of you would do this," Lori said, stomping back to the counter, her platform boots thudding. "I'm not going to tolerate sulking gay boys, you know. No cat fights and bitchy silences, no crying in the toilets. If you two mess it up, Jude is still out of the band."

Luk grabbed the handle of his trolley, and dragged it down the aisles of records to the back of the shop.

"Why not me?" Luk asked. "Jude's your friend."

Lori kicked open the door to a storage room and pointed into it. "In there. Jude can't play for shit. All he can do is sing and jump around while looking good. You, on the other hand, are some kind of guitar god. Stash your trolley and guitar, and get out of here before my boss gets back."

Luk shoved his trolley into the tiny room in amongst the empty cardboard boxes and damaged display cases, then balanced his guitar on top.

"Are you really angry?" Luk asked.

Lori shrugged. "I dunno, hon. It all looks doomed to me, but I might just be pessimistic about love."

Luk could still feel his cheeks burning, and Lori laughed and gave his shoulder a gentle shove. "Go, quickly. I'll see you later, when you collect your gear."

Luk grabbed his pack from the rack beside the door and bolted.

It was too much. Everything was too much.

When Luk banged on the door of Monlo's, Lori rushed up to let him in, grabbing his arms and pulling him in. "Are you busy tonight?" she babbled. "Please tell me you're not flying to London or having surgery or something."

Luk had been planning on staying home, not going to the Hydey, not getting drunk or trashed, and not sleeping with Jude, so he felt confidently able to say, "Nothing like that. Why?"

"Rick's got a night's work, as a sound tech for the Rod Stewart mega-concert tonight. Licks has gastro and Robbo has been arrested. Mark, who manages Delicate John, wants us to play Delicate John's spot instead at the Railway Hotel tonight. I need to ring him back, confirm the booking."

"Fuck."

Lori nodded, her fingers digging into Luk's arms where she was still hanging onto him. "We have to play a full set, that's twenty minutes, including intros. Can we work up that much material in an afternoon?"

Luk counted tracks in his head, adding up the minutes. They could legitimately play 'Not the Only One,' it was Lori's song. Then they had another three tracks, Jude's and Luk's songs, plus Lori's other song. Only Lori's other song wasn't ready.

Not enough. There was original material, then there was playing homage to rock royalty...

Would Alix and Maddie give them permission to use 'Jackrabbit' without having to pay royalties? They could ask Alix, who was singing to himself behind the bar, making the espresso machine squeal.

If they could put it together during the afternoon, in Lori's garage, then they'd have enough for a full set.

"What about gear?" Luk asked. "We don't have the kind of amps or speakers that we'd need to play the Railway."

"Rick said we can just borrow Delicate John's set up, as long as we don't set fire to it or use it as a deposit on a kilo of hash or anything."

Luk nodded, grinning at Lori. "We can do it. Book us in."

Lori squealed, just like the espresso machine, then said, "What am I going to wear?"

"I'm not your fashion consultant," Luk said. "It's all I can do to dress myself most days. Go make the call, while I ask Alix a favor."

Jude banged on the door, five minutes later, and Luk watched Lori run the length of the café to let him in. Jude waved at Luk, and Luk nodded back.

Alix nodded nostalgically. "I remember Maddie being like that," he said. "When we got the call to say we were going to cut our first single."

"So, no problems with us using 'Jackrabbit' tonight?" Luk asked.

Alix shook his head. "I'll ring Maddie and tell her, just to amuse her. The complexities of copyright still escape me, after all these years, but I'm sure that she and I, and the two deceased estates, still hold 'Jackrabbit' outright."

Luk watched Jude peel Lori off him and walk across to the espresso bar, where Luk was scribbling notes on a waiter's pad.

"Hi," Jude said, leaning against the bar.

"Um, hi," Luk said.

Jude touched Luk's cheek, just with the back of his knuckles, then leaned forward and kissed Luk chastely, a brief brush of lips.

"No," Lori said, clamping one hand on Jude's shoulder. "Not now. Too much work to do. Leave Luk alone, he has to finalize the song arrangements, and you have to tell me what to wear tonight."

"Go set up your drum kit," Jude said. "And stop panicking."

Lori poked her tongue out at Jude, and he pushed her gently back toward the stage.

"How have you been?" Jude asked.

"Lori gave me heaps," Luk said. "Then I got the whole parental lecture thing for staying out all night. Apart from that, yeah, I've been fine."

Jude nodded, and when he leaned forward, the kiss was still gentle, but there was nothing chaste about it.

Luk took a deep breath in when Jude pulled away, just to stop his head from spinning.

"Not sure where we'll wind up tonight," Jude said. "Since the Railway is in Fremantle, probably at Lori's place. Do you want to share a mattress?"

Luk had been going to say no; he'd been considering it seriously, in the privacy of his bedroom, when he should have been writing essays for uni. Was it worth the drama? Was Lori right, and Jude would have to leave the band?

"Yeah," Luk said, because Jude's hand was resting on his, where he was holding the pen, and damn, but Lori hadn't been there, and hadn't known what it had felt like.

"Work!" Lori shouted. "Stop making out and work!"

"Who made you the boss?" Jude said, grinning at Luk for a moment, but he lifted his hand and left Luk to finish working on the arrangement of 'Jackrabbit' while Jude and Lori set up for the gig.

The sound gear, packed into the back of Rick's van, was pretty much unbelievable, even by Luk's standards. Every single amp or sound board, every speaker stack and stomp pedal, had a small metal plaque engraved with the words 'Bedford Senior High School' attached to it.

"I can't believe everything is stolen," Luk said to Jude as they slid the microphone stands into the van, right against the roof.

"'Borrowed' is how Licks described it," Jude said.

"The Sex Pistols stole all of their mikes from David Bowie," Lori said, handing another mike stand to Jude. "Something Licks likes to remind people of. He also says the school should be proud to see their musical equipment put to such good use now, since it sure wasn't being used well when he was in high school."

Luk shook his head, and glanced at Jude. "Well?" he said. "Aren't you going to say something about using stolen gear on our gig?"

Jude shrugged. "We don't have time for me to do that. If we're opening, we need to move fast to get set up. Are you ready to go, Lori?"

"Do I look ready to go?" Lori demanded.

She was wearing a toweling bathrobe.

"Then get dressed, Duchess," Jude said.

Lori ran toward the house, the robe flapping around

her bare legs, and Jude called after her, "And wear shoes you can walk in!"

The late afternoon was peaceful, without the burning heat of the previous Wednesday, and Luk leaned against the side of the van and looked at the sky. The sea breeze was howling in, blowing thin clouds to tatters, and it was blissfully cool. A much better night for a gig; the crowd wouldn't be quite so aggro, and none of the band would pass out from heat stroke.

Jude pulled Luk in for a long kiss, one that made Luk half-hard, mouths joined wetly, then Jude said, "Wanna go hurry the queen up?"

"Why me?" Luk asked. "Shouldn't you do that? Girl stuff worries me."

"Girl stuff?" Jude asked, laughing, his arms around Luk.

"You know, lipstick and shoes and that sort of thing."

"Tell her she looks great, even if you're lying," Jude said. "Consider it part of your duties as a band member."

Luk bounced up the steps, and through the open front door. He knew which was Lori's room from the week before, so he knocked on the bedroom door, then pushed it open.

"Hurry up," he said. "Jude is fretting."

Lori was sitting on her unmade bed, hunched over, aluminum foil and a metal tube in her hands, smell of burning in the room.

"Shit!" she said. "Knock, you fucker."

"Um, I did," Luk said.

"Want some?" Lori asked, holding out the metal tube. "I've got half a hit left."

"You're smoking meth?" Luk asked, backing up involuntarily. Fuck, he was out of there if it was meth.

"Don't be stupid," Lori said. "It's just a little smack."

Luk shook his head. "Thanks, but no thanks. Are you ready?"

Smack didn't scare Luk the way meth did, but that didn't mean he was going anywhere near the stuff.

Lori crumpled up the foil, and shoved it and the tube into the paper bag on the bed. "Just gotta put my boots on, hon," she said.

Luk left Lori crouched beside the bed, peering under it and pulling shoes out of the mess, and went back out to where Jude was waiting beside the van.

"Is Lori nearly ready?" Jude asked.

"I think she's about done," Luk said, hauling open the driver's door and clambering in and across to the middle of the bench seat, hand brake between his knees.

Jude slid into the driver's seat and slammed the door. His hand rested on Luk's thigh, curled loosely over the curve of Luk's thigh muscle, and the contact made Luk smile.

"Nervous?" Jude asked.

"Nope," Luk said. "I've been to gigs at the Railway, and if we're opening, the only other people there are going to be the staff and the people in the other bands."

Jude laughed. "You're right. I hadn't thought of that. Besides, we're good."

"Are we?" Luk asked.

Jude's hand squeezed, sliding higher. "Yeah. It's one thing to play a café, with a tiny sound board and speaker stack. You wait until we get in front of Delicate John's stacks and start pumping out some noise."

"I've always wanted to do that, to really make a lot of decibels."

Jude's hand was over Luk's groin, rubbing, and Luk closed his eyes. "You did that on Wednesday night," Jude said.

The passenger door was wrenched open and Lori said,

"Oh, for fuck's sake, stop groping."

Jude didn't move his hand, not for a couple of seconds. "Ready, Your Highness?" Jude said.

Lori, wearing painted-on jeans and a bra, and carrying a bag of clothes and a pair of boots, said. "Fuck you, Jude. Just drive."

Jude raised an eyebrow at Luk, and started the van.

Perhaps Luk should tell Jude about the smack.

Perhaps he shouldn't.

They were early enough that Jude could park the van beside the pub, and if Luk hadn't been nervous before, he suddenly was. The service carpark was a solid row of band vans, trucks and wagons, and around the vehicles milled musicians and hangers-on, girlfriends and wives, all carrying gear.

Luk slid out of the driver's side door and went around the van to open the passenger door for Lori, who was still doing her boots up and waved Luk away.

"Fuck," Luk said to Jude, at the open rear doors of the van. "Have you seen the other musos?"

Jude nodded, dragging out a bundle of mike stands and handing them to Luk, then grabbing Lori's electronic drum kit. "They're all ten years older than us. Let's go find out where we bump in."

The rear doors to the venue were open at the back of the carpark, and that was where the other musos were heading, carrying amps and stacks, so Luk followed Jude there.

Inside the door, the other musos were stacking their gear on a pool table and the floor beside the stage. "Wow," Luk said, looking at the stage. They were going to be there, any moment.

A sound tech, wearing a headset and carrying a clipboard, looked at them and said, "Who the fuck are you?"

"We're The Tockleys," Jude said. "We're booked to open, filling in for Delicate John."

"That's right," the tech said, looking at his clipboard. "You're not opening; you're up third, in Delicate John's place. Put your gear there." He pointed at a patch of floor beside the pool table.

Someone behind Luk bumped into him, and said, "Get out of the fucking way."

Luk moved fast, setting the mike stands down where the tech had pointed before anyone else felt the need to hurt him.

"Third?" he squeaked to Jude.

Jude slapped him on his back. "Look at it this way: at least Lori will be dressed by then, and over whatever it was she used."

The two of them carried their gear into the venue. The speaker stacks were four times the size of the rehearsal stacks they used, and took the two of them to carry. Jude was right; they were going to make some serious noise.

Their amps went beside the stacks, then their guitars, the borrowed instruments from Maddie. Coils of cables, Lori's kit, and the mikes and stands.

Jude threw his arm around Luk's shoulder and hugged him as they surveyed the pile. "It's still less than everyone else," Luk said, glancing at the other musos with their equipment.

"Just think of your gorgeous guitar," Jude said. "They're all just compensating because your guitar is bigger than theirs."

"We should get out of the way," Luk said, as a large man with a larger beard hefted a six stack speaker single-handedly past them.

Lori was finally dressed when Luk and Jude went back to the van, at least, as dressed as she intended to get.

Jude looked in the passenger door, where Lori was

applying lipstick by ambient light. "We're bumped in. You ready to go in?"

"We're set up?" Lori said, winding her lipstick closed and tossing it into the bag between her feet.

"We're playing third, in Delicate John's slot," Jude said. "After The Limpets, and before Body Count."

"Third?" Lori said. "They do know it's us, don't they?"

Luk nudged Jude and pointed at the side of the pub. The bricks had been plastered over and painted black to form a rough blackboard, and the night's gigs were scrawled on the black, in giant letters: Wampos, The Limpets, The Tockleys, Body Count.

"They know it's us," Jude said.

The three of them stood in the carpark, Lori shivering a little in the evening air, and stared at the side of the pub. Someone wolf-whistled Lori as they drove past, and she flipped two fingers at them in response, without looking away from the pub wall.

"Vodka," Lori said. "I need vodka, and I bet Luk does too."

The Railway Hotel was almost empty when Lori led them in. "Get a jug of beer," Lori told Luk. "And a couple of glasses. I've got to go and do stuff, and I'll meet you in the beer garden."

"Stuff?" Luk asked Jude, leaning over the front bar, twenty dollar note and his ID in his hand.

"Not that sort of stuff," Jude said. "Rick's ex-girlfriend is here, I saw her when we carried the gear in. I suspect Lori is planning to jab a stiletto heel into her foot, or be all superior about the band. I'd stay out of it."

"Bloody hell," Luk said.

The barman checked his ID and took his order, then handed him change and the jug of beer and glasses.

"What else don't I know about the personal politics

of the band scene here?" Luk asked Jude, following him through the deserted lounge bar beside the stage and dance floor, where Wampos were doing sound checks.

The beer garden -- concrete pavers, bare pergolas and struggling ferns -- was less empty, with half a dozen of the tables occupied by either the people who had been in the carpark before, or their doubles.

Jude sat down at an empty table, away from the others. "What don't you know?" he asked. "The whole wives and girlfriends thing is painfully complex, and I don't pretend to understand what's going on. I am relieved to tell you my ex-lover isn't here, so that's one disaster averted."

Luk poured himself a glass of beer from the jug, carefully tipping the glass to avoid a frothy head. "Your ex is in a band?" he asked.

Jude shook his head. "No, he's a sound tech around the place." He touched Luk's hand, where Luk was drawing lines in the beer he'd spilled on the table. "Luk, people might tell you things, about what happened when he and I broke up."

Luk shrugged, remembering the faces peering through the window at Lori's place. "It doesn't matter, really. Don't worry about it."

"It matters to me."

Lori stalked across the beer garden and slid into a seat at the table. "Fucking bitch," she said. "Pour me a beer, Luk."

Luk filled an empty glass with beer and pushed it across the table to Lori, who pulled a small bottle of vodka out of her bag and added a splash to her beer.

"Want some?" she asked.

Luk glanced at Jude, who was leaning back in his seat so he could watch the stage through the open doors to the lounge bar, where Wampos were making their amps squeal.

"Thanks," Luk said, taking the bottle and adding a slug to his beer, then passing it back. "Who's a fucking bitch?"

"Rick's ex. She's in the Ladies, showing off some piece of glass on her hand, talking about how Kendo, or whatever his name is, bought it for her with his first royalty check from his album."

"More likely from a big deal," Jude said, patting Lori's shoulder. "Ignore her, she's got no style, and she can't even play an instrument. You've got your own band."

Lori's face lifted. "Yeah, you should have seen her when I told her that."

Inside, someone shouted, "One, two, three, four," and feedback shrieked through the Wampos' speaker stacks.

Luk leaned sideways, craning his head to look around Jude at the four members of Wampos, who were playing to a lounge bar empty of people, apart from a table of what looked like their partners.

"That should have been us, playing to an empty room," Jude said.

Lori shrugged. "No guarantees there'll be anyone in there when we do play," she said.

"Let's go listen to Wampos," Luk said, standing up and picking up the jug and his beer.

Jude nodded, and there was something in his smile that made Luk warm inside, warmer even than the vodka.

"Good idea."

Lori trailed behind them, spilling her beer as she flopped into one of the sticky lounge chairs. The music was loud, and the band was not good, raucous and out of time, the lead guitarist so inept that Luk had to work at not wincing. The Tockleys were a thousand times better.

A woman walked past between Wampos songs, carrying a full jug of beer, pausing long enough to stare at Luk and say, "Hi, Jude."

"That's her," Lori shouted against Luk's ear, as the Wampos launched into another three minutes of sound abuse. "Rick's ex."

Luk turned around to look at the woman. Her hair was cut short, the fringe no more than stubble on her forehead, but apart from that, she was a clone of Lori.

"You're much prettier," he shouted back.

Lori patted his cheek. "I'm keeping you."

Halfway through The Limpets' set, Lori pointed a painted fingernail at Luk, then Jude, then over at the pile of gear beside the stage.

Jude nodded and stood up, waiting for Luk.

Luk looked around the lounge bar, where a few dozen people had drifted in during the set, then stood up, his knees unsteady. Fuck, it was time for them to set up. It was almost time for them to play.

Chapter Nine

The Limpets finished, to louder applause, and Luk nodded at their bassist as he jumped down off the stage.

The bassist said, "Want to give me a hand with my stack, speed things up?"

Luk jumped up onto the stage after the bassist, and found himself under glaring lights, looking out over the lounge bar, the hum of conversation and clink of glasses rising in the room in the break between sets.

"This one, mate," the bassist said.

Luk grabbed the other side of the stack the bassist had used and hefted the weight. It was real, the weight of the stack and the smell of spilled beer were proof enough.

It took a couple of minutes to clear the stage of The Limpets' rig, then Jude and Luk began to lift the Delicate John stacks onto the stage, while Lori propped mike stands in place and uncoiled cables.

The amps balanced on top of the stacks, and Luk hooked up the guitars, checking the bridge and neck pickups were on and the gains were cranked up, while

Jude and Lori set the drum kit up.

A minute later, no more, and someone handed Luk a glass of beer and said, "Check the pick-ups, starting with the drums."

"Thanks, mate," Luk said to the sound tech, the one who wasn't Jude's ex. Right, drums. "Lori, check your rig, one pad at a time."

Lori slid onto the stool behind the drum kit, settling her headset over her coiled braids, spinning drumsticks in one hand.

She tapped across the pads, all three toms, both zones on the snare, the kick drum and the hi hat, then the cymbals, while Luk tweaked the gain on her sound board and Jude relayed instructions from the sound tech.

Then it was Jude's turn, sliding the strap of Maddie's mahogany Maton over his head, and if anyone in the crowd had recognized what the guitar was, then they'd be wetting themselves with envy. It was in tune, Luk had made sure of that before he'd packed the gear away that afternoon, so when Jude strummed the sliding chords from the opening of 'Not the Only One,' the sound from the stack was so sweet and true that it made Luk's eyes water.

"Mike check," the soundie called, and Jude leaned into his mike.

"Checking."

"Now the bass."

Luk pulled the strap of Maddie's Fender Jazz over his head, settling it across his hips, and someone whistled from behind the stage lights. There were enough guitarists out there that someone should pick a perfect vintage Fender on sight, even if they missed the more obscure Maton.

Luk pushed his thumb against the strings, listening for the hum in the amp to transmit to the stack, then played the matching chords to Jude's test, just for completion.

The sound, coming through the six stack speaker behind him, was fucking perfect, no distortion at all.

"Check," Luk said, leaning into his mike.

The soundie called, "You're good to play."

Behind Luk, Lori spoke into her headset. "We're The Tockleys, and this is my fucking song."

Her stick tapped on the edge of the snare, echoing through the stack, counting them into 'Not the Only One.'

Luk kept his voice back, letting Jude and Lori sing, but he rode his guitar right into the song over the top of Lori's drums, filling the gaps in Jude's dodgy chords, the noise pouring out of the stacks behind them so loud that it drowned everything out.

They played it straight and clean, just like they'd rehearsed, with no bridges, Lori singing her verses, Jude on top for the chorus, two melody lines. Jude bounced on the balls of his feet, covering his side of the stage, colliding across into Luk, sharing his mike.

Sweat ran into Luk's eyes, and it took everything he had to keep playing, to keep making the sound come out of the stack behind him, straight from his fingers, straight from his gut.

It was a huge feeling, as big as being with Jude had been, roaring into the end of the song, Jude and his guitar dropping out for the last two bars, so it was just Lori and Luk, pounding into the beat, pulling it closed.

The amps hummed through the stacks with a faint crackle, and Lori's stick tapped the snare, straight into Luk's song.

Luk flew through the opening chords, making the old Fender sing, Lori working hard behind him, Jude bouncing beside him, not getting in his way or messing the melody line up. Then the three of them were shouting the first verse.

"Can anybody here see me
standing right in your face?
I'm shouting out your name
just trying to claim my space."

People were on the concrete floor in front of the stage;
Luk could just make out their shapes through the glare of
the stage lights. People were actually on the floor, moving,
to Luk's music.

"Do you want me to go?
Should I just fade away?
I'm not gonna make it that easy
I'm gonna make it some day."

They ran through the first chorus, then Luk grabbed
the first bridge and did what he'd always dreamed of
doing; he played his own music as loud as he could, foot
on the stomp pedal, wringing everything he could out of
the Fender, the amp and the stack, and out of himself.

He fell into the next verse, out of breath, and a little
embarrassed to discover he was hard, just from the noise.
Jude sang, using Luk's mike, and Luk could see the sweat
darkening Jude's T-shirt and clumping his hair.

"Go on, see right through me
adopt your usual blank stare.
Pretend that you don't know me
I know that you don't care."

The three of them sang the next chorus, then Luk
wailed through the second bridge, the noise vibrating
through his body, and if he hadn't gone home with Jude
that week, if he hadn't tried that, then playing would have
been the best the thing he'd ever felt.

Luk stepped back on the stage at the end of the bridge, dragging his guitar pickup cable over, so he could stand beside Lori while Jude sang the last verse.

"I know you think that I'm worthless
well, I want a better life.
I know you don't think that I'm capable
well I don't think that you're right."

Lori didn't glance at Luk; she was focused completely on the song, and on her kit, her hands flying the sticks over the pads, pounding the beat. She was streaked in sweat and make-up, and Luk could completely understand why she'd dumped her shirt before she'd climbed on stage, and was wearing just a bra. Of all of them, she was working hardest.

Final chorus, and Luk bounded up to the front of the stage to share Jude's mike, keeping his guitar clear of any of Jude's random bounces.

"Do you want me to go?
Should I just fade away?
I'm not going that easily,
Today's gonna be my day."

This time, they ended with a crash, four bars out from the verse, and Luk had to pull back from the mike to stop the amp from picking up his breathing. He held up a finger to Lori, to stop her from plunging straight into the next song, and grabbed the beer someone held up from the dance floor, past the lights.

The beer was icy cold and bitter, going straight down Luk's throat, and he drank half the stubby and crouched down to hand it back, into the crowd.

The crowd. They had a fucking crowd of people, right

there, in front of the stage.

Jude tossed the plastic bottle of water he'd just drained off the stage toward the storage area, and bounded across to Luk. The arm he slung around Luk's shoulder was slick with sweat, and for one terrifying moment Luk thought Jude was going to kiss him.

Then Jude was gone, and Lori was counting them in, slower that time, to Jude's song.

Luk didn't have to sing at all, that was all for Jude, but the playing was all his, as Jude swung his guitar around, behind his back, and grabbed the mike with both hands.

It wasn't the right song, in Luk's opinion, not for the gig, or the set, but they hadn't had anything else arranged and ready, so they'd have to make the most of it, and just hope the crowd put up with the slower tempo and phrasing.

Jude's voice was roughened, a little raw from singing Luk's song, and coming through the stack behind Luk, it sounded even better than usual.

"Visions of you dance on the water," Jude sang, and Luk got it, for the first time, got the whole fucking song.

Jude was singing about his ex, the sound tech, and some of the crowd would know that, just like Lori had. And Luk had been an idiot, and not liked the song, and changed the music.

Jude wasn't bouncing, so Luk could watch him, the spotties shining on him, catching the strands of hair escaping from his plait, and the muscles and sinews in his forearms moving as he shifted the mike.

Luk's bass wrapped around Jude's voice, and Lori's drums were like a heartbeat in there, and it might not have been hardcore, but it was still fucking good.

At the end, Lori didn't pause, she gave just gave them a bar of clean 6/8 taps, then a 4/4 lead into 'Jackrabbit,' while Jude scrambled to get his guitar back in place.

"Sing along, you bastards," Lori shouted, and the three of them jumped into 'Jackrabbit,' the crowd roaring along with them, making so much noise that Luk could hear them, even over the speaker stacks.

The crowd screamed, and Luk thrashed his guitar through the bridges, jumping on his stomp pedal, his heart pounding in his chest, voice hoarse from shouting the choruses, hard again from the adrenaline surging through his blood.

When he glanced back at Lori, she was bashing away at the pads, elbows flying, winding herself up for the huge finish, as they came out of the final chorus.

Jude dropped the melody line, leaving just Luk and Lori. Luk howled the final chord, holding it hard, and Lori pounded the pads, leaving the cymbals ringing over the hum in Luk's ears.

And it was over.

Luk's hands were clumsy, unplugging the pickup cable for his guitar and pulling the strap over his head, his fingertips tingling and numb, and he shook them to try and get the feeling back.

He was just glad his T-shirt was hanging loose, out of his jeans, because he had the feeling his hard-on wasn't going to quit, not until he did something about it. Jude bounded past Luk, guitar in his hand, and he slapped Luk on the arse on the way past.

Luk switched off the amp, killing the sound to the stack, and pulled the leads free.

Body Count was big enough to have roadies, huge blokes with beards, who jumped on the stage and helped Jude and Luk lift down the stacks and amps.

"Good sound," one of the roadies said to Luk. "I drove a truck for Ratatosk, back in the Eighties. Took me right back, hearing 'Jackrabbit' again."

"Thanks," Luk said, sliding a mike out of the mike

stand, then unplugging the cable from the amp. "And thanks for helping clear the stage."

"No worries, kid," the roadie said.

Thirty seconds later, Luk slid Jude's guitar into its case and closed it, then looked up at Jude and Lori, who were dismantling the drum kit, packing it flat.

Lori had pulled her shirt back on, but it still hung open, and her hair and make-up were a mess. Jude's hair stood up in clumps, and his T-shirt was stuck to him with sweat. Beside them, on the stage, Body Count were setting up, beginning sound checks, and the crowd in the lounge bar was a buzz in the background.

"We did it," Luk said.

Lori slid the main panel of drum pads into the case and sat back on her heels, on the sticky carpet, shaking her hands. "We more than did it, babe."

Jude grinned, folding the drum stand flat and slotting it into the case, then closing the case lid. He stood up, helping Lori to her feet.

"Want to go make yourself gorgeous, Lori?" Jude said. "While Luk and I drag the gear to the van? Then I think we might need a celebratory kebab."

Lori glanced at herself in a smeary mirror advertising a poisonous soft drink and vodka mix and grimaced. "Bloody hell," she said. "This is a full rebuild job."

It took Jude and Luk several minutes to carry the stacks and amps out to the van through the empty carpark, the noise of Body Count's opening song carrying out of the pub as a dull roar.

Jude slammed the van door shut when Luk had slid the mike stands in on top of the guitars. He grabbed Luk's arm when Luk turned to head back into the pub.

"Wait," Jude said.

"I'm dying for a beer," Luk said. "And I'd like to hear Body Count."

Jude's hand slid down Luk's arm, to his wrist, and he stepped closer, backing Luk against the grubby paintwork of the van.

His other hand touched Luk's throat, the fingers stroking under Luk's chin. "I got the impression, when we'd finished the set, that you had something else on your mind. Beer and a band, or we could get in the van…"

"Here?" Luk said, which was stupid, because the carpark was empty, apart from them and a few dozen cars.

Jude's hand let go of Luk's wrist and found the front of Luk's jeans. "Yeah, here."

Jude slid into the passenger seat of the van first, Luk scrambling in after him, slamming the door hard to make it stay closed.

There wasn't much room, and Luk's elbow connected solidly with Jude's ribs, but after a bit of clambering, Luk managed to kneel astride Jude's thighs.

Luk's ears were still ringing from the gig, and he was coming down from playing into weariness, but the first kiss, with Jude's hands sliding up under his T-shirt and over his ribs, took it all away.

When Luk broke the kiss just to breathe, Jude slid his hand down to squeeze Luk's arse through his jeans. "What do you want?" Jude asked, his hand moving to the front of Luk's jeans. "Want to come?"

"Yeah," Luk said. "Need to, really need to."

"Me, too," Jude said, his fingers undoing Luk's button fly. "Fuck, I want to suck you so much, but I don't think I can here."

Jude's fingers were inside Luk's boxers, touching his cock, feeling so good, and Luk jammed his mouth back against Jude's, kissing hard. Jude's jeans undid easily, their hands colliding as they jerked at each other urgently.

Luk couldn't keep kissing, couldn't concentrate

enough for that, not with what Jude was doing to him, and with the feel of Jude's cock in his hand. He rested his face against the musty and cracked vinyl of the seat back, Jude's mouth against his neck, and tried not to come right at that moment.

Jude's legs twitched underneath Luk, and he growled, then there was wet stuff in Luk's hand, running between his fingers, spreading everywhere. Jude's hand on Luk's cock tightened, stroking harder, and Luk couldn't hold back a moment longer, he was coming too, banging his head on the roof of the van, hanging onto the back of the seat, shaking the seat.

Luk slid off Jude carefully, into the driver's seat, and when Luk glanced at Jude, he looked drained, completely exhausted.

"You okay?" Luk asked.

Jude took a deep breath and nodded slowly, then glanced down at his hand. "Can't waste it," he said, lifting his hand and licking his fingers.

Luk looked at his own hands. Yeah, they'd made a mess. Was he ready? If he was planning on letting Jude suck his cock later that night, and maybe doing it to Jude, he'd better be.

First lick, tasting someone else's come.

Which tasted exactly like his own. What was he expecting? Vanilla? Raspberry?

Someone rapped on the passenger side window, and Lori grinned through the glass at them. "Get dressed," she called through the glass, waving money in her hand. "We've been paid."

"Oh, fuck," Luk said, wiping his hands on the vinyl of the seat, then buttoning his jeans in a hurry.

Jude chuckled, stretching his legs out so he could zip his jeans back up. "Don't worry about Lori. She understands."

Lori was fully dressed, new make-up on, and her hair hanging in two loose plaits, when Luk slid out of the driver's side door and walked around the front of the van.

Jude popped the passenger door open and jumped out.

Lori looked Jude up and down, in the light spilling out of the pub. "That's gross," she said.

"Fuck," Jude said, looking down at his T-shirt.

Yeah, that would be where Luk had come.

Jude turned around and dragged his T-shirt over his head, then pulled it on again inside out.

"That's better," Lori said.

"At least you didn't interrupt us," Jude said.

"Nah," Lori said. "I waited for the van to stop shaking."

"Who gets the money?" Jude asked, and Luk could have hugged him for changing the subject.

"My band," Lori said. "My money."

"You're broke, and you'll fritter it away on beer and pot," Jude said.

"And you're broke, and will spend it on rent and lentils," Lori said.

The pair of them looked at Luk.

"Are you broke?" Lori asked.

"Um, guess not," Luk said. "I get an allowance."

"Spoiled brat," Lori said, and she handed three fifty dollar notes over to Luk. "Twenty dollars of that is for kebabs tonight, which is a reasonable band expense. The rest is for blank CDs, or whatever we decide on."

The three of them stood in the carpark, the roar of Body Count coming out of the pub, and Lori said, "You should know, both of you, that we completely fucking won that gig. If you hadn't been in the van fucking, you would have heard what people were saying. They loved us. They loved 'Not the Only One,' done our way. They loved Jude's song. They loved Luk's song. And we're going to play 'Jackrabbit' every fucking time, because that was amazing."

Jude shrugged. "I dunno, Lori. My ego's doing just fine; I think I'd rather be making out with Luk."

"And that's another thing," Lori said. "When I was putting on my green stick, there were these girls in the loos, and they were talking about Luk, only they didn't know his name. Seems our Luk was really enjoying performing, especially when he took his Fender off at the end."

Luk shook his head. "No way. No fucking way."

"Gotta remember, all the girls in the crowd are a meter lower than us on the stage," Lori said. "Different sight lines. I spend all my time Rick's playing perving at his crotch."

The Railway Hotel was near the docks, the buildings all small factories or warehouses, with few streetlights, which Luk didn't realize until he'd stalked down the road, away from the pub, leaving Lori and Jude standing in the carpark.

He didn't actually care where he went, he just wanted to get away from that fucking hotel, and from Lori and her teasing. He didn't want anyone commenting on his sex life, or his penis. He'd had enough.

He didn't get far, just around the corner and down the block, past a car wreckers and a boat yard, before Jude called out from behind him, "Hang on, Luk."

Luk stopped, and turned to watch Jude lope down the street toward him, his sneakers slapping on the road.

Jude was breathless when he skittered to a halt in front of Luk, and he didn't say anything for several seconds.

"Well?" Luk finally said. "Aren't you supposed to talk me into going back or something?"

"Actually, I ran after you to stop myself from throttling Lori," Jude said. "But you don't need to tell her that. She was just being malicious, telling you about the girls. That was completely unnecessary."

"I feel so stupid."

"For getting off on performing?" Jude asked. "I think it's fucking hot, myself. If I'd known, I'd have been hard too. I will be, next time, just thinking about you."

"What about the people watching?" Luk asked.

Jude stepped closer, right into Luk's space. "Does that matter?" Jude asked. "Does it matter if the straight girls and the queer boys watching are getting all hot from thinking about your cock, or mine? Lori can play the drums in a lace bra, flashing her tits, and it's just good stage presence. How is this different?"

"I don't want them to see me hard," Luk said.

Jude's hands were gentle, on Luk's shoulders. "Then I guess I'll have to suck you off, just before we get on stage, to make sure you're not horny."

"You'd do that for me?" Luk asked.

Jude's T-shirt smelled of come when Luk leaned his head against Jude's shoulder. Jude's arms wrapped around Luk securely. "Believe me, it won't be a hardship," Jude said. "Something I'm keen to show you as soon as possible."

Lori didn't say anything when Luk and Jude walked back to the van, just clambered into the passenger seat with a flounce, winding the window down and wrinkling her nose at the smell in the cab.

Luk thought she was being overly-dramatic about the smell, given that the van stunk of dog and wet carpet, but mostly of petrol, already, but he didn't argue with her over it. It was good to sit squashed against Jude, Jude's hand on his thigh in between gear changes, and drive into the heart of Fremantle on a Saturday night.

The city was teeming with people, the pubs completely

full, restaurants and cafés crowded, the streets packed. Jude parked the van in a way that Luk suspected was deeply illegal, jammed between a tree and a rubbish bin at a playground.

The souvlaki bar on High Street was crowded, all the tables full, so they collected their kebabs and wandered out onto the street.

Luk, mouth full of lamb yiros, pointed at the two jugglers who were working the crowd of drunks outside a pub, one with a loud hailer, the other persuading a member of the crowd to throw knives at him.

"We should do that," he said.

"Get drunks to throw knives at us?" Jude asked, chewing on his falafel kebab and stepping out of the way of the brawl that was about to erupt between two nightclub bouncers and the patron they'd just evicted.

"No, busk," Luk said. "You know, get a license, turn up here with some portable gear, play some tracks and flog our CDs, once we've got them."

Lori flicked raw onion on the ground from her beef souvlaki. "Fucking brilliant," she said. "When Robbo busks with his ukulele, he makes enough to pay the rent for a month." She looked speculatively at Luk over the paper wrapper of her kebab. "Reckon you could play the ukulele?"

"What?" Luk said.

"Or something like that, you know, something a bit different," Lori said.

"Lennon played the banjo," Jude said.

"Lennon played a guitar tuned like a banjo," Luk corrected. "What's the tuning on a ukulele, anyway?"

"Fuck knows," Lori said. "I live with one, and I've yet to hear proof of any tuning at all."

Jude tossed the empty paper wrapper from his kebab into a bin and wiped his mouth on the back of his hand.

"Are we done here?"

Lori poked a long fingernail into the remnants of her kebab and nodded. "Let's go home."

Chapter Ten

The front verge of Lori's house was cluttered with cars, most of them newcomers, so Jude parked the van as close as he could manage. They'd just have to lug the gear the rest of the way.

Lori squealed, kicking the passenger door open. "Rick's home, and Robbo's new girlfriend's here! She must have bailed him!"

Jude dragged the hand brake on, letting his hand linger on Luk's leg. "Do you want to crash here? I think the last train has gone already, so the only way back to my place would be to try and persuade Rick to lend me the van."

Luk was silent, but Jude could almost hear him worrying.

"I think everyone here already knows we're kind of together," Jude said. "If that helps. They either watched the whole mess on Wednesday, or Lori has filled them in on whatever assumptions she's made."

"Fuck," Luk said.

"So, the bit where we share a mattress isn't going to surprise anyone," Jude said. "It might confirm a rumor, but no more."

"It's kind of scary," Luk said.

"It's fucking terrifying, in my opinion," Jude said. "C'mon, let's unload the van."

When Jude hauled the rear doors of the van open, Luk said, "Hang on, you've been gay for years."

Jude caught the mike stands that slid off the pile of equipment and handed them to Luk, pausing to drop a brief kiss on Luk's mouth. "You scare me, not them. Reckon you can take your guitar as well?"

By the time Luk and Jude had hauled and lifted the stacks and amps back into the storage room, Jude was as sweaty as he had been on stage. He locked the van and hung the keys on the hook in the kitchen. The shower was running, and Luk had disappeared, so he guessed Luk had beaten him to the hot water.

Rick leaned against the kitchen doorway, bottle of bourbon in his hand. "Want some?"

Jude shook his head. He could see why some of his fellow Straight Edgers got tattoos of giant crosses on their hands, since no one seemed to remember he didn't drink, not until they wanted to be driven somewhere. "No, thanks, mate."

"Lori said the band had a good gig," Rick said.

"It was," Jude said. "She was awesome, just amazing on drums."

"She's alright," Rick said. "For a chick."

"She's talented," Jude said.

Rick shrugged, and Jude pushed past him. He wasn't going to argue with a drunk.

The bathroom was empty, so Jude locked himself in and peeled his sweaty clothes off. More than sweaty. Next time, he'd remember that Luk shot when he came, and make sure he got his hand in the way. Or his mouth. Now, there was a thought to make him want to get out of the shower as quickly as possible.

The sound from the back verandah, of Robbo jamming on his ukulele and someone, possibly Lori, on bongos, was muted when Jude closed the door of the store room behind him. The room was in darkness, apart from the street light that shone through the uncurtained window, and Jude wasn't sure that the light in the room even worked.

That didn't matter, not when he could make out the shape of Luk sitting cross-legged on the mattress.

Jude tossed his shoes behind the door and pulled his T-shirt off, dropping it on an amp, before sitting beside Luk.

"What did you mean?" Luk asked. "In the van..."

Jude lay back on the mattress, his hand on Luk's back through his T-shirt. "You hadn't realized you weren't the only one who was scared by this, had you?"

Luk slid down into Jude's arms. "Why?"

"It feels like it's all twisted together." Jude wrapped both arms around Luk, pulling him closer. "This, and the music, and The Tockleys, none of which I've got any kind of control over. Scary stuff."

"Yeah." Luk's arms wound around Jude's neck in the dark. "I think I understand now. This whole thing is crazy. You just seem like you're so together."

Jude slid a hand under Luk's T-shirt and across his belly, just to feel the yielding, smooth skin there. "I'm just calmer than Lori," Jude said, his lips against Luk's cheekbone. "Which is not difficult."

Luk's mouth tasted clean, making Jude very glad he'd remembered to bring his own toothbrush. Luk kissed him back, hard and eager, just like in the van, and Jude lifted his mouth for a moment. "Take your T-shirt off?"

Luk pulled his shirt over his head, and the feel of his warm skin against Jude's was heaven. Jude stroked Luk's belly, just to feel the flutter of muscle under the pad of fat, then drifted his fingers around Luk's nipples, tracing a figure eight.

Jude kissed Luk, then slid down the mattress a little. Luk's fingers found Jude's shoulders and arms, and his fingers dug in a little as Jude's mouth closed over his nipple.

His nipple hardened between Jude's lips, and his breath caught, enough for his chest wall to jerk under Jude's chin.

Jude sucked harder, fingers rubbing Luk's other nipple, listening for Luk's breathing, trying to find the right pressure, the right touch, the right way to press the flat of his tongue against the bump of flesh.

Something was right, because Luk said, "Fuck, yeah, that's going straight to my cock."

Jude chuckled, Luk's nipple held carefully between his teeth, and Luk squirmed, saying, "Ouch, take it easy."

"Sure, babe," Jude said, kissing Luk's nipple gently, then sliding down the mattress further. Luk didn't need any encouraging, reaching for the fly of his jeans and undoing it, then pushing his jeans off quickly, kicking his feet free, then pushing his boxers down, too.

Luk was onto something. Jude undid his own jeans and shoved them down, losing his boxers at the same time.

"I feel suddenly nervous," Jude said. "Like I'm representing the entire gay community here, and I'd better put in a good showing."

Luk laughed, but he sounded as nervous as Jude felt. This was silly; Jude had blown enough men in his life to be complacent about it, and he doubted Luk was going to be overly fussy, if anything they'd done so far was an indicator.

Fuck, Luk was hard, his cock pulsing faintly when Jude

slid the head into his mouth, and just kept on sliding. Jude was up to the task of representing the gay men of the city, if it meant he got to give Luk the blowjob of his life.

Luk gasped, and Jude held his breath, keeping all of Luk's cock in his mouth and throat, using his cheeks and swallow to keep the pressure on. It was possible Luk would come right then, which would be amusing, but -- by definition -- not anti-climactic.

Luk didn't come, and Jude slid enough of Luk's cock out of his mouth to be able to breathe comfortably again, then began a slow-suck-slide that had Luk moaning immediately.

There was enough saliva and pre-come, loose on Luk's belly and Jude's face, that Jude had plenty of options for making his fingers slippery. He cupped Luk's balls carefully, just for the feel of how tight they were, and let his thumb push against the skin behind Luk's balls.

Luk's cock in his mouth was just about the hottest thing Jude had ever felt, the way Luk's hips rocked, jabbing his cock in harder, the sound of Luk groaning.

This time, Jude was ready for Luk, grabbing Luk's cock with his free hand to hold it steady, backing off with his mouth, swallowing hard and keeping swallowing until Luk had finished coming.

Jude licked off the last drops of come that had leaked onto Luk's belly, and crawled back up the mattress to flop down beside Luk, waiting for Luk's breathing to stop rasping in the darkened room.

When it sounded like Luk might be able to speak again, Jude said, "Well?"

"Well, what?" Luk sounded amused, like he was smiling.

"Are you going to report me to the gay police?"

"Fuck," Luk said. "Fuck, no. That was... Can you do that again? Now?"

"I guess, in theory, I could," Jude said, grinning too. "Though there's something else that's on my mind."

Luk's hand touched Jude's hip, slid across to his cock. "I can feel. Want me to help?"

A helping hand would do, though Jude had been hoping for something a little more. "Yeah." Luk's hand curled around Jude's cock at the base, squeezing firmly, and it made Jude gasp. "Yeah, that's good."

Luk's face suddenly loomed over Jude, in the gloom, then he was gone, pushing Jude onto his back, crouching over him.

It wasn't comfortable, half off the mattress, the gritty floor boards cold under Jude's shoulders, but he wasn't going to stop Luk, not for that. Jude stroked Luk's back in the darkness, then ran his hand down to the smoothness of Luk's hip. He'd be able to reach Luk's arse, his arm was long enough, and it took considerable willpower not to grab Luk there.

Luk was tentative, touching just his lips to the head of Jude's cock, then slowly taking the head into his mouth. Jude could hear the rest of the household out on the back verandah; Rick was laughing loudly over the sounds of crashing and the dog barking, and Lori shouting.

"Yeah, that feels wonderful," Jude whispered. "Feels so good."

Fuck, it did feel good to have someone sucking his cock again, their mouth wet and slippery, their tongue sliding around the head. Jude was already turned on from going down on Luk, from being with Luk, and it wasn't going to take much, no matter how cautious Luk was being.

Luk's hand let go of Jude's cock, and Jude spread his thighs, hoping Luk would take the hint. Luk did, squeezing Jude's balls, then dragging his nails over the skin behind them. Jude didn't know if Luk meant to touch Jude's arse, or if it was a fumble in the dark, but one of Luk's fingers slid down into the crack of Jude's arse. Pins and needles shot through Jude's body, adding to the feeling of Luk's mouth, wet and hot.

"Close," Jude warned. "Gonna come."

Luk didn't take the hint; either he didn't care, or he didn't hear. Jude groaned deeply and fell into the exquisite relief of coming into someone's mouth, of being able to let go and surrender.

He crawled back onto the mattress, almost too tired to manage even that, and Luk dragged the blanket over both of them.

"Did I do that right?" Luk asked.

Jude slid an arm around Luk, pulling him closer, nuzzling against his shoulder. "You were perfect."

Something smashed, loud and sharp, in the house, and Luk jerked in Jude's arms, then Lori's voice shouted, "You fucker!"

Rick shouted, "Bitch," and there was another crash, more splintered wood than broken glass.

"Do you think...?" Luk whispered.

"I think we should stay here, out of everyone's way," Jude said. "If Lori sounds like she's hurt, I'll go out and see if I can help, but if they're just fighting, we need to stay out of it, at least until she sobers up."

A door slammed inside the house, and water ran in the bathroom.

"Relax," Jude said. "I think they're all going to bed."

Luk did relax, moving closer to Jude, tension dropping from his shoulders, his breathing slowing. Jude closed his eyes and tucked his knees in behind Luk's. Fuck Lori and her domestic dramas. The Delicate John household should play nice, for one night, out of respect for Jude's burgeoning sex life.

The dog barking woke Jude, early enough that the light coming through the murky glass was gray and pale.

141

Someone inside the house shouted, "Shut the fuck up, stupid dog!" and the dog subsided into silence.

Jude was more than comfortable. He'd rolled over during the night, and Luk was curled up against his back, radiating delicious warmth under the blanket. The air in the room was early-autumn-cool enough to make Jude appreciate this, just from a comfort point of view, even if Luk hadn't been pressing a generous morning erection against Jude's arse.

Fuck, Jude was glad they'd fallen asleep naked, because the feel of Luk's cock rubbing against one of his buttocks was going to be keeping him in sexual fantasies for a damned long time. He moved, shifting one knee, and Luk's cock slid into the crack of his arse.

Delicious friction, teasing Jude's imagination, just from the slightest pressure. Jude's cock was so hard it hurt, and Jude risked moving enough to shift his hand and squeeze himself.

Luk snuffled sleepily, and his hand slid around to grip Jude's hip bone. Yep, Jude was sprung, getting off on an accidental rub.

Luk rocked his hips, rubbing the length of his shaft against Jude's arse, and Jude gasped.

"I'm dreaming, aren't I?" Luk whispered.

"Yeah," Jude said. "But so am I." He must be; inexperienced Luk couldn't have worked out what to do to blow Jude's mind, not so quickly.

Jude spat into his fingers and reached around behind himself, spreading saliva over Luk's cock, his fingers lingering over the hard flesh.

Luk's hand left Jude's hip, and Jude heard Luk spit as well, then Luk shifted his cock a little and rubbed slippery fingers over Jude's arse.

Whimpering was something Jude tried to avoid; there was no way to do it, even during sex, and not have it come off as helpless and desperate, but fuck, he was helpless and desperate, too turned on to stop the noises he was making.

Luk was making noises too, in his throat, while his fingertips circled Jude's arse. If this was how Luk touched his guitar, then no wonder his music was so fucking good, because he was playing Jude, pulling feeling after feeling out of him, touching harder, becoming bolder.

"Fuck, I can't believe I'm doing this," Luk whispered, and the tip of one finger eased into Jude slowly.

Jude buried his face in the pillow, trying to muffle himself as Luk moved closer, hitching one leg over Jude's, leaning his chest across Jude's back, shoving the solid length of his cock against the cheek of Jude's arse.

More spit, and Jude's fingers lingered, spreading the saliva, encouraging Luk to push in further, making sure it was real, that he wasn't imagining Luk touching him.

Breathing hard, his hand starting to shake, Luk pushed a second finger in, so that the burn made Jude hiss, just until the two fingers were inside him, rocking and pushing.

Luk's cock was jabbing into Jude's buttock in time with Luk's fingers, and fuck, but Luk had worked it out, worked out what was inside Jude's head, what he wanted.

"I want to fuck you," Luk said, his mouth against Jude's ear. "But I don't know how to."

"I haven't got anything with me. Have you got a condom?" Jude said, his teeth gritted. If he didn't get a fucking medal for this, he was going to want to know why.

"Fuck, no," Luk said.

Medal. A big shiny medal. Some kind of award.

Jude moved, getting himself out from under Luk before Luk decided to take things further, getting Luk's fingers out of his arse, shoving Luk onto his back.

"What?" Luk asked, then Jude sucked his cock, deep-throated him in one sudden move, and just kept on sucking hard.

Stronger men than Luk had failed to resist that, and Luk didn't have a chance, grabbing Jude's hair, jamming his cock in harder, coming helplessly.

Deep-throating horny young guitarists who shot hard was something else there should be medals for, or at least some kind of public recognition. Jude was going to be hoarse for a week. At least he got the consolation prize...

In the gray light, Jude took hold of Luk's hand, and said, "Like this."

He spat on Luk's fingers, then knelt on the mattress and guided Luk's hand between his thighs. Like this, with Luk's fingers curled inside him, Jude had both hands free to touch his own cock, to ease the ache.

Luk's other hand closed over Jude's hands, and he was already so close, so wired from the feel of Luk's fingers in his arse, that it was more than Jude could take, and he was coming.

The mattress beside Luk had never looked so good, and Jude fell forward onto it, too boneless to move. He should pull the blanket up, at least, but it seemed like far too much hard work, besides, Luk was lovely and warm...

Somewhere in the house, a mattress squeaked rhythmically, and a bed frame collided with a wall repeatedly. Luk chuckled, but Jude couldn't raise the enthusiasm to agree with him. Sleep mattered more.

When Jude managed to open his eyes the next time, the light through the window was bright and the mattress beside him was empty. That was alright; he could wake up without Luk, as long as he could do it slowly.

He could smell toast somewhere else in the house,

and maybe even coffee. Coffee would be good, because there were times when he liked to forget he didn't drink caffeine. Jude rubbed a hand over his bare chest, then sniffed his fingers. A shower first would be polite.

Jude pulled on his jeans and retrieved his boxers from the top of the six stack, along with his backpack, then wandered out into the hallway, heading for the shower. The back door of the house stood open, and he could see Luk sitting on the back verandah, playing someone else's six string.

Shower, toast and coffee, then some music with his lover.

The shower was as dreadful as always, spraying indifferent water, barely enough to rinse off under. Jude pulled on boxers and jeans over his wet skin, and a clean T-shirt, then dragged the band out of his plait. It took a few minutes to work the knots out of his hair and redo the short plait, then brush his teeth, but he felt human afterward.

More than merely human, he felt fucking fantastic. Just laid. Satisfied.

On the back verandah, Jude sat in one of the sagging armchairs opposite Luk, coffee in one hand, and vegemite on toast in the other.

Robbo and Luk were jamming on ukulele and guitar, while a girl Jude didn't know listened. Jude nodded at Robbo and the girl, then smiled at Luk, who grinned back.

The girl might have stepped out of one of Luk's descriptions of his thwarted attempts at relationships with women. The young woman smiled at Jude and held out a pack of clove cigarettes, which he refused. She brushed flecks of ash off her black sweater and sucked at her cigarette with lips painted scarlet.

Luk and Robbo finished whatever they'd been jamming

-- it had been in a time register that had made Jude's brain hurt -- and Robbo said, "This is Brianna. Brianna, this is Jude. He plays lead guitar in The Tockleys."

"Caught your set last night," Brianna said. "At the Railway Hotel. Just lovely, like a transcendent moment in time."

"Thanks," Jude said, not daring to meet Luk's gaze, in case either of them laughed. "Are you friends with Robbo?"

"Brianna posted bail for me," Robbo said. "Lovely of her, since no one here could scrape together the cash."

"What did you get arrested for?" Jude asked. "Or is that a rude question?"

Robbo was crazy, but not in the self-destructive way the rest of Delicate John were, so it was probably safe to ask.

"A simple misunderstanding," Robbo said. "A small matter of some figs in a tree, and me wanting them, and failing to understand property law with regards to trespass and ownership of figs. I'm sure it can be cleared up, now someone has actually paid my bail."

"You got arrested for stealing fruit?" Jude asked.

Robbo shrugged.

"'The proper way to eat a fig, in society,'" Brianna intoned, and Jude knew she was quoting D. H. Lawrence's poem, *Figs*, but that didn't make it any less hysterically funny.

Luk started laughing, and turned it into a spluttering cough, so Jude handed over his mug of black instant coffee.

"There you go," Jude said sympathetically.

Robbo, who had possibly spotted a social disaster looming, cut into any further poetry recitals from Brianna and said, "Want a guitar, Jude? I'm sure there's another acoustic around somewhere."

The spare acoustic was battered and out of tune, and Luk took it off Jude and handed him the tuned one, to speed things up. Jude, who had to use a tuning fork to tune his electric guitar, didn't bother resisting. Besides, if Luk could tune a guitar in thirty seconds, based on a test chord and the feel of the strings, then he should be allowed to show off in front of young women called Brianna who quoted D. H. Lawrence at random.

"Do you like ferrets?" Jude asked Brianna.

"What?" she said.

"Ignore him, he's been awake all night shagging," Robbo said. "Now, shall we explore something in strict tempo, my dears?"

"Thank you," Jude said. "From the bottom of my strict tempo heart."

Lori wandered grumpily onto the back verandah, wearing panda pajamas and carrying a mug of coffee, at the end of a song.

"Morning, Wallaby," Robbo said cheerily.

"Who was fucking at six this morning?" Lori asked.

Jude lifted his hand, as did Luk. Robbo put his hand up and Brianna did, too.

"Oh, for fuck's sake," Lori said. "It was six on a Sunday morning. Couldn't you all have waited?"

"I think I speak for all of us here when I say, 'no,'" Robbo said. "Sorry."

Lori pulled out the exercise book she had tucked under her arm and tossed it at Luk. "My songbook, Loud Sex Boy. Want to work up some more arrangements before rehearsals this week?"

"It wasn't me making all the noise," Luk said, picking up the exercise book and sliding it under his knee. "I'm not the one with the full-on vocal projection here."

Jude found himself being stared at by four people. "What?" he said. "So? I've had some classical singing training, sure. Doesn't mean it was me screaming my head off, does it? It certainly wasn't us trying to take the side of the house out with a bedframe, was it?"

"Bastard," Robbo said. "Another set?"

"I'm going back to bed," Lori said. "To have loud sex."

Jude looked at Luk. "Want to keep playing? I need to head home soonish; I've got stuff to do this afternoon."

"One more," Luk said.

The train into the city was crowded enough that they had to stand, guitar cases propped in the wheelchair bay, backpacks beside their feet. Jude leaned back against the side of the carriage, and he knew he was staring at Luk, but he didn't seem to be able to stop.

It might have been the anonymity of the full train carriage, or leftover from the night before, but Luk leaned against Jude, one arm around his waist.

Jude didn't say anything; he'd take what he could get in the way of public contact with Luk.

At the train station, Luk slung his pack over his shoulder and picked up his guitar case.

"I'll see you at rehearsal," Jude said, juggling his pack and holding his guitar out of the way of a woman with a stroller and two kids.

Luk nodded, but didn't walk away, and Jude wondered how long they were going to stand around on the train platform, and if he should just give in and ask Luk back to his house for an afternoon of wild sex.

"See you," Luk finally said, and he moved, but not away. He reached up and kissed Jude, a quick brush of his lips, then he was gone, up the escalators with the crowd.

Jude stood on the platform until the crowd cleared

and the back of Luk's pack disappeared out of sight.

Damn. He should have gone with the afternoon of wild sex option.

Chapter Eleven

M addie held the door to the sound studio open for Jude. "He was here a moment ago," she said. "Then he went back to his place to get his acoustic and some arrangements he was working on."

"Thanks," Jude said, setting his guitar down on the couch in the studio. "I'll go find him. Which house is his?"

Maddie pointed. "That way, hon. There's a path, through the garden."

Jude found the gap through the bushes between the houses that Maddie had mentioned.

The driveway at Luk's family's house was empty, but the sliding door to what looked like the kitchen and dining area was open, so someone was home. Jude rapped on the door frame.

A teenage girl wandered into the kitchen, carrying an empty plate, and she undid the security screen and looked Jude up and down.

"What?" she said.

"Is Luk here?"

"Lucien!" the girl bellowed. "There's someone to see you!"

Jude looked down at her, and she shrugged. "Guess his door is closed. It's the one with the Lennon poster on it, down the hall."

It wasn't hard to find Luk's room, and Jude knocked on the door on John Lennon's chin, where it was cradled in his hand.

He could hear Luk playing, through the door, and Luk's voice called out, "Fuck off, Penny."

"It's me," Jude said, opening the door.

Luk's room was awash with clothes, books and papers, the bed unmade, the desk drowning under more mess, the walls covered in posters. Luk bounded off his bed, his acoustic guitar in his hand, and pulled Jude into the room, shoving the door shut behind him.

Luk put the guitar down on the floor at the same time as he slung his free arm around Jude's neck, mashing their mouths together, and they tumbled onto the bed, thudding the mattress against the wall.

"Missed you," Jude said, his mouth against Luk's neck, and Luk grunted, possibly in agreement, or possibly because Jude's hand was shoved between their bodies, undoing Luk's jeans.

The door opened, and Lori said, "That's disgusting."

"Fuck!" Luk said, scrambling out from under Jude, pulling his zip back up, and when Jude sat up, the teenage girl who'd let him in was standing behind Lori, in the hall, mouth and eyes wide open.

"Penny!" Luk said, and he was gone, off the bed, pushing past Lori, chasing the girl down the hall.

Jude sat on the edge of the bed, and Lori leaned against the door frame.

"Guess Luk just came out to his family," Lori eventually said.

"At least to his sister, assuming that's who the girl is."

"We could go over to Maddie's, set up for rehearsal, while Luk deals with this," Lori said.

Jude nodded, and he must have been staring at Lori's face, where her usually immaculate make-up was just a touch too heavy, because Lori lifted a hand to her puffy cheek.

"Don't you dare say anything," she said. "Not a word."

"Lori?" Jude said, standing up and reaching out a hand to her, but Lori pulled away and marched grimly in front of him to Maddie's studio. Jude let it drop, for the moment.

Luk followed them over into the sound studio ten minutes later, looking glum, his acoustic guitar in his hand.

"How's your sister?" Lori asked.

"Bribed into silence," Luk said. "Ecstatic at having leverage over me. Kind of horrified at what she saw. Can we not talk about this? I've done an arrangement for one of Lori's songs; do you both want to hear it?"

"Which one?" Lori asked. "Which one did you choose?"

"'Ascospore,'" Luk said. "I'll play the melody on the acoustic. You're all going to have to put up with me singing it, for now."

Luk sat down on a rehearsal chair, and checked the tuning of his acoustic with a chord.

"holding onto that memory of that
night that we kissed, and you held me there
with your hands in my hair
and you sighed
like you meant it.

"i cut myself with feathers because you
are so happy to see me bleed
you have this need
to hold me
all together.

"where in the world is this self-denial
it is a place on no map yet
i keep coming back
to this point
this beginning.

"we share pages of promises, written
in ink and twice crossed out
so there is no doubt
as to where
i am standing.

"all hard lines and hidden softness that i
cannot touch my desire is too
much so you require
this sense of control
this collar.

"so desperate for any semblance of
human attention that I let you stare
and pull my hair
and never cry
i don't mean it."

Luk's voice, when he wasn't trying to push himself,
was sweet and gentle, and the chord progressions in
the melody were eerie and haunting, nothing like what
they usually played, not even in Jude's song. The lyrics
themselves were disturbing, and when Jude glanced at

Lori, she was wiping her cheeks, her face turned away.

"What do you think?" Luk asked.

"That's an amazing song," Jude said. "Just wonderful, Lori."

"The words are mine," Lori said. "But I only gave Luk a chord list, nothing like what he just played. He wrote the music, not me."

"I know it's not our sound, really, but I think we should record this as an acoustic track," Luk said. "Jude and I could both play acoustics, Lori can add some bongos, and some other hand percussion. And maybe Jude should sing it; he's got the vocal range. What do you think, Lori?"

Lori nodded. "I couldn't sing it, not without crying, so it needs to be one of you two. You did just fine then, Luk, so you could."

"It's a bit emo," Luk said, putting his acoustic aside. "No offense, Lori."

"Fuck you," Lori said. "And I mean that in the nicest possible way. Of course it's emo, you emotionally-stunted adolescent."

Luk slammed the studio door on his way out, and Jude flicked the power off to the amp his guitar was plugged into and put his guitar down. "Not good, Lori," he said. "Think you could fuck things up any worse if you tried?"

"Fuck you, too," Lori called after Jude, as he left to find Luk.

Luk was sitting on the verge of Maddie's house, beside where Lori had parked Rick's van. Jude sat beside Luk on the grass. The streetlights were struggling on in the early evening, and Jude could hear at least four different TVs coming from nearby houses.

"Why the fuck is she such a bitch to me?" Luk asked. "Why does she have to do that? I really can't take that kind of shit from her any longer."

"All is not well in Lori-land," Jude said.

"She's using smack," Luk said.

"Yeah, I'd guessed. How are you feeling?"

"Fucking awful. I can't do this anymore."

"'This' is the band? Or 'this' is you and I?"

Jude had only to glance at Luk's face to know the answer: he was being dumped.

Jude drew his knees up and wrapped his arms around them. "Is that how you felt Sunday morning, when you wanted to fuck me?"

When Jude turned his head to look at Luk, Luk was staring at him.

"Deal with that, right now, because this is real. I'm real, you're real, what we do when we're together is about as real as it could possibly be," Jude said. "Have you been thinking about fucking me, imagining what it'll feel like?"

"Fuck, yeah," Luk said. "All I've been able to think about is what you felt like when I touched you, and the way you sounded."

Jude held out his hand to Luk. "This is not without meaning for me. I'm not going to drop any of that on you, except to let you know."

"I don't..." Luk took Jude's hand uncertainly.

"Let's just muddle through one mess at a time," Jude said, standing up and pulling Luk to his feet. Luk was standing close to him, close enough that Jude could smell the warmth of Luk's skin, and it made him want to kiss him.

Luk's fingers tightened around Jude's and he looked up at Jude. "Fuck, you're right," Luk said, and Jude didn't bother asking for clarification, not when Luk was backing him against the van, mouth hot and hungry against Jude's.

They needed to do something, and urgently, about

getting somewhere without cars driving past, and without Lori stomping around impatiently.

"Are we going to rehearse at all?" Lori demanded.

Luk pulled away from Jude and crossed the lawn to where Lori stood on Maddie's driveway.

"Listen here," Luk said. "If you treat me like shit again, I'm walking out of this band, and I'm taking my musical arrangements, loaned vintage guitars and borrowed sound studio with me. You don't give Jude any shit at all, so you've got to give me the same respect."

"If he leaves, I'm going, too," Jude said.

Luk glanced across at Jude, and Jude flashed him a smile.

Luk smiled back, and Jude was suddenly glad he'd told Luk he cared, because it wasn't something he wanted to hide, not right then.

"Alright," Lori said. "I'm sorry, Luk."

"Apology accepted," Luk said. "Shall we go rehearse, before any more catastrophes happen?"

At the door to the sound studio, Jude stopped Luk. "Come home with me tonight."

Lori's cymbals clattered and she glared at them.

Luk touched Jude's chest, his hand pressing against Jude's worn T-shirt. "I'm going to be prudent and say no, not tonight. I think disappearing might precipitate things at home, and I need to buy a little time there. Is that okay?"

Jude nodded. "Of course it's okay."

"What about Friday night?" Luk said. "At your place?"

Lori tapped her snare drum, counting herself into 'Not the Only One,' the percussion line completely familiar now.

Jude nodded and said, "You can stop, Lori, we've got the hint."

***

Jude had to admit that using Lori's shower had made him newly appreciative of the wonders of his own, with hot water bucketing out of the showerhead in an effective torrent, enabling the person using the shower to soap up and then remove the lather in a matter of seconds.

He shampooed his hair, then rinsed off. The timer hanging beside the shower said he had thirty seconds left out of his allocated three minutes, and Jude spent those blissful seconds with the water beating at his shoulders.

He wasn't sure what time Luk would turn up, or if they'd go out or just head to bed, but he'd showered off the day's sweat, and was probably ready for all of the options.

He shaved quickly, towel wrapped around his hips, then rinsed his face off and brushed his teeth.

"Hot date?" Sammie asked from the kitchen when Jude went back to his bedroom.

Jude looked at Sammie, who was also wearing only a towel, and seemed to be stirring a pot of brown goo. "Um, I'm hopeful. Why are you cooking mud while naked on a Friday afternoon?"

"It's hair dye," Sammie said. "And don't you dare tell anyone I color my hair."

"You're dyeing your hair?" Jude said. "Aren't you and Alison going to the center for the talk from the visiting monk?"

"Alison is going with that American exchange student she met last week, and I would have been in the way, so I'm staying home for my semi-regular encounter with henna instead."

"Smells, um, not appetizing."

"Promise I'll wash the pan up afterward," Sammie said.

Jude had gotten as far as his bedroom door when there was a knock on the front screen door of the house. Sammie squealed and dived for her bedroom, her towel clasped firmly to her breasts, which left Jude to answer the front door, wearing his towel.

He opened the front door and unlocked the screen to let Luk in.

"I like the dress code," Luk said, pushing past Jude, carrying his backpack and his acoustic guitar. "Hope you don't mind, but I came straight from class, rather than go home."

"Of course not," Jude said.

"What's that burning smell?" Luk asked when Jude opened his bedroom door.

"Hang on," Jude said. "Sammie! Your hair is on fire!"

Jude closed the bedroom door, shutting out the sound of Sammie swearing, and Luk slid his guitar and pack off his shoulders.

"Your housemate is burning her hair?" Luk asked.

"It's complicated, secret women's business," Jude said. "I could tell you, but you'd want to do something really macho afterward."

Luk smelled of chewing gum and sunshine and sweat, a heady combination that made Jude think it was a good thing he hadn't got around to getting dressed. Luk's fingers were gentle on Jude's back, tracing his ribs.

"Now you're just taunting," Luk said.

"What did you want to do this evening?" Jude asked. "We could go out, either to the Hydey, or just down the road for a bite to eat. Or we could just get naked right now, and worry about food later."

"Is there a reason we're even discussing these options?" Luk asked, laughing. "Honestly?"

"I'm being polite," Jude said. "At least, as polite as I

can be, given I'm wearing only a towel."

Luk grabbed Jude's buttock through the towel. "If you weren't trying to be polite, what would you be saying?"

The stubble on Luk's chin prickled Jude's palms when he cupped Luk's face in his hands. "Fuck, I want you, and I don't want to wait any longer."

"We're not going to have to stop this time?" Luk asked.

"Got condoms, got lube."

Jude brushed his lips over Luk's, then dropped to his knees in front of Luk. Luk smelled hot, of sweat and pheromones, when Jude unbuckled his heavy belt and unzipped his grubby jeans.

"Oh, yeah," Luk said, when Jude pushed down his jeans and boxers, freeing his hard cock so it sprang out.

"How long have you been hard?" Jude asked, looking up at Luk.

"For hours," Luk said, his hand stroking Jude's wet hair back off his face. "It hurts."

"Come for me," Jude said, and he slid the length of Luk's cock into his mouth and curled his hand around the base.

Luk's fingers wound into Jude's hair, guiding his head, and Luk rocked his hips, pushing his cock over Jude's tongue. When Jude glanced up, Luk was staring down, watching his cock disappearing into Jude's mouth.

"So fucking hot," Luk said.

Jude wanted to tell him: wait until you see your cock sliding into my arse; but he wasn't going to stop sucking Luk, not with the way Luk was gasping, bending forward over Jude, riding his mouth.

Jude had to hang onto Luk with both hands, holding him up, when Luk's knees failed him, and the pair of them stumbled backward onto Jude's mattress with a crash.

Luk started laughing, the kind of deep, slow laugh that

was about tension leaving and feeling safe, and it filled Jude with happiness as he clambered over Luk's knees and elbows, wiping the come from his chin, his towel long gone.

"That's better," Jude said.

"It's been a bad week," Luk said.

"Did your sister out you?" Jude asked.

"No," Luk said, shaking his head. "She's kind of tiptoeing around me at the moment, staring at me a lot. It can't last, and when it breaks, it's going to be bad. What happened when you came out?"

"With my family? I guess not much. I was eighteen when I told my mum. She said she already knew. My brother was away, overseas, at the time, and I told him over the phone. He wouldn't talk to me for ages, but when he came back again, he never mentioned it, and now he acts like it's no big deal."

"Your father?" Luk asked.

Jude shook his head. "Single parent family, so it was never an issue. I have no idea where my father even is. What do you think will happen when your sister blurts out what she saw?"

Luk shrugged, but Jude could see the fear creasing the skin around his eyes. "I can't do anything about it, not right now, except get you to persuade me it's all going to be worthwhile."

"Just think of Brianna," Jude said. "Peace at home, as long as you fuck Brianna for the rest of your life."

Luk shook his head, laughing again, and this time, it was the laugh of amusement. "She was unbelievable. What the fuck was she talking about with the figs?"

"It's a D. H. Lawrence poem," Jude said. "Which makes it all so much worse."

"Do you think she quotes poetry in bed?" Luk asked, and his breath caught as Jude slid a hand under his

T-shirt.

"She probably does," Jude said. "But, according to Lori, Robbo plays the ukulele in bed after fucking, so that's about even. You ready to stop talking?"

Luk pushed himself up so he was sitting up on the mattress, and pulled his T-shirt over his head. "Yeah, more than ready."

Dusk had turned into night, so Jude switched on the reading light beside the bed and watched while Luk unbuckled and unlaced his boots, then kicked them off.

"Do you want me to shower?" Luk pulled his socks off and tossed them across the room.

Jude shook his head. "Nah, you're just going to need another one afterward."

Luk stood up over Jude to slide his jeans and boxers off, and he was gorgeous in the muted light from the lamp, still wearing the last of his adolescence like a promise to be grown into, but becoming more of a man every moment.

"What?" Luk said, sprawling back down beside Jude, one leg tossed over Jude's, his hand finding Jude's cock, making Jude take a sudden breath in.

"Just thinking about you fucking me."

"Tell me what to do," Luk said. "Tell me how to make it good for you."

Jude reached over, beside the light. "These are for you," he said, holding up a box of condoms. "Mine, if you ever decide you want to try out being fucked, are on the bookshelf, just to make sure we don't get them mixed up."

"Why two boxes?" Luk said, taking the box out of Jude's hand and pulling a strip of condoms out.

"Different sizes," Jude said. "And here's the lube. Silicone-based, so really runny, which I believe you found out last time around."

"But this isn't what to do," Luk said.

"Remember Sunday? What you were doing to me? I don't need to show you how to get me so turned on that there's nothing I want more than to feel your cock inside me," Jude said. "I just need to make sure that this time we've got a condom within reach, so I don't have to stop you."

"Roll over," Luk said, tearing open a condom wrapper. "Because, this time, I'm not stopping."

Jude watched Luk roll the condom on, then turned over, lifting one knee, sliding a hand under his belly to hold his own cock. Luk cupped one of Jude's buttocks and kissed Jude's shoulder. The tube of lube popped loudly, then Luk's fingers, slippery and wet, slid down the crack of Jude's arse.

Luk took a deep breath, loud in the room, and Jude closed his eyes and let himself relax. Luk moved so his cock was pushing against Jude's hip, and he dragged his fingers around Jude's arse.

It made Jude shove his face into his pillow, just to stop from screaming, and Luk said, "Go on, I want to hear you make those noises again. I wanna hear you when I touch you."

Jude's window was closed, and anything Sammie heard through the walls of the old house would be her own fault for not going out like she'd said she would.

Pushing the pillow aside, Jude turned his head to the side so he could see Luk over his shoulder. "You want me to beg?"

"Do you want to?" Luk asked, and he pushed one finger in slowly, so that Jude had to grab at the mattress.

"Oh, fuck, yes," Jude said. "Like that, oh, more."

Luk chuckled. "Fuck, you're tight." His finger turned, twisting inside Jude, and Jude thrashed on the mattress, aware he was whimpering again, unable to do anything about it, not when Luk was easing a second finger in,

162

shifting his weight over so he was humping Jude's side.

Knowing this was when he'd stopped it all before made it so much sweeter, and Jude managed to make himself say, "Fuck, more lube, then, oh fuck, fuck me."

Luk's mouth was against Jude's ear, his breathing a roar, and he groaned deeply. "Yeah, 'kay."

Lube dripped on Jude's thigh, and Luk was lifting his weight over him in a confusion of legs and arms.

"Like this?" Luk asked, and it took a clumsy moment of sliding in the lube, then he was pushing in, not giving Jude time to adjust, or even breathe.

Luk held still, once he was fully sheathed, and Jude looked up a little, enough that Luk's lips pressed against his hair.

"Sweet..." Luk whispered. "This is perfect."

"Try moving," Jude whispered.

Luk lifted his weight, rocking forward, gently moving inside Jude. If Jude hadn't already fallen for Luk, he would have at that moment, just from listening to Luk's labored breathing as he tried to control himself and take it slow, make it last, make it good for them both.

Luk reached out, threaded his fingers through Jude's where Jude was hanging onto the edge of the mattress, and it began to build slowly, right from the soles of Jude's feet, tingling, then roaring.

Over him, Luk was driving into him harder, so that his sweat ran onto Jude's skin and his voice was raw against Jude's ear.

It was primal, out of control and wild, taking Jude when he came, shaking him to his core, leaving him to fall afterward, while Luk bellowed through coming.

Luk rolled off Jude, pulling out of him roughly, to collapse onto the mattress beside him.

Moving was hard work, and Jude was vaguely aware that Sammie, possibly in self-defense, was playing Britney

Spears loudly elsewhere in the house, as he slung an arm over Luk's heaving chest.

"So?" Jude said.

"Oh... oh..." Luk said, waggling fingers weakly at Jude. "Oh, fuck. I don't..."

"Incoherent is good," Jude said.

"Was that right?" Luk said. "Did you come?"

"That was fucking brilliant, and I came, with earth-shattering intensity, just a few seconds before you did," Jude said.

Luk grinned, and Jude could feel his own face was wearing a matching stupid grin, the blissed-out, sated smile of the just-fucked.

Chapter Twelve

The kitchen at Monlo's was empty, apart from the three of them who were gathered around a work bench, looking at the map Lori had spread out.

"Wongan Hills?" Luk said dubiously. "I think I've driven through there once, on the family camping holiday from hell."

"Is there really a pub at Wongan Hills?" Jude asked. "A pub that does gigs? It's just a dot on the map."

Lori shrugged. "I'm just telling you what Robbo told me. Delicate John is playing there tonight, and we can open for them."

Jude glanced at Luk, who still had the soft-smudged look he'd woken up with that morning, despite having got up early to go home and collect his electric guitar.

Luk shrugged. "Can we catch a lift with Delicate John in their truck and use their gear?"

Lori's shoulders sagged a little under her baggy sweater. "There's not a lot of room. I could ride with them, but not you two. And we should use our own amps and speakers, just because."

"Will Rick lend us his van?" Jude asked.

"That, I can get him to do," Lori said.

"We'll have to use today's lunchtime money to pay for the petrol," Jude said. "But if we get a hundred dollars for opening, then we still come out ahead, and I don't think we can turn down a gig. It'll be a two hour drive each way, but that's no big deal, as long as we don't hit a roo on the way home."

"So we're doing it?" Lori asked.

"It's a gig," Luk said, and Jude nodded his agreement.

He couldn't imagine they'd get a huge crowd, but Delicate John was a big enough act that it was just possible that every frustrated, head-banging farmer kid within a hundred-kilometer radius would decide to turn up for a night of beer and noise.

"Won't this be fun, boys and girls?" Jude said, folding the map up.

The pub was better than Jude expected, a substantial red brick building, with added-on accommodation running off to one side and an ample carpark. 'Wednesday darts!' the blackboard outside the pub shouted. 'Counter meals! Kids' meals free!'

The banner hanging from the upper floor balcony, fluttering in the late afternoon sun, made it all clear. 'Wongan Hills drag races this weekend!'

"Drag races?" Luk said, craning his head to look out of the passenger window as Jude turned the van into the crowded hotel carpark. "Look at the machines lined up here! That's a Ford V8, with a hood cut out, and a full spoiler!"

Jude, despairing of finding an empty bay in the carpark,

settled for parking the van immediately behind Delicate John's truck, which Lori had ridden up in. He'd been glad of the time alone with Luk, the chance to listen to Luk rambling on about music and his plans for the recording the band was going to make. It looked like the trip home that night was going to be all about hotted-up drag-racing cars, which might be more of a trial.

Luk undid his seatbelt and kicked the passenger door open. "What a great place," he said. "I don't remember it being like this."

Jude stood in the carpark and stretched. "Just replace the fancy cars with dust, see how exciting it is then. Let's go find Lori, see if she knows where we unload the gear."

The Delicate John players were in the crowded beer garden at the back of the pub, jugs of beer on the table in front of them, but no Lori was in sight. Rick didn't look up, but Robbo stood up from the table and walked over to where Luk and Jude waited.

"Hey," Robbo said.

"Where's Lori?" Jude asked.

Robbo looked uneasy. "Probably in the band's hotel room. She and Rick had a fight in the truck on the way here. She was pretty upset about it."

Jude grabbed Robbo's arm. "Has he hurt her?"

"Hurt her?" Luk said. "Does Rick hit Lori?"

"I don't know anything about that," Robbo said, "but he's speeding badly today."

"What's the room number?" Jude said.

The band's room was at the end of the block of added-on accommodation units, tacked on some time in the Seventies, and sliding rapidly into decay. Jude knocked on the room door, Luk hovering anxiously beside him.

"Why didn't you tell me?" Luk said, his voice low, as Lori opened the hotel room door.

"Oh, it's you," she said, turning back to fall on the rumpled bed covered in clothes, but leaving the door open.

Jude sniffed the sour air in the room, smelling vomit, and Luk's nose wrinkled.

Luk crouched down beside the bed, his face close to Lori's. "What have you taken, Lori?" Luk asked gently. "Are you alright?"

"I'm sick," Lori said. "That's all. Just had a drink."

Luk looked over his shoulder at Jude. "Want to go find some electrolyte replacement fluid? Failing that, vegemite on toast?"

Jude nodded, but he didn't leave. Instead he knelt down beside Luk and slid Lori's sweater sleeves up.

"Looking for track marks?" Lori asked, her voice brittle.

"No," Jude said, smoothing his fingers over Lori's pale skin, then pulling her sleeves down again. "I'm looking for bruises, love. I'll be back in a moment."

The front bar had Gatorade, so Jude grabbed two bottles and ran back to the hotel room, and found the room empty.

The bathroom door was ajar, and he could hear retching noises. Luk came out of the bathroom a moment later, wiping his wet hands on his jeans.

"What do you think?" Jude asked, his voice low, as he handed the Gatorade to Luk.

"There's a half-empty bottle of vodka on the floor beside the bed," Luk said. "That's enough to make me puke my guts out. How long until the gig?"

Jude glanced at the digital clock beside the hotel room bed. "An hour. Can you look after Lori while I set up the gear?"

"Shouldn't you do this bit?" Luk asked.

"I've never had a hangover in my life," Jude said. "I

suspect you know far more than I do about this side of things."

Luk's face was disbelieving. "Never? Never?"

"Never had a drink," Jude said. "Any puking I've done has been because of dodgy takeaway samosas."

"Luk!" Lori called, from the bathroom.

"Go and set up for the gig," Luk said. "Looks like I'm the one with the life experience, for a change."

Robbo, almost sober and definitely grim, helped Jude set up the assorted speaker stacks and amps that they'd salvaged from Lori's garage. The lounge bar was half full already, with a ragged crowd of drag-racers, mechanics and hangers-on, when Jude and Robbo balanced the mikes on the rickety stage.

"No sound tech," Robbo said. "I'll give you a hand to make sure everything is hooked up."

"It's not a good crowd, is it?" Jude said when Robbo helped feed the extension leads behind the stage to the power board.

Robbo shook his head. "Bad crowd, and there's an ugly mood in the air, too. Rick and Lori have been fighting all week, and I don't think I can stand it anymore."

"Gonna move in with Brianna?" Jude asked, jumping back up on the stage to flick the power to the amps on.

"If she'll have me," Robbo said. "If she'll have me."

"Poetry?" Jude asked, following Robbo off the stage with the intention of heading back to the hotel room to find Lori and Luk.

"She recites poetry, eats vast amounts of garlic, and keeps an incontinent budgie," Robbo said. "And yet, she has no rodents in her kitchen, and her sheets are clean. I could love her."

"Thanks for your help," Jude said.

"Not a problem, mate," Robbo said. "It was a chance to not notice what any of my fellow band members were pouring into their systems."

Luk opened the hotel room door when Jude knocked.

"She's putting on make-up," Luk said, his voice low.

"Is she going to make it?" Jude asked.

Luk shrugged. "She seems sober enough now."

Lori appeared in the bathroom doorway, dressed in jeans and a bra. "You can stop muttering about me. Do you think this looks alright?"

Jude looked Lori over, taking in the careful eyeliner, pinned up braids and boobs falling out of her bra. That seemed to answer his concerns about Lori hiding bruises.

"It's not a tits-and-all crowd, Lori," Jude said. "It's a drunk-and-nasty crowd, in my opinion."

"Everyone loves tits," Lori said, sitting down on the bed and pulling on her boots. "At least, everyone who's not a gay man."

Jude and Luk exchanged glances, and if Lori noticed, she didn't complain.

Beside Jude, Luk said, "Bloody hell," under his breath as they walked through the side door to the lounge bar, where they'd be performing.

Bloody hell was right. The crowd was loud, calling out to friends, hassling the waitresses, the shouts interspersed by smashing glasses.

Lori pulled her headset on and sat down at her drum kit, twirling her drum-sticks, while Jude switched her pickups on.

"Feeling okay?" he mouthed at her.

She shook her head, swallowing hard.

Luk stood beside Jude, while Jude pulled his guitar strap over his head, and Lori said, "We're The Tockleys, and this is my song."

The sound was dodgy, with the amp and speaker stack Lori and Jude were sharing flattening the sound out, and they had an echo in the room, coming off the art deco arched ceiling. Luk's sound was better, through his old amp and speaker set, but right then, Jude would have even welcomed help from his ex, Dave, if it could have fixed the sound system.

They finished the song, and Lori ploughed straight into 'Fade Away,' without giving Jude and Luk time to do anything about the amp and pickups.

At least it hid the fact that no one was going to applaud them.

Luk and Jude were singing the second chorus of 'Fade Away,' Luk working damned hard on the bass, holding it all together, when the percussion stopped cold, in an ugly clatter of snare, and the sound of Lori retching came through the speaker stack behind Jude.

"Play on," Luk mouthed, during the bridge, and it wasn't Jude's call, but he wasn't about to abandon Luk on stage.

Someone must have got Lori's headset off her, because the noises stopped, though the jeering from the audience didn't.

The two of them made it to the end of the song, no grand flourishes or fancy chords from Luk, and Luk shrugged at Jude and reached back to flick his amp off.

Lori was gone, hopefully back to her hotel room.

The two of them set about knocking down their gear, lifting amps, then speakers off the stage, leaving the mikes in place for Delicate John, getting as much distance between them and the audience as possible.

Jude kicked open the side door from the lounge bar to the carpark, ready to heft the speaker stack from Lori's garage out, when Luk said, "Fuck!" from the other end of the stack.

Rick and Lori were standing beside Delicate John's truck, Rick towering over Lori, menace in his voice as he said, "...bitch, we were going to perform that song."

Jude set his end of the speaker down, turning toward Lori, but Luk was faster, tossing the speaker down and hurtling across the gravel of the carpark, not slowing down, just running right into Rick and smashing him against the side of the truck with a huge crash, before both of them went down in a welter of flailing arms.

Jude was slower, since he wasn't intent on smearing Rick against metal, running up and grabbing Lori and pulling her away, dragging her back from where Rick and Luk were rolling in the dirt in the deep shadows between the truck and the souped-up dragster beside it.

"Stop!" Lori shrieked, struggling against Jude's arms, but not getting free. "Help!"

Jude couldn't not watch, couldn't make himself look away, as much as it sickened him to even think of Luk being hurt.

Delicate John band members appeared, running from the hotel room and the front bar, Robbo at the front, tearing up to Jude and looking down at Luk and Rick, who seemed to be slowing down, flailing less and shouting more.

"It was time someone thumped Rick," Robbo said, wading competently into the brawl, grabbing hands, then Luk's shirt, and pulling him off Rick.

Lori sobbed and squirmed in Jude's arms, but he didn't let her go, because he wasn't watching a second person he loved get hurt, not if he could help it.

"Not a chance, Your Highness," he said, against her ear. "Not until we know he's stopped throwing punches."

"Who made you the fucking boss?" Lori said, but she stopped struggling, and Jude loosened his grip to a hug, a close, secure hug.

"Children," Robbo said, moving Luk, who was wiping blood from his mouth, against the truck, before bending down to pull Rick to his feet. "Children, now why the argument?"

"Because that bitch played our fucking song!" Rick said, pointing at Lori. "And now we can't."

Luk strolled nonchalantly across to Jude and Lori, wiping dirt from his T-shirt, spitting blood onto the gravel.

"Are you alright?" Lori asked, and Jude reached out a hand to touch Luk's shoulder, to find Luk was trembling.

"Luk?" Jude whispered, his hand touching Luk's neck, then his cheek.

Luk smiled at Jude reassuringly, reaching out and sliding an arm around Jude's waist.

"It's my fucking song, you arsehole," Lori said. "Read the fucking copyright, next time you go to play it. I wrote it, and it's my song."

"The lady has a point," Robbo said. "And we are supposed to be setting up to play, right this moment. Shall we go and salvage this gig?"

Rick, aggression in his shoulders, shaped up to Robbo. "Fuck you," Rick said. "Fuck you, and her, and this stupid gig."

Robbo eased out of Rick's reach, toward the rest of Delicate John. "Set up, now," he said, his voice controlled. "Without Rick, if necessary."

Licks and Tank both turned to follow Robbo, and Rick said, "Fuck you, Lori," and followed the three of them into the lounge bar.

Lori sagged in Jude's arms, turning around to hug him, and Jude pulled Luk into the hug.

"Let's head back to the city," Jude said. "As soon as we've loaded the gear up. Are you hurt, Luk?'

"I don't seem to be," Luk said, looking over Lori's head at Jude in the yellow light of the carpark. "I don't think I hurt him, either."

"I'm mostly concerned with getting the hell out of here in Rick's van, before Rick remembers he lent it to us," Jude said.

The speaker stack Luk and Jude had dropped looked intact when they tossed it in the back of the van. Luk's speaker and amp was next, then Lori's amp, Lori's drum kit, the two guitars, and they were done.

Jude backed the van out of the carpark, just as the noise of Delicate John's first song started. They weren't playing 'Not the Only One.'

The road toward the city was empty; the wheat farms the road ran through were dark, apart from the occasional distant light from a farmhouse. The van headlights caught the flickering movement of roos in the darkness, but none of them bounded across the road. Lori was quiet, and when Jude glanced across the cab of the van, the dashboard lights were bright enough that he could see Luk had his arm around her, hugging her.

Jude squeezed Luk's thigh, then flexed his hands and settled himself more comfortably at the wheel, checking the gauges on the dash again.

The petrol gauge, instead of reading half full, was falling fast, and the reek of petrol was stronger than ever.

"Damn," Jude said, dropping speed.

"What is it?" Luk asked.

"Did you notice, when we left Wongan Hills, how far it was to Goomalling?"

Lori stirred. "What's wrong?"

"Forty-eight kilometers," Luk said. "Why?"

Jude slowed the van back down, through the gears, pulling it over on the side of the road, and putting it into reverse. "We're closer to Wongan Hills than Goomalling, and we're about to run out of petrol."

"You put fuel in," Lori said. "Half a tank."

The red fuel light of doom came on, and Jude kept the touch of his foot on the accelerator as light as he could, trying to eke out the fuel.

"That smell of petrol," Jude said, slipping the van into neutral as soon as it topped the hill, and letting it coast down the other side. "That smell would be a leaking fuel pump or line."

The van stuttered to a halt, part way up the next hill, and Jude let it roll off the road, into the rough scrub beside the road, then turned the ignition off, killing the lights.

"What now?" Luk asked.

"We can stay here until it's light," Jude said. "Or we can walk in the dark back to Wongan Hills, buy some petrol and some duct tape, try and get the van going, or arrange a tow back to Wongan Hills."

"How far is it?" Lori asked.

Luk said, "We've been driving about seven or eight minutes, at eighty kilometers an hour, maybe a bit less than that because of the speed restrictions coming out of Wongan Hills. Then we turned back, for about a kilometer. How do we all feel about hiking six or seven kilometers in the dark?"

"Less than that," Lori said. "We got stopped by the booze bus, on the edge of town. That'll take a kilometer or two off the walk."

Jude nodded. "Good point. They can probably call the tow truck for us."

The booze bus, a police checkpoint set up just for the drag-racing event, was stopping every car that left Wongan Hills that night, breathalysing the drivers and arresting the drunks. Jude had been sober, of course, but the police had already impounded a row of vehicles, the drivers sitting beside the modified bus on folding garden chairs, looking forward to a night in detention somewhere after a bus ride back to the city.

Luk shrugged. "I'm fine with that, but I've got comfortable shoes on."

Lori planted a foot heavily on the van dashboard. "Today was a Doc Marten day, and I'm deeply grateful for it."

Jude locked up the van while Lori pulled on her sweater, and the three of them started off through the cool evening air.

It was pleasant, walking under the crystal clear skies, the Milky Way a huge sprawl of stars above them, the Southern Cross hanging heavy in the sky whenever Jude glanced back over his shoulder. There were no other cars around, not heading toward Wongan Hills, and the occasional car in the opposite direction whooshed past in a flash of light and a roar of souped-up engine.

The scrub beside the road smelled of peppermint and wattle, and the gravel crunched underfoot. Luk was quiet, his boots scuffing in the dirt, and Jude could hear Lori humming under her breath, but couldn't place the song.

Lori ducked into the scrub to pee, and Jude hugged Luk, breathing in the smell of fresh sweat and warm skin.

"Don't do that again," Jude said quietly. "Don't get involved in a fight with a bully like Rick."

"He was going to hurt Lori; I had to stop him," Luk said.

"I'm not arguing with you about that," Jude said. "If you hadn't, then I would have. It was the bit afterward, where you were fighting with him, that was unnecessary. Please don't do that again."

The half-light from the stars wasn't enough for Jude to be able to read Luk's face clearly, but Luk's hand on Jude's cheek was gentle.

Lori rustled out from bushes, doing up her jeans, and Luk dropped his hand, then the three of them walked again.

If the others were bored by the beauty of the night, they didn't voice their thoughts, and Jude was willing to let the moments, the steps and the time wash past him in a walking meditation on companionship and love.

An easterly wind sprang up, coming over the last hill, the spotlights of the booze bus below them, Wongan Hills a splash of lights beyond. Jude did up the buttons of the shirt he'd pulled on over his T-shirt, shutting the cold air out, and Lori slid her hand through his elbow.

"Fuck, I'm tired," she said.

"Nearly there," Jude said. "Lean on me, for the last bit."

Lori's hand squeezed his arm. "Gonna be leaning on you a lot for a while," Lori said.

Jude patted her hand, and they followed Luk down the hill, toward the booze bus.

If the police officers were perplexed by three punks wandering in from the darkness, then they didn't show it.

"Evening, people," the officer in charge said. "Out for a stroll?"

"Evening, officer," Jude said. "Our van's broken down, partway to Goomalling. Any chance of some assistance?"

The female officer who had breathalysed Jude said, "I remember you, and your van. I'm not surprised the van has broken down; it was definitely not roadworthy. I should have taken it off the road."

"It seems the universe has agreed with you," Jude said, glancing back at Luk and Lori.

Luk was hanging back, looking sullen, and Lori hid behind him.

Damn. He could understand Lori, who presumably was carrying paraphernalia in the van or her bag, but Luk should have nothing to be sullen about.

The officer in charge swung a torch on Luk's face and whistled. "Nice black-eye, and it looks fresh. You people are having an exciting evening."

The female police officer stepped forward. "It should be quiet here, Sarge, until the pub closes. I could run them into town, to the roadhouse there, see if the tow truck will go pick the van up."

"I think the van has split a fuel line," Jude said. "I can fix it with some tape and a can of fuel. Even if I can't, then I can hand feed the carbie, if I can get some fuel back out to the van."

"Drive the kids around," the officer in charge said. "We can't have people wandering around in the dark after they've asked for help; it's the sort of thing that looks bad at a coronial enquiry."

"Um, thanks," Jude said.

The female officer pointed at one of the pursuit cars parked beside the booze bus. "Come on, before Sarge changes his mind."

Jude, Luk, and Lori sat in the back of the police car, Lori hunkered down in her seat belt, trying to look invisible, while the officer drove back into Wongan Hills, past the pub. Jude could hear the noise from the pub, of Delicate John playing and people drinking.

"Looks like a big night at the pub," Jude said to the police officer.

"Not my problem," the officer said. "I'm assigned to traffic duty tonight. There're officers here from Moora to keep control of things in the town."

The road house was closing up for the night, but the attendant looked up from dragging the signs in when the police car pulled into the forecourt, lifting a hand in greeting.

"Evening, officer," the attendant said, leaning into the driver's window. "I've shut the compressor down for the night, but I can power it back up if you need some fuel."

"These people are having car problems on the Goomalling road. You got a can of fuel they can buy?" the officer asked.

"And hose repair tape, for a fuel line," Jude said, going to open the car rear door and finding it locked.

"Sorry," the officer said. "Secure lock is on."

The officer flicked a switch, the doors clunked, unlocking, and Jude climbed out of the car.

"Can you get me a cold drink?" Lori asked, and when Jude looked back in the car, she had her head on Luk's shoulder.

Jude nodded, and followed the road house attendant into the small store.

It looked like whatever ego-driven chest-beating had been going on between Lori and Luk might just have been settled by Luk rolling around in the dirt with Rick, smacking him. It was enough to make Jude smile.

Chocolate for everyone, a can of fuel, a cold drink for Lori, and a roll of fuel line tape. The Tockleys sure knew how to enjoy themselves after a gig.

The cop drove out to the van, munching on the bar of chocolate Jude had bought her, the police car's powerful headlights illuminating the wheat paddocks beside the road, the distance that had taken them an hour and a half to walk whizzing past in a few minutes.

"I think the van's close, over the next hill," Jude said, leaning forward.

The police car slowed, and the officer said, "Uh-oh."

"What?" Jude said, as the police officer flicked on the pursuit car's hazard lights.

"Don't supposed you left your van doors open, did

you?" the officer said.

"No," Jude said. "I locked the van up."

"Fuck!" Luk said. "No! Oh, God, no!"

The squad car stopped in front of the van. The van doors were ajar, the front windscreen obviously smashed.

Jude undid his seatbelt, Luk swearing and pushing beside him, urging him out.

As soon as Jude was out of the car, Luk shoved past him, running to the back of the van, Jude and Lori behind him.

"No!" Luk shouted. "No! The gear's gone!"

The rear doors of the van stood open, and the police officer shone her torch in over their shoulders, showing the rear of the van was empty apart from a couple of grubby sleeping bags and a power board.

"Fucking hell," Lori swore. "My drum kit!"

"The guitars!" Luk said, grabbing Jude's arm. "Don't you understand? Maddie's guitars are gone!"

The police officer was speaking into her radio, talking to someone, and she looked up and said, "What's been taken? Can you tell me?"

"Twenty thousand dollars' worth of vintage guitars," Luk said, and Jude could hear he was crying. "Oh, fuck, what are we going to do?"

"Twenty thousand dollars?" Jude said. "Twenty grand? The guitars were worth that much?"

"A '71 Fender Jazz in pristine condition? And a mahogany Maton from the 60s? What did you think they were worth?"

"I've called it in," the police officer said. "There's a police tow truck on the way, from Moora. You'd better all come and sit in the squad car while we wait for it to show up."

Jude reached out a hand, to touch Luk's shoulder, but Luk shook his hand off.

"That's the end, then," Lori said. "The end of The Tockleys."

Chapter Thirteen

Luk sat out the front of the Moora police station, a blanket around his shoulders, his hunched silhouette visible in the light spilling out of the police station.

Inside, Lori sat on a bench in the waiting room, a mug of tea in her hands. "Let him calm down," she said. "I need to talk to you about something."

Jude sat back down, beside Lori. "About Rick?" Jude asked.

"Indirectly only," Lori said. "I want to ask you to do something for me, something special and, I guess, a little bit religious or something."

Jude put an arm around Lori's shoulders. "What's wrong?"

"I'm pregnant."

Lori looked at Jude when he didn't say anything. "It's alright; you don't have to work out how to say something polite. I'm going to have a termination, it's all arranged and everything, for tomorrow. Will you come with me?"

"Of course I will, hon," Jude said. "Do you need

money?"

"You've been watching too many movies; terminations don't cost anything here. There's something else I need you to do," Lori said, and when she glanced up at Jude, her eyes were brimming with moisture. "Will you say a prayer for the baby? I don't think I can, and I don't know who else to ask to do it."

"I can do that for you, and for the baby," Jude said. "There's a guardian, like a saint, for unborn babies who are lost."

"Does your religion... It's not one of the crazy ones, is it?" Lori asked. "You're not going to tell me I'm evil, and that sort of thing?"

Jude tightened his arm around Lori's shoulder, and waited until the night duty officer had walked past them out to the carpark for a smoke.

"I'm out of my depth here, Lori," Jude said. "I'd have to ask one of the women I share a house with what the current interpretation of the teachings was, and how Buddhist feminist thought examined the issue. I think the existence of a saint is probably a sign of tolerance, a compassionate response to a human need."

"But what do you think?" Lori asked.

"Lori, I'm a gay man who doesn't eat meat or wear leather. This is possibly a place we don't want to go. That doesn't mean I won't hold your hand, and hug you, and love you. Have you told Rick?"

Lori nodded. "Last week. He got angry at me, all because one night he was too trashed to wear a condom."

Jude touched Lori's cheek, the one that had been swollen, when she looked up at him.

"The bastard," Jude said.

"Can I stay with you, just until it's over?"

"Of course you can."

Lori drank from her cup of tea, then leaned against

Jude, and Jude watched Luk tighten the blanket around his shoulders and wave away the night duty officer.

The Tockleys were over, and whatever grief he was feeling at that, whatever his concerns were about Luk slipping away from him, it was all nothing, on the scale of things. Even the theft of the guitars was insignificant, compared to getting Lori through.

The taxi dropped Luk off in front of his house, but he didn't dig his keys out of his pockets, not yet. First, before he showered even, he needed to see Maddie.

She knew. The police had phoned her from Moora, as soon as the day shift had come on duty. Luk hadn't heard the conversation, so he didn't know how angry she was.

It didn't matter; he owed it to her to apologize in person.

He stood at Maddie's front door, listening to the door chime play the opening chords of 'Jackrabbit,' feeling like crap. He hadn't slept, his face hurt, he owed Maddie twenty thousand dollars, and The Tockleys were over. And Jude... Jude had barely said goodbye to him, when they'd got off the bus from Moora in the city.

Jack opened the front door, and unlocked the screen.

"Lucien, come on in. Maddie's in the kitchen, if you're looking for her."

Luk followed Jack through to the kitchen, where Maddie was sitting at the huge marble table, newspaper in front of her, coffee mug and pot beside her.

"Lucien!" Maddie said, belting her bathrobe tighter. "You look like shit. Get the boy a coffee mug, Jack, and something to eat."

"I can't stay," Luk said. "I just wanted to apologize in person for the theft of your guitars. I don't know how I'll do it, but I'll repay you the money."

Jack put a coffee mug and a carton of milk beside Luk and pushed on his shoulder, guiding him down onto one of the chairs.

"Stop being all noble," Maddie said. "The guitars were over-insured, and I never played them anyway. It's not like it was my old Gibson. Besides, those things have got my name engraved all over them, inside the metalwork. As soon as they hit the professional market, I'll get them back."

"You're not angry?" Luk asked.

Maddie pushed the coffee pot closer, and Luk reached out and grabbed the handle.

"Hell, no," Maddie said. "It's not like it hasn't happened to me, too. There was the time our bus got torched, in Tamworth. We lost everything -- uninsured, of course. And then Alix had a gorgeous '56 Maton Starline, which he took with him when we went to Japan to play the Budokan gig. Customs impounded it when we came back into the country, said it had worms in it or something, and it would have to be destroyed."

Luk poured himself coffee, and added milk. Jack put a packet of Tim Tams in front of him and sat down.

"Then there was the time you toured with The Who, when they did that reunion tour," Jack said.

"I'd forgotten that," Maddie said, chuckling. "That would be all the drugs. Yeah, a hot tip, young Lucien, never lend Pete Townshend a guitar, especially a gorgeous Les Paul you love."

"I doubt that the occasion will ever arise," Luk said.

"I'm glad you dropped in," Maddie said. "We wanted to have a word with you."

Luk looked up, Tim Tam in his hand. "What about?"

Jack leaned forward. "It's kind of personal, but we're worried about you. I was down the pub, escaping from the endless nagging at home--"

"Just clean up a little, that's all I ask," Maddie cut in.

"As I was saying, I was having a beer down the local, and Cliff Barker, who lives in that ugly place up the street, was there."

Luk nodded. "I know the Barker kids. One of them goes to school with Penny."

Jack paused. "Don't take this the wrong way, Lucien, but Cliff was saying that his kids reckon you're gay. And he said he'd driven past here, last week, and you'd been snogging a bloke against a van out the front."

Maddie and Jack were watching Luk, waiting for him to respond, as he fumbled for words. "Jude... in the band, he and I... we're together. Or we were, but now the band's broken up..."

"So, you are gay?" Maddie asked gently. "Do your parents know?"

Luk looked up from the table. "I have no idea if I'm gay. Jude's the first bloke I've... And Penny knows, but I don't think she's told Mum and Dad yet. They're not going to take it well; you know what they're like."

"I do, indeed," Maddie said. "My frequent conversations with your father on the subject of the evils of the rock and roll lifestyle are one of the high points of my life."

"You can come here," Jack said. "Day or night, it doesn't matter. If you need somewhere to go, you come to us."

"Now we've embarrassed you by asking about your sex life, why don't you tell us how you got that black eye?" Maddie said.

Luk shrugged. "There's this bloke, in another band, and he was threatening Lori. So I hurt him, at least I hope I did."

"Lori? Lovely Lori who bosses you and Jude around

unmercifully?" Maddie asked. "I hope you broke his face."

"I doubt I did," Luk said. "But he didn't get to touch her, not that time." He stood up. "I should go home, have a shower, get some sleep and do some work for uni. Thank you, for being so understanding about everything."

Maddie leaned across and patted Luk's arm. "That's alright, babe. Put an ice pack on your face, it'll stop it from hurting so much."

"Good luck with your boyfriend," Jack said when he let Luk out of the front door.

When Luk let himself into the kitchen, he found himself face to face to with his mother.

"Lucien, dear," she said. "What happened to your face? Where have you been?"

"I got punched," Luk said. "And I spent the night at the Moora police station."

"And Friday night? Where were you then?"

Luk opened the fridge and took out a can of soft drink. "Do you want to know? I'm nineteen; there are some things you might not want to ask about."

"Do you want to tell me?" Luk's mother asked, her hand on Luk's arm. "You can, if you want to."

"I was with my lover," Luk said, popping the can of drink. "At his house."

Luk didn't hang around to find out what his mother thought of that. He slammed his bedroom door and dragged his chest of drawers across the door, just to make sure no one could get in.

He was tired, really tired. He'd been awake for well over twenty-four hours, ever since first light the morning before, and he hadn't slept much that night, either. He and Jude had fucked, then showered together, then gone out for food. Then they'd fucked again, long and hard, and if the first time had been good, that time had completely blown his mind, kneeling over Jude, watching Jude's face while his cock slid into Jude's body.

Luk wrenched his boots off and tossed them on the floor, then dragged his T-shirt off. His jeans slid down and he fell onto his bed, hugging his pillow.

Weird stuff was going on with Lori, though. She'd cried on the bus to the city from Moora, holding Jude's hand. Luk had wanted to cry, too, until he knew that Maddie understood about the guitars, but it had been more than that.

He drank from the can of soft drink, ignoring his mother's tapping at his bedroom door.

"Lucien?" his mother called. "Lucien, dear? Can we talk? Please?"

She didn't sound angry, just upset, and Luk felt suddenly bad about having just dropped it all on her.

"Hang on," Luk called, putting his can of soft drink down and reaching for his jeans.

He dragged the chest of drawers back out of the way and opened his door, letting his mother in.

She shut the door behind her and looked disapprovingly at the mess in his room, but didn't say anything, not until Luk had shifted his acoustic guitar off his desk chair so she could sit down.

Luk sat on the edge of his bed opposite her.

"Lucien, dear," his mother said, her voice trembling a little. "Did you mean... that thing you said before?"

Damn, Luk should have pulled a T-shirt on too, because he was sure he had marks from Friday night.

"Yeah. I'm seeing someone, a man."

His mother blinked. "Have you always been...?"

"Gay?" Luk asked. "No, he's the first man I've been with. Before this, it's always been girls."

"Are you... alright? Do you... need anything?"

"I'm fine, Mum," Luk said. "Right now, I need to

sleep."

"I won't tell your father." Luk's mother stood up, stepping over books to reach the door.

"That's probably for the best," Luk said.

Luk's mother opened his door, and Luk said, "Penny knows."

She nodded, and closed the door behind her.

Luk didn't bother dragging the chest of drawers over again.

Lori hesitated in the doorway of Jude's room, and Jude winced when he remembered what the room had looked like the last time he'd seen it.

"How about you have a shower while I clean up in here?" Jude asked. "Or a bath? Our bath is relatively clean, and the water is hot."

"Well," Lori said, shaking her head at the room. "That's answered a question I was never going to ask. Show me the bath, big boy."

Lori locked herself in the bathroom, and Jude dashed back to his room to survey the damage. Condom strip on the bed. Used condoms, empty tube of lube, condom wrappers -- all strewn across the floor. His sheets were in a tangled heap, and were liberally smeared with lube and come.

Jude opened his window, letting fresh air into the room, and tidied up quickly, throwing away the mess and putting the box of condoms away. He stripped off his sheets and pillowcases, tossing them into the washing machine, then quickly remade his bed with his one remaining sheet.

It would have to do.

Sammie wandered out from her bedroom, and Jude grabbed her and pulled her into the kitchen, closing the door.

"Wassup?" Sammie asked sleepily, putting the kettle on.

"I have huge favors to ask of you and Alison," Jude said. "Lots of them."

"Damn, hon. Favors, and keeping us awake on Friday night. This had better be good."

"You remember Lori? Goth girl in the band?" Jude asked.

Sammie nodded, rubbing at her face. "And?"

"She's here, and she needs to stay for a while."

"Oh," Sammie said. "A girl? Is she quieter than your boyfriend? You were a much nicer housemate when you were celibate."

Jude frowned at Sammie, and she crossed her arms.

"Lori's in a mess," Jude said. "A big mess. She's hiding from a nasty boyfriend."

"Bastard," Sammie said. "Of course she can stay then."

"There's more," Jude said. "She's got nothing with her. Can she borrow trackies from you, for today?"

"Guess so, though I hope I'm too inherently stylish to own anything as dire as trackpants," Sammie said. "I can find some clothes that will fit her."

"And I need to borrow your car, tomorrow during the day."

Sammie's smile dropped. "No way, no how. I don't lend my car; you know that, not even to you or Alison."

"Lori's having a procedure tomorrow," Jude said.

Sammie was a smart woman; she was quite capable of putting it all together.

"Damn, some men need to be sorted out," she said. "Of course you can use my car. She's skinny, isn't she? I'll dig out some clothes for her."

The kettle whistled, and Sammie reached for a cup,

rinsing it out under the tap.

"Jude?" she said.

"Yes?"

"Do something about the bastard, will you?"

Jude went to speak, and Sammie glared at him.

"Don't you dare recite doctrine at me. I don't care," Sammie said. "I really don't care. When someone is being hurt like that, it gets inside their head, twists them around, so they can't see anything clearly. They're not participating in the relationship, they're being tortured."

Jude stared at Sammie, who pointed a very determined finger back at him.

"You can put aside your deep-seated beliefs," she said. "And get over yourself. This is not something that someone who died two and a half thousand years ago gets to pass an opinion on. Once the nastiness starts, I don't care how inter-related things are. The person it's being done to just gets crushed by it. Don't you want clothes? So Lori can get out of the bath?"

Sammie left her peppermint tea soaking and disappeared into her bedroom, then came back a moment later and handed Jude a pile of clothing and a packet of sanitary pads.

"She'll need them tomorrow," Sammie said.

Lori, dressed in Sammie's yoga clothes and with her hair hanging loose, sat on Jude's mattress, mug of peppermint tea in her hands, watching Jude pull on boxers under his towel.

"So your housemates are okay with me staying?" Lori said.

"Sammie is," Jude said. "Alison is either still asleep or not here." He hung his towel on the back of his door and pulled a T-shirt on, then sat down on the mattress beside Lori.

"This is a drug-free household, Lori," he said. "You

can't use anything here. You do understand that?"

"I haven't got anything with me," Lori said. "It's all gone now."

"Are you coping?" Jude said, tucking Lori's hair behind her ear.

"I'm not jammed on anything," Lori said. "Honestly. I feel really gross, but that's from the hormones, and maybe a little from not having scored for a couple of days, but I'm not shaking or anything. I'm really tired, and I just want to cry, but I don't think I can anymore."

Jude took the mug of tea out of Lori's hands and put it down on the floor beside the mattress. "Sleep for a while. Then we can talk some more."

Lori curled up on the clean sheet, on her side, and Jude pulled the blankets over her, then lay down himself, his arm around her.

She didn't go to sleep, not right away.

Jude didn't, either. He played back Sammie's words in the kitchen, looking at them again, trying to see inside them.

"You have to leave him," he said, his words hanging in the room.

"It's not that easy," Lori said. "You wouldn't understand. You just up and left Dave, didn't give him a chance to explain anything. I love Rick too much to do that to him."

Jude flinched mentally at Lori's words, but didn't argue with her. Maybe she was right, and he hadn't loved Dave enough.

Lori waved reassuringly at Jude through the glass of the phone booth on the street near Jude's house. Jude waved back, but didn't try and work out what Lori was saying from her expression or lips.

She was phoning Robbo, in theory, to try and persuade him to cover for her at Loud People the next day. If Robbo was at Brianna's, then Lori talking to him would be easy; if he was home, then Rick would be around, and the whole process would be complicated.

Jude watched a man jog past, two dogs on leads bounding beside him, and then watched the traffic lights at the end of the road run through two cycles before Lori stepped out of the phone booth.

"How did that go?" Jude asked.

"He's going to work for me," Lori said. "The delay was him trying to find my work keys in my room without waking Rick, who is sleeping off the analgesics the hospital gave him for his broken ribs."

"Ribs?" Jude said. "I guess Luk had worked up a fair bit of momentum before he got to Rick."

Lori shrugged. "At the moment, I find that I really don't care."

Jude nodded. "Do you want to go back to the house? I need to make a call, too."

"Can I wait with you?" Lori said. "Your housemates scare me."

"Sammie and Alison? Scare you?"

"They're so... earnest," Lori said. "So proper. Don't they ever mess around?"

"I guess they're pretty earnest people," Jude said.

Lori leaned against the tree where Jude had been waiting, and Jude ducked into the phone booth and pulled the scrap of paper Luk had given him out of his pocket. It said 'Lucien' and a number.

A woman answered the phone, and Jude said, "Hi, may I please speak to Lucien?"

The woman's voice said, "Oh, oh, of course, I'll just get him." Footsteps, and a rapping on a door, making

Jude think of John Lennon, peering solemnly through glasses. "Lucien, dear, there's a friend on the phone for you."

A moment later, Luk said, "Thanks, Mum. Hello?"

"Hi, there, this is Jude."

Luk's laugh was breathy and nervous. "Hey, there."

"Did I ring at a bad time?" Jude asked.

"It's been a big day," Luk said. "I told my mum this morning. She's a bit freaked out."

Jude leaned against the glass pane of the phone booth and propped the door open with his foot, letting some fresh air in. "Are you alright? That's a huge thing to have done."

"I guess. I saw Maddie and Jack, first thing. She's not upset about the guitars, which is a relief. Then I told Mum, and crashed out for a few hours. Woke up, showered, ate all the food in the house, and now I'm looking at the work I haven't done for uni. What about you?"

Jude looked across at Lori. "I've been looking after Lori. Got some sleep."

"Can I see you soon?" Luk asked. "During the week?"

Jude smiled. "Yeah, that'd be good. I don't know how long Lori is staying with me for, but we could meet up for a meal in the city, after work and uni, one day."

"Is this how it's done?" Luk asked. "Is this right?"

Jude thought of Friday night, and being fucked into the mattress by Luk. "It's working for me. How about you?"

"Yeah, 's good for me. Friday was more than good."

"Friday was amazing," Jude said, his voice low, his shoulders turned so Lori couldn't see his face. "Luk..."

"Was it?" Luk asked.

"Yeah, and just thinking about it is doing things to me," Jude said. "Things that--"

Lori tapped on the glass of the phone booth, and Jude stopped. Her eyes were bleak, and she looked pale and washed out, with the kind of shakiness that heralded another bout of vomiting.

"What?" Luk said. "This is not the time to stop."

"I have to go," Jude said. "I've got someone banging on the phone booth door, wanting to use the phone."

"Other people have real phones," Luk said. "Phones at home, or mobile phones on prepaid plans. And email addresses. I have no idea how you and Lori function!"

"Love to argue with you, babe," Jude said. "Another time? I'll call you again, arrange to have a meal with you, okay? Bye."

"Bye," Luk said, and Jude put the phone down and got out the booth, just as Lori started dry-retching into the nearest garden bed.

"Peppermint tea," Jude said, rubbing Lori's bony back through her borrowed T-shirt. "Sammie assures me that you need peppermint and ginger tea. I'm not sure how Sammie knows this, but I'm not arguing with her."

Lori let Jude lead her back to the house.

"Fucking hell," she said when he sat her on the couch in the living room, while Sammie and Alison bustled around, putting on the kettle and finding a bucket. "How do women do this for real? This is vile."

Sammie elbowed Jude aside and handed Lori a mug of tea. "Either be useful, Jude, or get out of the way."

Lori held out her spare hand, and Jude sat on the couch, beside her. "He is useful," Lori said. "Possibly not as useful as Luk, who beat up Rick, but he's still worth hanging onto."

Alison nodded approvingly over the top of Lori's head, and the smirk on Sammie's face as she strolled back out to the kitchen was decidedly vengeful. Jude was learning a lot about his housemates, and the limited application of

Buddhist precepts when it came to looking after another woman in trouble.

"What?" Lori said, looking up at Jude.

"I was just being glad I'm gay," Jude said.

"Too right," Lori said. "You never have to deal with any of this messy reproductive stuff."

"It's not that," Jude said. "It's more that I never want to have to face Sammie and Alison when they're like this."

"Do they play instruments?" Lori asked. "They belong in a girl band."

Lori put the hot water bottle aside and pushed herself upright off Jude's mattress. "No, I'm fine to walk, really. It's just like period pain."

Jude handed her Alison's trackpants. "If you're playing the menstrual cycle card, I'm not arguing anymore. Are you sure you want to call Rick? Is this what you want to do?"

Lori pulled the trackpants on and stood up, only a little wobbly on her feet. "I just want to talk to him."

While Lori was in the toilet, Sammie grabbed Jude's arm, pulling him into her bedroom. "I can't believe you're letting her do this," Sammie hissed.

"What am I supposed to do?" Jude asked. "I can't stop her physically, if she really wants to go back to him."

"You're her friend; you have to talk some sense into her."

"I've tried," Jude said.

"Then try harder," Sammie said. "If you really care for her."

Lori had to hold onto Jude's arm to walk to the phone booth, despite her protests of feeling fine, and Jude covered her hand with his own.

"Please don't do this, Lori," he said. "I'm worried about you, about Rick hurting you."

"I need to be with him," Lori said. "That's all. Don't worry about me. Now this is over, things will be better."

Jude nodded, smiling reluctantly down at Lori. He'd tried, and tried again. It would have to do.

When Lori sat on the front steps of Jude's house, waiting for Rick to collect her, Jude sat beside her.

"This is for you," he said, holding out a necklace, a strand of glass beads on a thread. "It's called a mala."

"Oh," Lori said, taking the beads. "It's beautiful, thank you. What does it mean?"

"It's for counting prayers."

Lori slipped the necklace over her head, pulling her plaits through the string, then slid it inside her shirt, out of sight.

"I'll keep it safe." Lori slid an arm around Jude, hugging him. "Thank you, for everything. Say thank you to Sammie and Alison for me too."

Robbo's sedan turned into the street, Rick at the wheel, and Lori stood up. "No van; it must still be missing a windscreen."

"Or impounded," Jude said.

Lori waved from the footpath as she got into the sedan, and Jude watched her lean across and kiss Rick.

Chapter Fourteen

The food hall was half-empty, making Jude easy to spot amongst the office workers grabbing a meal on their way home from work. Luk set his guitar case and pack down on an empty chair at the table Jude was sitting at, and slid into the seat opposite Jude.

"Hi," Luk said, and Jude's answering smile made Luk's belly squirm in a good way.

"Hey, there," Jude said, waving a fork at the plate of curry and rice in front of him. "I was starving, so I grabbed a meal already."

"I'll get something in a moment," Luk said. Jude was wearing his work T-shirt with the insignia of a shopping center maintenance company on it. "Good day at work?"

Jude shrugged. "As good as any day involving collecting shopping trolleys in carparks ever can be. It wasn't hot, and it didn't rain, and that's about all I ask for. How was uni?"

Luk shrugged too. "I've handed in all the work I had due, which is where my break even point is. How is

Lori?"

"Get your meal," Jude said. "Then I'll bring you up to date. Lori said to tell you everything, or you'd complain we were shutting you out."

Luk grinned. "Yeah, well, I kind of had misunderstood a lot of things when I accused her of that."

Luk came back with a steaming plate of Chinese food, loaded with noodles, rice and lumps of deep-fried goodness drenched in sugary sauce. He was hungry.

"Lori?" Luk asked around the first mouthful of noodles and rice he shoveled in.

"Lori has been at my place, but has gone back to Rick. She had a termination on Monday."

Luk stared at Jude over his fork.

"Hence all the throwing up," Jude said.

"That's, um, something," Luk said.

"And you broke some of Rick's ribs when you slammed him against the truck. I'm not sure how Rick feels about any of this, but I'm guessing he doesn't consider any of us with affection."

"His ribs?" Luk said. "Shit. I didn't know I'd hit him that hard. How did he manage to perform afterward?" He was just a little proud he'd done that much damage to Rick, who completely deserved to be hurt, but Luk suspected that letting Jude see that might not be a good idea. Jude probably thought retribution was evil.

"Chemicals, I'd guess," Jude said. "He probably didn't feel anything until the next day."

Under the table, Jude's knee brushed against Luk's, the sudden contact making it hard for Luk to swallow the lump of fried dough he was chewing. He moved his legs, making proper contact with Jude's calves, and Jude's gaze held Luk's.

"Tease," Jude said, his voice low, then he went back to eating his curry.

Luk ate quickly, his mind mostly on the feel of Jude's legs under the table. Something had happened inside him to get him to this point, and he still hadn't really worked it all out. A month before, if someone had told him he'd be sleeping with another man, or even meeting him for a meal somewhere public and getting all turned on from rubbing legs with him under the table, Luk would have scoffed at the idea.

But it had happened. He'd fucked Jude more than once, they'd sucked each other off, and Luk was hanging out for the next time they could get together, horny as anything, more desperate than he'd ever been for any girl.

The two women in office clothes who were sitting at the other end of the table from Jude and Luk picked up their trays and left, and Luk had a quick look around them.

No one was close.

"I think I'm gay," Luk said. "Obviously, I've been giving the matter some thought, and I keep coming back to this."

Jude put down the chunk of potato he'd skewered with his fork. "I can understand that you've been thinking about it. Want to tell me about it?"

Luk pushed his plate aside and leaned across the table, and the smell of Jude's curry was pungent. "Since we got together, I've not done anything, except maybe drink or smoke a little, nothing more, but it still feels like every nerve-ending in me is on fire, burning me up. My body, it's raw and hungry, so that even my clothes hurt, and that's nothing compared to what's inside my head, to what I've been thinking and imagining."

Jude shoved his plate aside too, and his hands covered Luk's. "Yeah?" Jude sounded like he had on Friday night, when Luk had fucked him. "What are you thinking about?"

"Right now? What your face looked like, when I was inside you. I can't be sitting in a food hall on a Wednesday afternoon, going crazy with remembering how you looked when I fucked you, if I'm straight, can I?"

Jude lifted one of Luk's hands up to his mouth and kissed the palm, then put it back down again. "Probably not. Do you feel any different for working this out?"

Luk was distantly aware of some old woman staring at them disapprovingly over her cappuccino, but he ignored her. "I feel like running around, shouting it to people. I want to tell everyone that I'm so fucking happy, that I feel like I'm alive at long last, not just an observer any longer, but that life is finally happening to me.

"I should be upset that The Tockleys are over, because I bought that dream. I should be worrying about someone contacting Alix to say we won't be at Monlo's this week. I should be freaking out about what happens when my father finds out. There's so much that a few weeks ago would have crushed me, but I don't feel crushed."

Jude's mouth curved in the sweetest of smiles, reminding Luk that Jude was fucking gorgeous, with minute gold flecks in his brown eyes. "I think I know how you feel. Have you had enough to eat? Do you want to get out of here?"

"Where do you want to go?" Luk asked. "Loud People? Is Lori working?"

"I think she is. We should talk to her about the gig at Monlo's. If she isn't, then Robbo will be, and he'll let us use the phone there to call Rick's mobile, for free."

"But Rick hates us," Luk pointed out.

"Robbo can make the call, and get Lori on," Jude said.

"I've finished," Luk said, standing up so suddenly that he yanked his hands out from Jude's grasp. "Loud People has a store room."

Jude's gaze was on Luk's crotch, and he said, "Really? Let's go."

Lori was behind the counter at Loud People, packet of chips and a magazine in front of her, ignoring the late afternoon customers browsing the racks of imported vinyl records.

She looked up, and her smile was as painted on as the rest of her face. "Luk and Jude, what are you two doing here?"

"Come to see you," Jude said, leaning across the counter to kiss Lori's cheek. "Luk has reminded me we need to talk with you about some details. Have you heard anything from the police about the missing equipment yet?"

"Nothing. Rick's got his van back, complete with a broken windscreen and an unroadworthiness work order, but that's all."

"What do you want to do about the gig at Monlo's?" Luk asked, propping himself against the counter.

"What can we do?" Lori said. "We have no gear."

"That's not quite true," Jude said. "I still have my old electric guitar."

"And my acoustic is an Ovation Legend, and has sweet bridge pickups," Luk said.

Lori shook her head. "I've got no gear, and I doubt Licks will lend me even his practice drums. The Tockleys are over, but if you both want to keep playing the gig, just as yourselves, then that's fine by me."

"This isn't going to cause problems if we do, is it?" Jude asked.

"Am I going to bear you both a grudge? Am I going to sulk? I couldn't give a fuck what the pair of you do," Lori said. "Go and clutter up someone else's shop."

Luk pulled himself upright, ready to leave, but Jude

just smiled at Lori. "Love you too," he said. "Talk to you soon."

On the steps outside Loud People, Luk said, "Do you think you're up to it?"

"What? Singing Beatles covers while you play acoustic? I can do that."

Luk looked at Jude speculatively. "How well do you play acoustic? I heard you play at Maddie's once, at our first rehearsal, but can't really remember. You could play my acoustic, and I could get something out of your electric. I might even be able to make it stay in tune, if I can fix the tuning somehow."

"I haven't touched an acoustic in years," Jude said. "Apart from that time at Maddie's."

Luk pulled his guitar case off his shoulder and shoved it at Jude. "Go on, right now. Let's hear what you can do."

"You're kidding?" Jude said, taking the guitar case reluctantly. "You want me to play this?"

"Dare you," Luk said, sitting down on the concrete steps, his face level with Jude's knees.

Jude sat down on the step below Luk and unclipped the guitar case. The traffic on the street above was a muted roar, and the sound of The Damned leaked out of Loud People through the door. The guitar case was pushed behind Jude, cushioning his back from the concrete wall, and he set Luk's Ovation on his lap.

"It's standard tuning," Luk said. "There're no hidden tricks."

Jude nodded, and he tried a couple of chords, managing not to flub a simple G, then a C.

The Ovation had a gorgeous tone, echoing a little in the stairwell, and Jude paused, then started to play, working through an unimaginative introduction, before beginning to sing.

"diva
give me rhythm
in diminished chords
work your throat
around my words."

The door to Loud People opened, and someone shouted, "Lori, turn the stereo off!" then people appeared at the doorway, listening.

"bloodbeat a drum
words roll your tongue
possession
possession."

Luk could feel he was flushing, and it wasn't with embarrassment, for a change. Jude had written a song, this song, and it was about him, or maybe for him, and a wave of something that Luk couldn't identify was washing over him, leaving him feeling like he had after they'd fucked; broken and safe and lost, all at the same time.

"lover
sing me forté
straining your voice
match my beat
create sweet noise."

Jude's voice, rising in strength, carried the melody, over the top of Jude's dubious playing, but Luk wasn't thinking of the chords, or the counterbeat hand percussion the rhythm was crying out for. Luk was just watching Jude's face and hands, hoping he wasn't about to cry.

"bloodbeat a drum
words roll your tongue
possession
possession.

"diva
sing us higher
on divine God-notes
feel the licks
and bring us home."

After the final chorus, Jude's hands stilled, the song faltering rather than ending, and the three or four Loud People customers in the doorway applauded.

Jude didn't look at them; he didn't shift his gaze from Luk's face. "Well?"

Luk had to clear his throat to get his voice to work. "That was amazing."

"You liked it? You don't want to redo the chords? Tell me that it's crap?"

"Fuck, no," Luk said. "Maybe I'll tweak the introduction eventually, if you'll let me, but not now."

Jude slid the guitar into the case, then handed it to Luk as they stood up, and his eyes were turned away.

"Please, don't go," Luk said. "I'm worried I'm being an idiot here, but I have no idea what to say. That song... It's the most beautiful song I've ever heard."

"Do you think so?" Jude asked.

Luk had his hands full, so he dropped his backpack onto the steps and brushed his palm against Jude's cheek.

"Yeah," Luk whispered, then he leaned forward and pressed his lips against Jude's, because his heart was banging against his ribs so hard it hurt, and he wanted somehow to show Jude how the song had made him feel.

They stayed like that, lips just touching, while one of the customers from Loud People pushed past them, then Jude pulled away.

"You're not the only one that's on fire," Jude said. "I feel like that, too."

Jude was smiling in the single fluorescent light over the stairwell, and Luk slid his hand round behind Jude's neck, pulling him closer. "Who you calling a diva?" Luk whispered.

"You," Jude said. "Only you."

Luk wandered through the early evening city to his bus stop without noticing anything. The shops were all closing, restaurants and bars opening up for the evening, the walkways crowded with office workers going home. He slid the earpieces of his music player into his ears, but didn't even bother switching it on, not when he had Jude's song running through his head, over and over.

The bus was crowded, and he had to stand all the way home, but he didn't care. He didn't care about anything, not right then, except what had happened, and what was going to happen. Rehearsal the next evening, after uni, when he could see Jude again. Maybe fuck him, too.

Luk was deeply involved in speculation as to whether he could afford to buy a secondhand amp and speaker for Jude's guitar from his small savings when he slid the kitchen door open.

"Lucien?" Luk's mother called out. "Is that you?"

"Yeah," Luk called, turning to go down the hall to his bedroom.

"Lucien!" Luk's father bellowed. "Come here!"

Luk dropped his backpack, and set his guitar down carefully. "On my way."

His father was standing in the formal living room, the one they never used, and Luk's mother was perched nervously on one of the monstrous couches.

"Sit!" Luk's father ordered, pointing at another couch. "I want to talk to you."

Luk sat, trying for the right mix of innocent nonchalance, and his mother wouldn't meet his gaze.

"What about, Dad?" Luk asked.

"I've heard... certain unsavory rumors about you. About your personal life." Luk's father, still wearing his tie and suit jacket from work, loomed over Luk.

"Dad, I can't be held responsible for every stupid rumor that someone starts," Luk said, trying to keep his voice steady in spite of the adrenaline pouring into his bloodstream. It wasn't irretrievable, not yet, but it would become so at any moment.

"More than rumors," Luk's father said. "Someone saw you... kissing another boy on the Hades' front lawn."

"You know these modern girls," Luk's mother said, and his father turned to look at her. "The way they dress."

"They dress like starving prostitutes," Luk's father said. "Not like boys."

"Not the uni students that Lucien is friends with."

"Don't, Mum," Luk said, standing up. "Yeah, Dad, I'm gay. The rumors are all true. I was kissing my boyfriend on Maddie's front lawn. I don't want to hide this any longer, not even from you."

Luk's father's face blotched, red and pale, and his mouth worked soundlessly, just for a moment, before he bellowed. "Gay! No son of mine is a poofter!"

The blow, when it hit, was open-handed, sending Luk sprawling backward across the couch, his face burning with pain, tears leaking from his eyes. He could hear his mother shouting, and Penny screaming, then his father shouted, "Get him out of this house now!" and the front door slammed with a boom.

Luk's mother crouched over him, and Luk fended off her hands, wiping his eyes and pushing himself back onto his feet.

"Don't, Mum, just stop. I'm alright." He knew what he had to do; he'd been planning it out in his head.

He felt numb, apart from where his face was scalded. He went to his bedroom and began stuffing clothes into his spare pack, adding the books he needed for uni, and his personal notebooks of songs. His laptop went into the back of the pack, and he opened his bedside drawer and took out the money he'd been stockpiling, pilfering from his mother's housekeeping jar in the pantry over the past couple of weeks. He had The Tockleys' money, too, in his wallet.

His mother hovered in the doorway, crying, and he hugged her. "I'll be fine," he said. "I'm going to my boyfriend's place."

She pressed a bundle of money into his hand. "That's all I've got on me. I'm so sorry, Lucien."

Luk kissed her cheek. "Look after Penny."

The door to Penny's room pushed open, and Penny was face down on her bed, crying. Luk put down the pack he was carrying and crouched beside her bed.

"I'll be fine," he told her. "You don't have to lie for me anymore."

Penny sniffed and nodded, wiping her nose on her pillow. "Okay."

Luk slid a baggie out of his pocket and across the bed to her. "You get my stash, because I can't take it with me to Jude's place. Don't smoke it all at once."

"Your boyfriend is hot," Penny said, slipping the baggie into her jeans pocket. "I can see why you fancy him."

"He is, isn't he?" Luk said. "I have to go now." He kissed the top of her head. "Take care of Mum."

Luk slung both packs over his shoulders, picked up his guitar case, and walked out of the house.

Maddie answered her door, reading glasses on her nose, trashy detective novel in her hand.

"Lucien, come on in. We heard the shouting, thought you might be over. Are you alright?"

"Is that Lucien?" Jack called, from further back in the house.

"It is, and bring the ice pack," Maddie yelled back. "Put your stuff down; let's get you a stiff drink, and get something on your face."

Luk set his guitar case down, then his packs, and followed Maddie into the kitchen, where Jack was wrapping an ice pack in a small towel.

"Damn," Jack said, holding the ice pack out to Luk. "Slap that on you. The last black eye has only just faded, and you've got another one."

"Drink!" Maddie said to Jack, and Jack pulled a tumbler out of the cupboard.

Luk touched his face tentatively where his father had struck him, feeling the swelling and tenderness, then put the ice pack against his face and sat down at Maddie's table.

Jack pushed a tumbler with an inch of golden spirits in it across to Luk. "It's whisky," he said. "Get that into you, then we can talk."

The whisky slid straight down Luk's throat, smoother than vodka, burning into his stomach, and he put the glass back on the table.

"Good to see you drink like a bass guitarist," Maddie said. "Now, what can we do to help?"

"Can you drive me somewhere?" Luk said. "To Jude's house?"

"Is that it?" Jack said. "I think Maddie was hoping for something a little more dramatic, like ramming your father's fake sports car with our four-wheel drive."

"Or spray-painting it," Maddie said. "I could enjoy that. And the taxation department has a dob-in-a-cheat line. Getting him audited would feel good, too."

Luk had to smile, despite the way his cheek was swelling under the ice pack. "You can take the chick out of the rock band, but not the rock band out of the chick?" Luk asked.

Maddie chortled, setting herself off on a bout of gasping and wheezing, until Jack handed her an inhaler.

"Smart kid," Maddie said, once she could breathe again. "Are you sure we can't help more?"

Luk shook his head carefully, in case it started hurting more. "Just take me to Jude's."

Chapter Fifteen

Maddie parked her car outside Jude's house. Luk leaned forward over the back seat, and held out the ice pack he'd been using. "Thanks, for everything."

"Keep the ice pack, dear," Maddie said, pushing Luk's hand back. "For the next time someone punches you."

Luk undid the back door of the four-wheel drive and found Jack waiting, ready to take his packs. "I'll take them," Jack said. "I think Maddie wants a word with young Jude."

"I do, with both of you," Maddie said. "And I'm curious to see how an ambitious guitarist lives these days."

"You need to see Lori's house for that," Luk said, reaching into the back seat for his guitar case. "She has rats, and I don't mean the kind that live in a cage and run around on a little wheel."

When Luk knocked on the front door, Sammie's voice said, "Who is it?" from the other side.

"It's Luk."

The door opened, and Sammie unlocked the screen door, while peering at Maddie and Jack.

"This is Jack and Maddie," Luk said. "Is Jude here?"

"Sure," Sammie said. "What happened to your face?"

Jude appeared down the hall, pulling a T-shirt over his head. "I heard, Sammie."

Sammie backed into the kitchen, her wide eyes indicating she'd just worked out who Maddie was. Jude hugged Luk quickly, then turned him around under the hall light to look at his face.

"Who did this?" Jude asked. He looked up at Maddie and Jack. "Do you know?"

The hurt on Jude's face was too much, and Luk grabbed his arms. "I'll tell you later," Luk said. "I need somewhere to stay."

Jude's arms wrapped around Luk, pulling him against Jude's chest. The smell of Jude's skin and the soft cotton of Jude's T-shirt against the icy numbness of Luk's face was too much. Jude had written a song for him. He'd been thrown out of home. His face hurt. It was all too much.

Jude kissed Luk's forehead, and Luk hung onto him, trying to stop crying, while people bustled discreetly around him.

"Don't fight it, love," Jude murmured. "You're safe now."

Luk finally took a shuddering breath in and pulled away, turning to wipe his face with his hands.

Jude's hands, on his shoulders, were almost enough to start him crying again. "Maddie and Jack are in the kitchen," Jude said. "I'm going to go rescue them from Alison and Sammie." Jude's mouth pressed against Luk's neck, just for a moment, then he was gone.

Luk slipped past the open door to the kitchen and

washed his face in the bathroom. In the mirror over the sink, the skin over his cheekbone was swollen and bruised and splitting, and his eye was closing up. Two black eyes in a week; he was earning his punk credentials in a hurry.

When Luk walked into the kitchen, Alison handed him a mug of hot water and green bits that smelled like toothpaste, and Sammie gave him the chair she'd been sitting on.

"It was lovely meeting you, Maddie and Jack," Alison said.

Sammie nodded enthusiastically. "A real honor."

The two girls left the room, and Luk put his mug on the table, beside plates holding the remains of dinners of noodles and tomatoes.

"I'm feeling dreadful about not having done more," Maddie said. "It's obvious, in retrospect, that Lucien's home life was hideous, and was only going to end like this."

Luk went to speak, but Jack said, "Don't bother, kiddo. There's no point in fighting her, not when she's determined."

"That's right," Maddie said. "So, I'm stepping in. Meddling, even. I've heard Luk play often, and he's better than almost anyone I've known. Lori is a darling, and Jude is cute, and can sing well enough to be commercial. I'm proposing to put The Tockleys in my studio, with some borrowed gear since yours has all been stolen, with Jack doing the mixing, and we'll burn some recordings, get your music out there. Consider it my apology for not stepping in before things got this bad."

Luk glanced at Jude, and said, "Thank you, so much. We'll have to talk to Lori, obviously, before we can accept your amazingly generous offer."

"Let the girl continue to believe she's in charge," Jack

said. "You'll get more peace in the end that way."

Maddie glared at Jack. "You and I are going to have a chat about that, boy."

Jack grinned. "Shit, I'm in strife now. We should go, before this gets any more embarrassing."

When they'd gone, and Luk's packs and guitar were in Jude's room, Jude took Luk's hand in his. "What do you need? What can I do?"

"Can we go to bed?"

Luk sat on the edge of Jude's mattress, reaching down to unlace his boots, and in the half-light from the reading lamp, Jude knelt in front of him.

"I'll do that," Jude said, lifting Luk's hands off. He undid the knots at the tops of the Luk's calf-high boots, then loosened each lace all the way down, his face a shadow of concentration. Then he slid each foot out, putting the boots beside the bookcase.

Luk stood up, standing over Jude, and unbuttoned his jeans, then pushed them down. He'd thought he'd be too shattered, too worn out, but his body was remembering how Jude had knelt in front of him before, sucking him.

Luk pulled his T-shirt off and pushed his underwear down, stepping out of his clothes so he stood naked.

"How do you feel?" Jude asked, standing again, pulling his own T-shirt off.

A few weeks ago, Luk would have thought that was a stupid question to ask someone with a hard-on, because the answer was obvious, but he wasn't the same person he had been then.

When Jude was naked, Luk touched Jude's chest, feeling the beat of his heart and the rise of his breath. "I feel like this is turning back into the best day of my life again."

Luk lay down and Jude knelt over him, his hair falling loose down around Luk's face when Luk pulled the band off the end of Jude's plait and freed his hair.

The kiss was gentle on the side of Luk's face that didn't hurt, then Jude moved down Luk's body, licking his skin, pressing kisses, making Luk gasp. The feel of Jude's tongue on his cock, hot and slippery, was enough to make Luk jerk his hips, needing more, needing all of Jude's mouth.

Jude looked up, and said, "Luk?"

"Huh? Yeah?"

"Wanna fuck me?"

"Is this a trick question?" Luk asked. "Of course I do."

"I mean now," Jude said. "Right away."

Luk had good manual dexterity. He got the condom strip out of the box, and the condom out of the wrapper, in a quarter of a beat. Getting it on took longer, and Jude had to help Luk get the condom round the right way.

"Gimme the lube," Jude said, kneeling up on the mattress, and Luk tossed it to him.

A quick pass with the lube over Luk's cock, and Jude clambered over Luk. "You've got to be quiet," Jude said.

It wasn't fair, saying 'You've got to be quiet' to a man, then lowering down him, tighter than anything Luk had ever imagined, impossible and beautiful and perfect. Luk clamped his mouth shut, grabbing hold of the bedding, then Jude's thighs, while Jude slid down his cock, all the way.

"Breathe," Jude whispered, leaning forward so his face was over Luk's and his cock was trapped between their bellies. "Breathe, or you'll pass out."

Luk didn't dare answer, because any response was going to start out witty and wind up with him shouting the house down as he came.

Jude moved, rocking his hips slowly, making Luk thrash

around under him, teeth gritted desperately, grunting and gasping inarticulately. It all mixed up inside Luk's head; the way he'd felt on the steps of Loud People, the fear of things exploding at home, the pain and shock of being hit again, the relief of being able to hang onto Jude while he cried, and the excruciating pleasure of having his cock deep inside Jude and feeling Jude grinding against him. It twisted inside him, burning him, so he had to hold onto Jude, just to push in as hard as he could, while he came.

"Easy," Jude whispered against his ear, reaching between their bodies to grab the condom as Luk slid out.

Luk was breathing too hard to ask Jude anything, but when he touched his side, it was slippery with Jude's come, wordless reassurance that Jude had needed it, too.

Jude's rumpled sheets smelled of perfume when Jude dragged the bedding over the pair of them and turned the light out.

"Smells girly," Luk said, as Jude's arm slid around Luk's waist, pulling him closer in the darkness.

"Lori," Jude said. "No time to wash my sheets."

Luk shifted, rolling over so the sore part of his face was off the pillow, and he was closer to Jude. "Don't care. Don't care about much, not at the moment."

Jude kissed Luk's forehead. "Go to sleep, gorgeous. Some of us have to go to work in the morning."

"This is a vegetable," Sammie said, waving the piece of broccoli on her fork at Jude. "Some people eat them."

"This is a vegetable, too," Alison added, pointing at the yellow squash on her plate. "Most vegetarians eat vegetables."

"Jude doesn't eat vegetables?" Luk asked. "How does

a vegetarian not eat vegetables?"

"Carbohydrates are my friends," Jude said. "If rice is good enough for the entire population of India and China, then I can live on it, too."

"I'll think you find the population of China and India eats the occasional vegetable too," Sammie said.

"I eat potatoes," Jude said. "They're a vegetable."

"Anyway," Alison said. "Luk not only eats vegetables, he cooks them. We love you, Luk."

"Good," Luk said. "Does that mean I can stay?"

"And that was the question on the table, before Luk served up dinner," Jude said. "And distracted you both."

"You can stay," Sammie said. "Right, Alison?"

Alison nodded, then swallowed the mouthful of broccoli she was chewing. "Absolutely. You say you wash dishes, too?"

"House rules," Sammie said. "They actually say each person has to deal with their own kitchen mess, and this is a kitchen-nagging-free household."

Luk looked at the sink, which was stacked with dirty dishes. "I can see that. You don't have rats, do you?"

"No rats," Alison said. "Jude is scared of rats. He'd be prepared to actually put down baits, which just goes to show how poor his grasp of the first precept is."

"What?" Luk said.

"The first precept is not to take life," Jude said. "This is an observant Buddhist household, and we strive to follow the five precepts, which include no drugs or alcohol."

"I got rid of my stash before I came here," Luk said. "And I've not smuggled a steak in, either."

"We have to work out how the rent gets divided," Sammie said. "It shouldn't be four ways, because Luk and Jude share a room."

"But they both use the communal spaces," Alison said. "Like the kitchen and the bathroom."

"Do the maths," Luk said. "How many rooms in the house? How many of those rooms does each person access exclusively, and what proportion do they share?"

"Three bedrooms," Jude said. "Living room, kitchen, bathroom and laundry. The outdoor space probably counts, too. Can you do that sort of calculation in your head?"

Luk rolled his eyes at Jude. "We all access five communal spaces equally; we just need to assign a proportionate value of the rent to that access."

"Half," Alison said. "How does that sound?"

"Reasonable," Sammie agreed.

"So we each pay one eighth of the rent for the shared space. Sammie and Alison then pay a sixth each, for their bedrooms, and Jude and I pay a twelfth each, for our room, since we share. The utilities get split four ways."

The three of them looked at Luk, and he said, "What?"

"Write it down, before any of us forget that," Alison said. "And no loud sex when people are trying to sleep or eat, especially no loud sex in the shower."

"It was once!" Sammie said. "Once only, and do you think anyone will let me forget it?"

"It was while I had people over for dinner," Alison said.

"Monks," Jude added.

"The acoustics were impressive," Alison said.

Luk stared at the three of them. "You know monks? Actual monks?"

"Lovely people," Alison said. "Very easily amused."

Sammie had gone as red as Luk sometimes did, and he felt sorry for her.

"I went to Centrelink today before uni, to apply for social security benefits," Luk said. "Like Sammie suggested I do, before the bruising faded. They agreed I was in crisis, and couldn't possibly go home again, and let me have an independent youth allowance, despite not being eligible."

Alison nodded. "They get embarrassed when people turn up after being beaten up. It makes them look bad, or something. How is the face?"

"Sore," Luk said. "No one would sit next to me on the bus. I must look scary or something."

Alison and Sammie both started laughing, and Luk said, "What?"

"Luk, you're a punk," Alison said. "You're wearing a Sex Pistols T-shirt, and you've got chains on your jeans and boots. Aren't people always scared by how you look?"

Luk laughed, too. "I hadn't thought of that."

After dinner, while Sammie and Alison clattered in the kitchen, actually washing some of the dishes up since Luk had cooked for all of them, Jude and Luk practiced.

The Ovation looked gorgeous in Jude's hands, the rosewood front glowing against his skin, his hands remembering how to move over an acoustic. He was better than Luk had expected, better than the day before had led Luk to believe he would be, but that would be Luk's fault for putting Jude under so much pressure without warning.

Jude's electric guitar was a dog, on the other hand. It needed new capstans urgently, to stop the tuning pegs from sliding loose almost immediately. Tuned, it sounded tinny, and Luk was frankly horrified that Jude ran it through an ancient CD player for solo practice. Luk could replace the capstans the very next day, but an amp and speaker was going to take work.

They played through the standard Beatles songs, the ones in ordinary time signatures, with Luk calling the chords for Jude while playing the lead melody himself. It was basic musical skills, playing one thing while thinking another, and Jude only needed to be told once.

After an hour and a half, when Luk was retuning the lead guitar yet again, Jude said, "Can we stop? I don't think I can take in any more."

Luk put the lead guitar aside on the floor, and took the Ovation off Jude. "Sure, we can stop rehearsing. You comfy there?"

Jude had two pillows behind him, and was leaning back against the wall to one side of the mattress. "Yeah. Why?"

Luk crawled over the mattress to sit between Jude's spread knees. "Because I wasn't."

He leaned back against Jude, and settled the acoustic across his lap.

"That better?" Jude asked, his breath tickling Luk's scalp.

"Much," Luk said. "Now, be quiet, I want to concentrate."

Arnold's 'Guitar Concerto, Opus 67' took total concentration, and even the feel of Jude, his warmth and the slow steady reassurance of his breathing, slipped away under the demands of the piece as Luk worked through it, letting the music come from his memory, trusting it would all be there when he needed it to be.

His hands moved by themselves, faltering occasionally, but when he came to the end, Luk was content with his performance. It was a monstrous piece of music, endlessly complex, but he had time to work the bugs out before he had to perform it for uni.

Luk put the guitar aside on the bed and stretched his hands and arms, rolling his shoulders. Jude's arms slid around his waist, hugging him, and Jude said, "I'm sorry I ever called you a diva. That was fucking brilliant."

"It wasn't perfect," Luk said. "It needs more work,

but I'm glad you liked it. I was a brat about your song 'Fall Back, Retreat,' and completely deserve worse things than to be called a diva. I'm surprised you had anything to do with me after that."

Jude nuzzled the side of Luk's neck. "The problem there is that you're completely hot, and no matter how obnoxious you were, I still wanted you."

"Really?" Luk asked, his breath catching as Jude's hands slid under his T-shirt, almost-tickling across Luk's belly, up to his chest.

"If you only knew some of things I've fantasized about doing to you..." Jude whispered. "How desperately I wanted you..."

"Yeah?" Luk asked. "You hid it well."

One of Jude's hands pushed lower, to the front of Luk's jeans. "Yeah. Down the beach, that day, when you stomped off to sulk... Your arse in wet boxers... I was so hard for you then."

"You were?" Luk asked, as Jude's hands undid Luk's jeans.

"Yeah. I had to swim off, just in case Lori decided that hanging onto me was easier than swimming. Take your jeans off, and grab the lube."

Luk kicked his jeans and boxers off. He reached across and found the lube while Jude stripped off, then Jude sat back where he'd been before and patted the mattress in front of him.

"But I can't touch you," Luk said, settling back, between Jude's knees.

"Later," Jude said. "If you want to. Give me the lube, and it's your turn."

The feel of Jude's hand, slippery with lube, on his cock was enough to stop Luk from talking for a moment. "Oh, fuck," Luk said. "Yeah. That day, on the way to the Hydey after the beach, you had your hand on my thigh, and I was so fucking hard. I think if you'd touched me then like you are now, I would have come instantly, I wanted you so much."

Jude's other hand cupped Luk's balls, then slid lower, spreading lube, and it felt good, hot and a little weird. One of Jude's fingertips rubbed across Luk's arse, and Jude said, "Did you? Do you know how difficult it was to leave, that night? Do you have any idea of how turned on I was?"

The finger eased into Luk's arse, slowly, and Jude's other hand worked Luk's cock harder and faster, so Luk had no chance of answering, not with the feelings rushing through him, hot and sharp inside.

"Oh," Jude moaned against Luk's ear. "Yeah, like that, come for me, babe, wanna fuck you so much."

It was too late, Luk was too close to coming; he couldn't stop himself from thinking about Jude's thick cock being inside him, pushing into him. Jude's finger was doing something to him, driving him crazy, and Luk dug his heels into the mattress and tipped his head back onto Jude's shoulder, while his body just exploded, it felt so fucking good.

Jude hung onto Luk while he stopped shaking, kissing his neck, wiping the come off his chest and licking it up.

"I need to come," Jude said, once Luk was managing to breathe without gasping. "Think you can move enough for me to get a hand behind you?"

Could Luk move? Pitching forward, onto the mattress, seemed the safest option, then Luk rolled onto his back and held out an arm for Jude.

Jude lay down beside Luk, propped on one elbow, the other hand wrapped around his own cock. His face twisted, and his knees jerked, then he was coming over Luk's belly.

It took maneuvering to get them both under the

blanket, then Luk reached out and switched off the light.

Lying in the dark, rubbing at the dried come itching in his pubic hair, Jude's arm around his chest, Luk said, "Did you mean that?"

"Mean what?"

"About wanting to fuck me."

Jude moved closer, tangling his legs with Luk's. "If and when you think you want to try it, I can't think of anything I'd rather do, except have you fuck me."

Luk could hear the wind picking up outside, rattling the loose tin on the old house's roof, shaking the windows a little. The last of the summer was finally gone, and autumn had arrived.

"I want to try it soon," Luk said.

Chapter Sixteen

Robbo was behind the counter at Loud People when Jude pushed the door open after he'd finished work the next Monday.

"Hello, dear possum," Robbo said, his voice raised over The Cramps playing over the sound system. "How's my favorite trolley stacker?"

"Robbo, you mad man, how are you? Not incarcerated?" Jude said, leaning against the counter. "I'm fine, though I'm in search of Her Royal Highness, and you are obviously not her."

Robbo minced a little in imitation of Lori behind the counter, then turned the volume down on The Cramps, which, in Jude's opinion, was only an improvement. "My court appearance is not for a few weeks, so I remain on bail, and indebted to the adorable Brianna until then. The lovely Lori didn't front for work today, so when the boss turned up here to do the banking and the place was locked up, he called me in to work in her place."

"Is she alright?" Jude asked. "Is she ill?"

"According to Rick, when I rang him, she is grievously

hungover, and hates the world. I am content to merely hate the parts of it that didn't bother phoning in sick for work. Mind you, a little bit of employment might persuade the nice magistrate that I'm not a no-good malcontent, and should be given a nice community service order. What did you do to get away with a community service order when you got busted being buggered by Dave at Big Day Out?"

"I asked the head of the Buddhist Society here to give me a character reference, and he turned up in his saffron robes and enthused about what a good Buddhist I was, and how he'd personally guarantee that I'd learned my lesson in modesty," Jude said. "The part where I had to explain to a monk what I'd actually done to be charged with public indecency was the tricky bit. There are rules about sexual misconduct, and trying to explain why I'd thought going for it in front of a few thousand people was a good idea was unpleasant."

"Ouch," Robbo said. "Does your monk hand out references to anyone, or would I have to actually convert first?"

"You'd have to make some effort first," Jude said. "Besides, what would you be converting from? I didn't know you were religious."

"The Church of Enlightened Self-Interest," Robbo said. "They don't do character references, unfortunately. Stop interrupting me, I've got to remember how to be nice to strangers."

A middle-aged woman, pinched and worried-looking, hesitated in the doorway of the shop, and Robbo waved a cheery hand at her.

"Come in, my dear," he called out.

"Oh," the woman said, approaching the counter. "I'm trying to find someone, and I don't know if I'm in the right shop even."

Robbo turned The Cramps off, which was the best track of theirs, and leaned over the counter. "Who are you looking for?"

"There's a girl, and I think she works here," the woman said.

"Lori?" Robbo asked. "Cute goth girl?"

"I don't know what she looks like, but I think Lori is her name," the woman said.

"She's off work sick," Robbo said. "She should be back at work tomorrow."

The woman's face paled, and she went to leave.

"Wait," Jude said. "We're her friends. Perhaps we can help you."

The woman turned back. "She's in a band, and my son, Lucien, is also in the band, and I don't know how to find him, and I was hoping she would help me."

Robbo stepped back, and said, "Jude, you get to take this."

"Did you want to sit down somewhere?" Jude asked Luk's mother. "Where we can talk?"

"Do you know where Lucien is?" Luk's mother asked. "Is he safe?"

"I'm Jude. I'm Luk's boyfriend. He's staying with me."

Luk's mother started sobbing, and Jude shared a glance with Robbo, then wrapped his arms around Luk's mother and hugged her.

Luk's mother sat at a table at the café two shops along from Loud People, drying her face on a napkin. "I'm so sorry," she said. "I've been so worried about him, and how to find him, and there you were, just waiting for me. My name's Anne."

The waitress put a mug of tea and a glass of lemonade on the table, then stomped off.

Jude smiled at Anne. "Luk is fine. His face is healing

up, and he's coping. How are you and Penny? He said you were both there when his father hurt him."

"That's why I wanted to find him," Anne said. "To tell him his father's gone. How could someone hurt their own child? Does he need money? Can I give you money to give to him?"

Jude stopped Anne's hand, where she was reaching into her purse. "Why don't you tell him about all this yourself? I think he'd love to see you, if he knew it was safe for you both."

"I'm glad he's got you," Anne said. "I don't care that he's gay, I don't care about anything like that, as long as he's alright."

"I think he's going to be just fine now," Jude said.

Luk slammed into the house, calling out, "Why is one of my family's cars outside? Who told them where I was?"

Jude caught up with him, in the hall. "Your mother is here, Luk. I brought her here."

Luk brushed Jude's hands off his arms and pushed past him into the kitchen, Jude following behind him.

"Mum!" Luk said, and Anne stood up from the chair on which she'd been perched.

"It's alright, Lucien," Anne said. "Your father's gone now."

Luk froze, and Jude retrieved the guitar case before Luk could drop it.

"And Jude was kind enough to bring me here, to see you."

Then Luk and Anne were hugging and crying, and Jude pulled the kitchen door shut and went to sit out the back, with Sammie and Alison.

"So," Sammie said, moving across on the blanket they all used on the paving, to make room for Jude. "You're losing your bedwarmer again."

"I doubt he'll stay away," Jude said.

He would miss having Luk there all the time. Weekends weren't enough, not with how he felt.

A few minutes later, Jude sat on his mattress, on sheets that smelled of sex, while Luk shoved his clothes into his pack.

"I'm glad, for you, and for your mum," Jude said. "She's a darling."

Luk shuffled across the floor, underwear in his hands. "I'll be back," he said. "Friday night? I think Mum is going to be fine, especially now she's met you."

"Friday night," Jude said. "And I'll call you before then, too."

"Fuck," Luk said, then he was in Jude's arms, hugging him, tipping both of them back onto the mattress.

"Your mum needs you," Jude said, burrowing his face against Luk's neck.

"I gotta go," Luk said, then he kissed Jude hard, scooped up his pack, and bolted out of the room, leaving the rest of his clothes behind.

Jude stayed where he was, on the bed, hugging a pillow, while Anne and Luk left.

Sammie tapped on his partly-open door a few minutes later. "What?" he called.

"Feel like breaking a precept?" she said, peeking around the door. "Alison has a secret stash of chocolate, for menstrual cramp and boyfriend problems."

Jude thought about throwing the pillow at the door, but some chocolate sounded like a good idea. "On my way," he said. "Can we watch a chick flick on Alison's TV, too? Something without any crying?"

"Jane Austen movie time!" Sammie called to Alison.

"Break out the bonnets and the chocolate, we're living it up."

Jude still felt lost, like he was incomplete, when he finished dragging trolleys around the supermarket car park the next afternoon, and he was annoyed with himself over it. It was one thing to be in love, but something else entirely to be moping around because he couldn't with be Luk all the time, and he should get the fuck over himself.

He needed someone else to tell him that, and there was no one quite like Her Royal Highness for popping balloons, especially romantic ones.

The music was off in Loud People when Jude pushed the door open, and Robbo looked up from behind the counter.

"I'm so glad you're here," Robbo said, and he sounded panicked. "Did you get my message?"

"No message," Jude said.

"I rang your mum in Melbourne, and she rang your housemate's mobile. And I rang Luk's home," Robbo said.

"I've not been home." Jude took a deep breath. "It's Lori, isn't it?"

"Yeah," Robbo said. "It's Lori. Oh, fuck, it's bad."

Jude got as far as the counter. "Is... is she dead? OD'ed?"

Robbo shook his head. "No. At least, she wasn't a couple of hours ago. Not an overdose. She's been in a car accident."

Jude grabbed Robbo's hand, and Robbo squeezed. "Was Rick driving? Is Rick alright?"

Robbo looked bleak. "Lori was by herself, that's all I

know. Rick is at home, with Licks, trying to straighten up enough to go to the hospital."

Fat tears slid down Robbo's cheeks, and Jude leaned across the counter and slung an arm around his shoulders.

The door opened behind them, and Luk's voice said, "Jude! You're here! Robbo, is there any news?"

Jude turned, and Luk ran straight into his arms, throwing himself at Jude.

Jude hugged Luk, hanging onto the feel of Luk's body, the warmth of his skin, until the phone rang.

"Good afternoon, Loud People," Robbo said, his voice sounding choked. "Mrs. Porter... thanks... thanks for letting us know. When Lori wakes up, can you tell her we all love her very much?"

Robbo put the phone down.

"That was Lori's mum. Lori is out of surgery, and will be in intensive care for a while. She's smashed up, but doesn't have head injuries. She's listed as critical but stable."

"We can't go to her, can we?" Luk said.

Robbo shook his head. "We can't do anything."

Jude said, "We can. I'm going to a temple."

Luk pulled a set of keys from his pocket and jangled them. "I'll drive. I've got Mum's car."

Jude directed Luk, who drove his mother's car with the kind of exaggerated caution that made Jude suspect he hadn't had his license long, to the temple on Guildford Road. It wasn't where Sammie, Alison and Jude usually went -- it wasn't even in the same Buddhist tradition -- but it was closest to the city.

"What do I have to do?" Luk asked nervously, following Jude into the front vestibule of the temple.

"Take your shoes and socks off," Jude said in a low voice. "Be respectful. Be silent. You'll be able to sit on a bench, around the outside of the temple. If there's no service on, one of the monks or nuns may speak with you. If he or she does, tell them about Lori."

Jude undid his sneakers and slipped them off, then stuffed his socks into them and put them onto a shelf.

He left Luk unlacing his boots, and passed through the double curtains into the hall of worship. The altar was in use, incense burning, and several monks were meditating silently at the front of the hall, but there was no formal service in progress.

Jude made his bow, and moved to sit partway down the hall, so he wouldn't disturb the monks.

His heart was choked with fear as he knelt. His mind was racing, panic and grief flaring through him, desperate longing for Lori consuming him. There could be no reflection, no practice, until he moved through the pain and fear.

He'd been raised Buddhist, his mother a hippy, so the process was there, engrained into him from childhood. Breathe in the pain; breathe out compassion. Breathe in grief; breathe out hope. Move through despair. Know it is not the end, just like death is a gateway, and time is an illusion. Be all times and things at once.

It took many breaths, many conscious efforts, to let go, to find the calmness, to still his pulse and mind.

Then Jude said the Heart Sutra, slowly and deliberately, the same as he had said for Lori's baby, the Sanskrit words translating into a reminder to travel the paths to connection with the world.

Twenty-eight times he said the words, while holding Lori in his thoughts.

He wasn't asking for intercession, or doing more than blessing her. He was reminding himself, Lori, and the Universe that she belonged, that she was part of this wondrous existence, and that he and other people treasured her, whatever happened to her.

At the end, when Jude stood slowly, bowing his thanks, some of the calm lingered.

Luk wasn't sitting on the benches around the temple, but one of the monks waved at Jude from a corner doorway, calling him over.

Luk was sitting in the temple kitchen, an industrial kitchen designed to cater for hundreds, with a young female novitiate dressed in white, and another monk in red robes, all of them drinking hot water from mugs.

The novitiate held a mug out for Jude. "Please, come sit with us."

"Thank you," Jude said.

"Did you find peace?" the novitiate asked.

"I did, thank you," Jude said.

The monk nodded, smiling broadly, and Jude couldn't help but smile back.

"Your friend has told us about Lori. We will add blessings for Lori to our service tonight," the novitiate said.

"Lori's family and friends appreciate your generosity," Jude said.

The novitiate put her mug down on the stainless steel workbench they were seated around. "If you will allow me to escort you both from the kitchen, I must prepare for evening service."

In the vestibule, after the novitiate had bowed and left them, Jude took his wallet out and put what he had in it into the collection box above the shoe rack.

"Do you have any money?" he asked Luk. "It's appropriate to make a donation, especially after an audience with a monk, like we just had."

Luk opened his wallet. "I've got The Tockleys' money on me."

"Put that in," Jude said. "I'm sure Lori's music money

should go to prayers."

In the car, Luk said, "Was that really an audience with a monk? He didn't say anything, and we just drank hot water."

"He's probably taken a vow of silence," Jude said. "The novitiate was there to speak on his behalf. She'd have that job because she was mostly able to predict what he'd want to say, anyway. And the hot water is because some monks fast from mid-morning to dawn."

Luk started the car and turned to look at Jude. "Can we go to your place and go to bed? I feel like crap, and I think all that's going to help is being with you."

Jude touched Luk's arm. "I should warn you I'm not going to want to fuck. But, if you just want to be held, then there's nothing I'd rather do than be next to you right now."

Luk pulled out of the temple carpark, his face lit by the dashboard lights. "What do you think happened to Lori?"

"She was drunk, or drug-fucked," Jude said. "And she wrecked the van. It probably wasn't very complicated."

Jude had seen Mrs. Porter, Lori's mother, once before, but she was almost unrecognizable now, her eyes swollen from crying, her face pale in sleep.

"Mrs. Porter," Jude said gently at the door to Lori's hospital room.

Mrs. Porter jerked awake on the hard plastic chair beside Lori's bed. "What?"

"I'm Jude. We met once before, at Lori's birthday lunch." Jude's eyes were on Lori's bed, where Lori lay motionless, her legs hidden by a framework draped in a sheet, tubes running into her arms, machines humming beside her. "Do you mind if I come in for a moment?"

Mrs. Porter stood up, unsteady on her feet. "Please do, Jude. If you could sit with her, just in case she wakes up again, while I get a coffee and something to eat..."

Jude sat on the plastic chair and touched the back of Lori's hand gently with his fingertips, where no tubes or bandages were.

"Lori, darling," Jude whispered.

Tears came, and Jude let them, let himself feel the grief in his heart that this had happened to someone he loved. He could own the pain, then let it go, because to deny it would be to deny what Lori was suffering.

Lori said, "Jude, I did something wrong."

Jude looked up, grabbing Lori's fingers, rubbing at his face with his other hand.

"Lori?"

But Lori was asleep. She hadn't moved, certainly hadn't spoken.

Mrs. Porter came back, and when Jude stood to give her back her seat, Rick and Robbo were standing in the doorway.

Rick didn't meet Jude's gaze, didn't acknowledge him at all, just stood like a zombie in the doorway, staring at Lori.

Robbo followed Jude down the hall, and the pair of them looked out a barred window, down at a concrete courtyard, gray cement under a gray sky.

"I found out what happened. She wrapped Rick's van around a tree," Robbo said. "It was a single car, straight road accident. She wasn't drunk."

Jude glanced at Robbo. "She was trying to kill herself?"

"That's the theory with single car, straight road accidents, isn't it?"

Jude looked back, down the hall. "This stops now. It's

Laney Cairo

my fault, for not speaking out before."

He walked back, down the hall, past Rick and into Lori's room, to where Mrs. Porter kept vigil at her daughter's bedside.

"Lori's been using heroin," Jude said. "You have to tell her doctors. And Rick has been abusing her, beating her. Get her away from him."

Mrs. Porter said, "What? Jude?"

Jude looked at Lori. "There's more, but she'll have to tell you herself. It's my fault. I knew all this, and I didn't help her enough. I failed her completely."

Jude walked out of the hospital into the first rain of the year.

It was a long walk home, but he needed to think, and to feel. The rain slicked his hair down his back and stuck his clothes to his body, chilling him. His wet socks rubbed his feet, chafing him. He was hungry and tired. What was any of this to what Lori had felt?

He'd made mistakes before, big mistakes even, but never anything like this. Lori was crushed, her body and spirit broken, because of his failure. He'd been so wrapped up in falling in love with Luk, and with the music they'd been making, that he'd turned away from Lori. He'd seen the bruises. He'd known she was using, and Luk had told him it was smack. He'd let her go back to Rick after the termination, with only a string of glass beads to protect her.

The long, wet kilometers to his house were bitter, and gave Jude no peace. It would take more than a cold walk in the rain to bring him calm.

Luk's sister, Penny, answered their phone, and even her teasing of Luk as she handed the phone over did nothing to lift a smile from Jude.

"How was Lori?" Luk asked. "Did you get to see her?"

"She was asleep," Jude said. "But I saw her."

"How did she look?" Luk asked. "Is she improving?"

Jude looked at the water trickling down the outside of the phone booth window, rivulets streaking through an entire summer's worth of dirt. "She's out of intensive care. I saw her mother. I need to talk to you, love."

"What's wrong? You sound grim? Is there bad news about Lori?"

"I need to go away," Jude said. "I won't be around for a while."

"How long?" Luk asked, sounding disappointed. "Where are you going? What's happened?"

"I love you," Jude said. "I hope you already know that. I'll still love you when I come back."

Luk was silent for a few seconds, though his breathing was ragged. "Please, Jude, tell me what's going on. I'm coming over, right now."

"Don't," Jude said. "I can't see anyone right now, not even you."

"You're crying, aren't you?" Luk said. "Why?"

"I'll call you when I'm able to."

Jude put the phone down, then picked it up again. Thursday evening services would just be over, so someone would probably answer the phone at the Dhamma Center.

Ajahn Mal came to the phone when Jude asked to speak to one of the monks.

"Jude, child," Ajahn Mal said, his voice soft and mellow. "You are in distress?"

"I am," Jude said, pressing his head against the glass of the booth, to feel the cool of the rain. "I'm in a difficult place. I need to step away from the pain and go on retreat."

"I'll make a call, tomorrow morning," Ajahn Mal said. "As soon as someone is in the office down there. You get yourself there, and there will be a pallet waiting for you, even if all the accommodation is full. You can sleep on the office floor, if need be."

"Thank you," Jude said.

"Remember, all pain is temporary, and you can choose to let it pass through you," Ajahn Mal said. "I don't need to lecture you about suffering. You know all this, you just need to be in a place that reminds you."

Alison and Sammie didn't bother arguing, which Jude was grateful for. "You've told Luk?" Sammie asked, as Jude counted out his rent on the kitchen table.

"I rang him," Jude said. "That's four weeks in advance. That's all I had in the bank. When my pay for the past fortnight goes in, I'll transfer some more across. If I stay on retreat longer than that, you can let my room out to someone else."

"Leave it tidy," Sammie said. "We'll just move anything you leave behind into the laundry if we have to."

The three of them sat in silence, for a few minutes, but it wasn't uncomfortable. Then Sammie said, "It helped me, to go there. It helped to stop talking in circles."

Jude nodded. "I can't stop the noise inside my head at the moment."

Sammie patted his shoulder. "Go to bed, Jude. I'll drop you at the bus station on my way to work tomorrow morning."

Chapter Seventeen

obbo propped his boots on the counter at Loud People, and Luk hopped up to sit beside his feet. "So, Jude has just pissed off?" Robbo said.

Luk shrugged. "He said he had to go away. I don't think that counts as pissed off."

"He's a noble chap in some ways," Robbo said, handing Luk the packet of Milk Arrowroots he was munching from. "Want to dunk?"

Luk took a Milk Arrowroot and dipped the end into the cup of tea Robbo had made him, then ate the soggy mess. "He is?"

"Oh, yes," Robbo said. "You should have seen him telling Lori's mum what an arsehole Rick was. Goodbye, Rick. But he does have form, when it comes to disappearing."

Luk said, "What?"

"No one told you?" Robbo asked. "How Jude didn't hang around at all when things went bad with his ex, Dave? Dave had some issues, but who doesn't? Anyway, Dave was trying to sort himself out, get himself clean, and Jude just bolted, disappeared for a couple of months, then wouldn't have anything to do with Dave."

"A couple of months?" Luk said. "Not just a day or two? He just disappeared? Where the fuck did he go?"

"No idea, my marsupial friend. It's possible Lori would know, but I don't know anyone else you could ask. Not even Dave would know, not that Dave would do anything to help Jude or Jude's bonk out anyway."

"Did Dave do anything to find him?" Luk asked.

Robbo shrugged, then accidentally dropped the last of his Milk Arrowroot into his cup of tea, where it dissolved. "Damn. I think Dave was too busy trying not to use to worry about locating a wandering lover. What is it you all see in Jude, anyway? I don't do blokes, so I must be missing something here, but he just seems kind of thin and intense and annoying to me. A decent enough friend, as long as you don't rely on him in a crisis."

"Lori relied on him," Luk said. "He helped her as much as she'd let him."

"And wasn't that wonderfully successful?" Robbo said, abandoning his squelchy mug of tea and reaching for his ukulele. "We've thrown Rick out of Delicate John, and are looking for another guitarist. You fancy playing with us? You were bloody good, jamming that morning at the house."

Luk shook his head at Robbo, who was strumming his ukulele in time with The Clash playing over the sound system. "You know, a few weeks ago, I would have jumped at playing with Delicate John, but right now, I have to go find a thin and annoying man."

Lori said, "No, it's alright, Mum, he's not one of the bad guys."

Luk put his pack and guitar down. "I'm Luk, I was in the band with Lori."

Lori's mother, who was blocking the door to Lori's hospital room, stood aside. "Alright, you can come in, young man, but you're not to give her any drugs, or pass any messages from That Man."

Lori held out a hand to Luk, and Luk took it gingerly, then leaned forward and kissed Lori's pale cheek. "How are you feeling?" he asked.

"In fucking agony," Lori said. "Thanks to Jude's wonderful outburst, which I don't actually remember, I can no longer have the real painkillers."

Luk looked at Lori's legs, which were covered in a mess of dressings and braces. "What did you break?"

"Both legs, in multiple places," Lori said. "Ribs, and my spleen was removed."

"Ouch?" Luk said.

"Ouch," Lori agreed. "It's good to see you. I know Jude's been in, because Mum told me, but I thought he would have been back since I woke up properly."

Luk looked down, at Lori's hand. "I need to ask you about that. Jude has run off somewhere, and Robbo said he'd done it before. Robbo thought you might know where he goes."

Lori said, "Oh? Like he did with Dave?"

"I didn't know anything about that until Robbo told me," Luk said. "Jude rang me up, a few nights ago. He said he had to go away, but that he'd be back."

He didn't feel the need to tell Lori about Jude saying 'I love you.' That was just a bit too personal. Luk wasn't sure how he felt about it himself, except that he kept playing it back in his memory whenever he missed Jude, and wishing he'd managed to say something back.

"So he didn't dump you?" Lori asked.

"Definitely not," Luk said. "No dumping. Do you

know where he goes?"

"Not a clue," Lori said. "What's that song he wrote, about breaking up with Dave?"

"'Fall Back, Retreat'?" Luk said.

"All I know is he wrote that, while he was away."

Luk grabbed his guitar case, and pulled his guitar out.

"Visions of you dance on the water," Luk sang. "Where my memory laps at me and soaks through my skin."

He sang on, through the first verse, to the line he'd been looking for in his memory. "My silence is worth it -- it's only my hurt."

His fingers faltered, and he looked up at Lori. "Damn, why didn't I think of that?"

"Why'd you stop?" Lori said plaintively.

"Because it's in the song, and it's in the bloody title. He goes on a retreat, where no one talks, like the monk."

"What monk?" Lori asked.

"The monk at the temple we went to," Luk said. "Where Jude prayed for you, when you were first hurt. The monk didn't speak at all, which was odd."

"I miss out on the best things," Lori said. "If it's a religious thing, Sammie and Alison will know about it. Go and ask them."

"I will," Luk said. "You're a darling, Lori. Get better, quickly, because I miss playing with you."

Lori shook her head. "I'm going home with Mum when I can leave the hospital. You and Jude, you can have The Tockleys, the pair of you. I've had enough."

Luk nodded. "Yeah, I can understand that."

Sammie looked at her fluffy bunny slippers, and Alison fiddled with the buttons of her pajamas, while Luk watched them across their kitchen table piled with dirty dishes.

"If Jude didn't tell you where he was going, then I'm not sure I can," Sammie said, finally.

Luk sighed, and reached for his guitar. "I kind of know where he is," Luk said. "Listen."

He played them 'Fall Back, Retreat,' the chords careful and the words clear.

"Um, wow," Sammie said. "That's amazing."

"That's Jude's song," Luk said. "He wrote it after breaking up with his last boyfriend, when he went on a silent retreat somewhere."

"The poisonous Dave," Alison said.

"So, tell me where the silent retreat is," Luk said. "I can probably find out for myself tomorrow, by working out which temple place the three of you go to and going there and asking, but it would be easier if you just told me."

"You have no reason to think Jude doesn't want to see you?" Alison asked.

Luk shook his head. "None at all."

"So why do you want to follow him, then?" Alison asked. "The pair of you haven't broken up, he just wants some time to recover from what has been a pretty horrible experience. Are you acting from your own needs? Who benefits from this?"

Luk looked at Sammie and Alison, and decided to tell them the truth. "He told me he loved me on the phone, and I was too surprised to say anything back to him. I don't want him to think I don't love him, too."

Sammie lifted an eyebrow at Alison, who nodded and said, "Who are we to stand in the way of true love?"

Alison nodded. "And he does cry when Mr. Darcy proposes the second time, so we know he's a sucker for this sort of thing."

Alison leaned back on her rickety kitchen chair and opened a drawer in the cabinet behind her, rummaging around. A moment later, she handed Luk a pamphlet.

"He's there," Alison said. "Map's on the back. Nearest town is Nannup, so if you catch a bus there, you can probably hitch out to the retreat."

Luk looked at the pamphlet and nodded. "Thanks," he said, standing up and reaching for his guitar.

"There're no buses until tomorrow morning," Alison said.

"I'm going to hitch all the way," Luk said.

Sammie stood up, hands on her hips. "Listen here, young man. While we're all in favor of romantic love, neither of us are going to let you walk out into the middle of the night to hitchhike four hundred kilometers. Sit down."

Alison nodded. "Absolutely. Sit down, and we will feed you. Then you can crash in Jude's bed, and Sammie will drop you at the bus station first thing in the morning. Call your mother, too."

Sammie nodded. "Call your mother. Absolutely. Well spotted, Alison." A mobile phone was pushed across the table, toward Luk.

Luk sat down again meekly. He knew better to argue, not when he was both outnumbered and outclassed.

Chapter Eighteen

Nannup was a small town, nestled between hills covered in deep forest. Luk shouldered his pack and picked up his guitar case, and glanced at the pamphlet in his hands. The retreat was on the Bridgetown road, and after blundering up and down the main street of the town, Luk asked for directions at the only petrol station.

"Bridgetown road?" the woman behind the counter said. "That way, past the bakery and the tea rooms." She pointed helpfully. "Where you going?"

Luk held out the pamphlet. "The Forest Retreat."

"Hang on," the woman said. She leaned forward so she could look through the open window to the service station forecourt and the main street, which was deserted.

"See the general store?" she said. "Over there? Someone from the retreat comes in every Wednesday to pick up supplies. Go over there, and ask if they've been yet. If they haven't, then you can get a lift back with them."

The girl at the general store stared at Luk. "What?"

"Has anyone from the Forest Retreat been in to pick

up supplies yet today?" Luk repeated.

The girl frowned, and Luk wondered exactly how busy she had been, if she couldn't remember a bunch of monks in robes collecting rice.

The door to the general store tinkled as it opened behind Luk, and the girl said, "No, because they're here now."

The woman in the doorway was wearing jeans and a plain T-shirt, and had the same haircut as Luk.

"Hi there," she said brightly.

"He's looking for you," the general store girl said helpfully.

"So I gathered. I'm Donna. How can I help you?"

"I'm Luk. I was hoping to get a lift out to the retreat with you," Luk said.

"Sure," Donna said. "Especially if you'll load the truck for me."

Luk and Donna stacked crates of supplies onto the back of the small truck she'd parked outside the store: packs of toilet paper, sacks of rice, boxes of porridge and fruit.

Luk hopped into the front passenger seat, his pack and guitar at his feet. "The retreat is full," Donna said. "If you were hoping to stay, you're not going to be able to."

"I just need to see someone who is there," Luk said. "Then I'll go."

Donna nodded. "You can talk to one of the Ajahns about it. I'm sure they can work something out for you."

Luk wasn't sure what the Ajahn could work out, either staying or seeing Jude, but Luk would take either option.

"So, you a Buddhist?" Donna asked conversationally, as the truck rattled along the twisting forest road, huge trees pressing in on each side.

"No, but my lover is," Luk said.

"Ah," Donna said. "I guess that's Jude, then."

She didn't say any more, just hummed to herself while she drove. She turned the truck off the sealed road, rattling it down a rough track through heavy forest that shut out most of the light, before bringing it to a halt in a clearing beside a cluster of mudbrick buildings.

Luk jumped down from the truck and helped Donna unload the crates, moving them into a store room off a primitive kitchen and dining hall.

"Everyone else is meditating," Donna said. "You can sit under a tree, out the front, and I'll let one of the Ajahns know you're here. Don't wander, don't speak to anyone."

"I've got the idea," Luk said.

He took his pack and guitar out of the truck, and found a small patch of overgrown grass where the forest and the rudimentary gardens at the retreat were fighting it out.

It was beautiful, sitting in the shade, listening to the sound of the forest, the trees whispering and creaking, the birds calling. Luk was tired; he'd not slept much the night before, not being back in Jude's bed again, and alone.

He might have dozed, or might just have been thinking hard, when a voice said, "You wanted an audience?"

Luk jumped to his feet, pressing his hands together and bowing like he'd seen Jude do to greet the monks at the temple.

The monk was a middle-aged man with a shaven head and a somber face, wrapped in orange robes. "Sit down again."

The monk squatted in front of Luk, settling himself cautiously on the grass. "I am Ajahn P, so called because my full name is unpronounceable."

"I'm Luk." Luk sat back down again. "I'd like to see

Jude."

"Jude is on retreat. Are you sure he wants to see you?"

"I'm willing to take my chances."

Ajahn P nodded. "He is not speaking, taking refuge from too many words and thoughts. If you see him, will you respect that?"

Luk nodded. "If that is what he needs."

The monk sighed. "I'm glad you've come. I hope you'll stay, for his sake. Come with me. Donna will instruct you in behavior here, since you are not familiar with retreat etiquette."

Donna looked from Ajahn P to Luk, and back again. "Alright," she said, sounding dubious. "Come with me, Luk."

She pointed at a corner of the store room, where they'd stacked the crates of supplies. "Rearrange the crates, make yourself some room in here," she said. "I'll get you some blankets. Put your guitar and bag here, and follow me."

She pointed at the blackboard in the kitchen. "That's the cooking and cleaning roster. Put yourself on it, for the amount you feel is reasonable. We eat our main meal in the morning, and observe the five precepts. You do know the five precepts, right?"

"You'd better tell me them again," Luk said. "Just to make sure."

"Don't take life, don't steal, no sexual misconduct, no lying, and no mind-altering substances," Donna rattled off. "In addition, don't approach anyone except myself or the monks. Music is for solo consumption only, respect people on the retreat who are observing silences, and don't be an idiot. You might want to make a point of wearing T-shirts without offensive slogans."

Luk looked down at his T-shirt. "*Do it Dog Style* is

the name of a classic punk album by Slaughter and the Dogs."

"Not a good message here, is it?" Donna said.

Luk pulled his T-shirt over his head, turned it inside out, and pulled it back on again. If it was good enough for Jude, it was good enough for him.

"Better?" he asked.

Donna thinned her lips at him. "Anyway. Meditation program is on the noticeboard in the main hall. They're doing a walking meditation in there at the moment, then solitary down by the lake, then meeting in the kitchen for a light meal. You can read the board while everyone is down by the lake, and join the group at dinner."

Luk re-stacked the boxes in the store room, making space for himself, then laid out the blankets Donna gave him. He hadn't showered for a couple of days, so after he'd watched the distant shapes of the people on the retreat move through the trees, away from the buildings, Luk went in search of the showers.

The main hall was empty, a plain room with a wooden floor, a pile of cushions in one corner. It had none of the finishes of the temple, none of the gilding and carving, just a plain wooden ledge holding a candle and a bowl of fruit.

Bathrooms and showers were in the main block, and Luk showered, resisting the urge to jerk off in the shower. He wasn't sure if it would make a difference, but he wanted to try, to show Jude he cared and he was making an effort to be part of Jude's world.

He hadn't packed a towel, but Lori's house had taught Luk that pulling clothes on over wet skin was completely acceptable. Luk had grabbed the clothes he'd left at Jude's house, which Jude had folded neatly and put in a pile on the bookshelf for him, so Luk did have underwear and T-shirts. Most of the T-shirts would have to be worn inside out.

Donna was in the kitchen, working, when Luk had finished showering, so he took a chopping board off the rack and found a knife, and stood beside her, cutting fruit.

People began to file into the kitchen, some talking quietly amongst themselves, voices low and muted, others walking alone.

Luk was watching the doorway to the verandah when Jude walked through, his head shaven, his hair gone.

Luk must have made a sound, because Donna looked up. "Go and see him," she said. "There's nothing that says you can't greet him."

Luk walked over past the two long dining tables with benches to where Jude was standing in the doorway, looking like he was trying not to cry.

Luk stood in front of Jude and held a hand out to him.

Jude slowly reached out and took his hand, and held it carefully.

"I know you're not speaking," Luk said. "I respect that."

Jude nodded, and his fingers tightened around Luk's hand, pulling Luk forward and into a hug.

They walked, side by side, through the forest and down to the lake. Luk had to shove his hands into his jeans to remind himself not to reach out to Jude, but he couldn't stop himself from glancing sideways at Jude, with his newly shaved skull gleaming in the light filtering through the trees.

The lake was perfectly still, mirroring the forest rising around it, the ferns growing down to the shoreline, the insects that swooped through the dusk above it.

Every time Luk went to say something, he squashed it, stopping himself. There was only one thing he needed to say, and he hoped that didn't need words, that he'd already said it, just by being there. Everything else could wait.

Jude's face, when Luk studied it, wasn't right, and it was more than just his hair that was missing. The music, the rhythm that made Jude bound around rehearsals or the stage like a demented rabbit, was gone. Luk didn't want to imagine trying to live without music inside him; he could understand Jude not wanting to talk until the songs came back.

Luk took Jude's hand where it rested on the dirt between them and held it, along with some of the dirt. "If the song has gone out for you, you can share mine," Luk said.

The bereft look in Jude's eyes when he'd stared at Luk was gone, and he looked like he had at the football oval, when they'd been dealing with the fallout from Luk Behaves Badly. Then the corners of his eyes creased, something like a smile flittered across his face, and he squeezed Luk's fingers.

A gong chimed, back in the buildings, and Jude gestured with his head.

Dinner was a bowl of diced apple and pear, eaten in silence at the long tables in the kitchen. After the plates were cleared away, mugs of hot water were passed around, and Luk could hear quiet conversation at the other table, but the table he was at stayed silent.

Luk washed dishes, the hot water and suds soothing and enjoyable, and Jude stood beside him, tea towel in his hands, drying.

Another gong chimed, and Donna touched Luk's shoulder. "Bedtime in ten minutes."

Luk nodded and followed Jude out onto the verandah. Jude took his hand, holding it for a moment while people moved around them, closing doors and switching off lights.

The moment stretched, and Luk closed his eyes, concentrating on the feel of Jude's fingers around his own. He could hear the rustle of Jude's clothes, and the faint rush of Jude's breathing.

Then Jude was gone, and Luk went back into the kitchen store room, his heart as full as any of the times he and Jude had fucked.

Luk slept deeply, waking before dawn to the sound of people talking in the kitchen. He went to the toilet, and paused on his way back through the kitchen, astounded. Four monks sat around the end of one of the tables, bowls of porridge in front of them, gossiping and chatting.

Ajahn P looked up and smiled at Luk, then turned his attention back to the animated conversation he was having.

Luk went back to his blankets, but didn't go back to sleep.

It took exactly one session each for Luk to work out that guided meditation was kind of relaxing and soothing, but that unguided meditation was boring and only good for composing songs in his head or catching up on naps. Walking meditation was somewhere in between, because at least Luk could be sure he wouldn't fall asleep. The little talks from the monks were charming and incomprehensible, being composed of contradictory statements that were then explained away. Luk stopped trying to understand them, and just listened.

On the third evening, while Jude held his hand on the darkened verandah before melting away to wherever he slept, Luk tightened his grip on Jude's hand, pulling him closer.

He could see Jude's face, above him in the gloom, and Jude was smiling, his teeth shining. He knew Jude was saying 'tease' but Luk didn't care, not when he could smell the sweat of Jude's body through his clothes.

Luk hurt with the intensity of his longing for Jude.

Jude's breath was loud in the darkness as he exhaled impatiently, and he bent forward and pressed his mouth against Luk's cheek for a moment, then he was gone.

Luk struggled with the requirement not to seek sexual gratification that night.

Something happened on the fourth day, something let go inside Luk, or maybe he just got so horny and desperate that he stopped resisting, because it all made sense.

The forest around the retreat dripped as cool rain fell, the water rattling on the tin roof, gurgling in the gutters. Frogs sang out in the gardens, and from the cisterns of the toilets. The sky was huge between the clouds, when Luk pegged the wet tea towels out on the line after breakfast, and it felt like time had stopped, the sun stationary in the sky.

Ajahn P's chat on dependent co-arising seemed like an essay on love, when Luk could see the curve of Jude's forearm and knee across the room in the corner of his vision. The guided meditation made Luk feel like he was floating, as high as a kite, only he was stone-cold sober. The walking meditation flowed and rippled up and down the main hall as Luk followed the steps of the woman in front of him. He merely avoided the solitary meditation, hiding in his store room with his guitar instead.

Donna's footsteps at the door made Luk look up, and he wondered if he should apologize for disturbing her when she pushed his door open a fraction.

"I just wanted to say how beautiful your music is," she said. "Would you mind if I left the door open, so I can hear better?"

"Isn't that against the rules?" Luk asked.

"The rules were invented to stop people from playing Abba loudly," Donna said. "Not whatever it is you're playing."

"Arnold's 'Guitar Concerto, Opus 67,'" Luk said. Just because he was missing uni didn't mean he was planning on ditching the entire semester, necessarily.

What Luk hadn't anticipated, when he walked out of the store room half an hour later to get a drink of water, was to find the four monks sitting in a row on one of the benches, mugs of hot water in front of them, obviously listening to his playing.

Ajahn P nodded politely to Luk, then all four monks went back to staring at the kitchen, where Donna was chuckling as she diced potatoes.

When Luk picked up his guitar, he didn't go back to 'Opus 67.' He played all of his own songs, instead.

The next night, when Jude took his hand on the verandah in their silent goodnight, he kept hold of Luk's hand until the verandah had emptied, and only the occasional light at a bedroom window indicated where someone was still preparing for bed.

Luk didn't know what Jude wanted, or what he had planned, but Luk was willing to take anything Jude offered, right at that moment.

The silence stretched on, and Luk realized that if only one of them could speak, he'd better show some damned initiative.

"My room?" Luk whispered, and Jude nodded.

The store room had no windows, and with the light turned off, the room was completely dark. Luk reached out for Jude, finding his arms, then his shoulders. Jude's breath was warm against Luk's neck, then his mouth was pressed urgently against Luk's throat, licking at Luk's skin.

Luk wrapped his arms around Jude's neck, pulling their bodies close, and he could feel Jude's cock straining at the loose trousers he was wearing.

Jude's mouth found Luk's, the kiss melting Luk so he had to cling to Jude to stay standing. One of Jude's hands was on the back of Luk's head, cradling him, and the other was cupping Luk's arse through his jeans, pushing their groins closer together.

In the darkness, Jude's skin was everything, his weight pressing Luk back against the wall, their feet clattering against a crate in the darkness.

"Please stay," Luk whispered.

Jude's breath, against Luk's ear, was an exhalation of frustration. "No, I can't. We can leave tomorrow, since I think I've proved that I now need you more than I need to work through my self-recrimination."

Then Jude let go of Luk, pulling back across the small store room, colliding with crates of food, and Luk could hear him panting in the darkness. Fuck, Luk was breathing pretty hard himself.

"I love you," Luk said. "That's what I came here to say."

"I knew that, the moment I saw you standing there, in the kitchen. Talk about taking the words away from someone. I'm going now, before my resolve crumbles any further."

The door opened and closed again, and Luk reached out for the wall behind himself and kicked at it in frustration.

Donna waved goodbye from the cab of the truck, and Luk gripped Jude's hand tighter. The bus stop was a tin shed with a bench, already occupied by backpackers and more genteel tourists, so Luk dragged Jude around behind the shack to where the forest was trying to take back the clearing and the shelter in a tangle of weeds and half-grown treelings.

Jude didn't need encouraging, kissing Luk over and over.

"How long until the bus comes?" Luk asked, as Jude sucked on the skin of his neck. "Can I get there first?"

Jude whispered, "Fuck, I want you."

Luk groaned, shoving a hand between their bodies roughly to grope at the front of Jude's jeans, then fumble with his own. "Fuck," Luk whispered. "Quick."

"I didn't mean right this instant. Don't undo," Jude said, grabbing Luk's wrist. "I've already been busted once for fucking in public, and I'm not going through that again."

Luk whimpered, and Jude kissed him again, gentler and slower. "Just hang on for a little longer."

The rumble of the bus arriving stopped Luk from complaining, at least until they got on the bus, pushing down the back for seats, and there was an 'out of order' sign hanging on the toilet cubicle door.

"Stop whining," Jude said, holding his arm out for Luk to sit closer to him. "Who's been on the retreat longer here?"

"But you've had practice," Luk said, moving across on the seat so he was sitting right against Jude. "Lots of it."

"And that makes it better how? Think of something else. Tell me about Lori. Did you see her before you left the city?"

"I did. She's going home to her mum when she leaves hospital. Says she's had enough of music, and we can have The Tockleys, if we want the band. And Robbo asked me to join Delicate John, but I don't want to, not if we can play together."

Jude took hold of Luk's hand. "Do you want to do that? Take Maddie and Jack up on their offer, record a CD?"

"The two of us?" Luk asked, and Jude nodded.

Luk thought about their music. "It won't be hardcore, more like edgy acoustic, and the sound will be thin, but some of that can be fixed on mixing. And I've been writing a lot of music, over the past few days."

"Play it all for me, when we get home?" Jude asked.

"After we've fucked," Luk said, and the woman on the seat in front of them choked on her soft drink. It was going to be a long trip back to the city.

Luk bounced from foot to foot while Jude unlocked the screen door, then the front door of his house. "Anyone home?" he called out, and no one answered.

Luk dropped his pack and guitar in the hall and grabbed Jude's arm. "C'mon," he said, and the pair of them tumbled through the door of Jude's bedroom.

Jude kicked the bedroom door shut, and started pulling off his clothes. "Forget your boots for now," he told Luk, falling on Luk still half-dressed, his hands working at the buckle of Luk's belt.

He was too low on the bed, so Luk wriggled backward up the bed, pushing his jeans and boxers down as he went, until they were around his knees. Jude stood up for a moment, kicking his jeans off, then he was over Luk, kissing him, grinding their cocks together.

"Hang on," Luk said, and he got his hands in between them and managed to get hold of both of their cocks, holding them both steady.

The feel of their cocks held together tightly, combined with the look of bliss on Jude's face and the fact that Luk was hornier than he'd ever been before in his life, took him straight over the edge, so hard that each throb of coming hurt inside.

Jude's cock slipped and slid in Luk's come, then he was shuddering, spreading come over both of their bellies, the smell of both of them thick in the room.

"You stopping at all?" Luk asked Jude as he kept rubbing, grinding his cock into Luk's hands.

"Do you want me to stop?" Jude asked. "Because it doesn't feel like you're going to either. Or do you just want to clean up a bit?"

"I want to take my boots off," Luk said. "Because I can't fucking move at the moment."

Jude smiled, and it wasn't his usual smile. "Let me help you there." He clambered off Luk completely, then lifted both of Luk's legs up, and over him. "Can you reach from there?"

"I guess," Luk said, reaching up for one of his laces. "It's not--"

He didn't finish the sentence, because Jude disappeared, out of sight behind Luk's knees and bunched-up jeans, and his hands were on Luk's arse, where it was sticking up in the air.

"Fuck!" Luk shouted, then something soft and wet and hot touched his arse. Something slippery. Something that felt like a tongue.

Jude made a noise, needy and desperate, and a finger slid against Luk's arse, beside Jude's tongue. "Take your damned boots off," Jude said, his voice muffled, then things got crazy, hot and electric and so fucking right.

Luk yanked at his boot laces, just enough to be able to drag each boot off, then he tossed each boot across the room with a crash. He got his jeans and boxers off, too, so he could actually move his legs enough to be able to look down and see Jude's scalp, with the fuzz of new hair growing on it, bobbing between his legs.

It felt like he was going to explode, it was so amazingly good to have Jude's fingers sliding inside him, and Jude's tongue against the outside of him, pushing and twisting.

"Please," Luk said, and Jude lifted his head.

"Yeah?" Jude asked, and Luk nodded.

Jude pulled his fingers out, then darted off the bed and across the room to the bookcase, to grab a box of condoms.

He knelt between Luk's knees when Luk put his feet back on the mattress. "Don't think about it," Jude said, ripping a condom packet open with his teeth, then rolling the condom onto his cock.

Fuck, Luk wasn't sure how he was supposed to not think about something that big going into his arse, then Jude squeezed lube onto Luk's cock. "Touch yourself," Jude said. "Can you do that?"

Luk rubbed the lube over his cock, then curled his fingers around himself. "Been practicing for years," he said.

"Lift your knees again," Jude said. "Just for a little while."

Fingers slid into Luk, spreading lube, teasing him, and Luk had a moment of feeling horribly inadequate for the way he'd touched Jude, if this was how he was supposed to do it. But then Jude knelt over him, holding his weight on one hand, the other pressing against Luk.

Something pushed against him, and just kept pushing, and Jude whispered, "Breathe, love. Can you do that?"

Luk unlocked his diaphragm, made his stomach muscles relax, and it happened, it all just happened.

"Put your legs around me," Jude said, his voice tight, and when Luk did, he could feel Jude was trembling.

Luk wound his arms around Jude's neck, pulling him down so Jude's weight was resting on him.

"Tell me," Jude whispered. "Tell me when you think you can bear for me to move."

Talking – thinking -- wasn't an option. Luk's brain

was jammed on 'thing inside' and wouldn't budge; it just kept looping back, over and over, as if he hadn't already fucking noticed. Fuck, his body was far smarter, knowing what to do, to hang onto Jude, move a little, then move more.

Then Jude moved, rocking, too, and it was all one huge, crazy feeling, too much for Luk to process or label, not even once Jude had shouted and come, then pulled out.

Jude sucked Luk afterward, in that amazing way he did, all the way down his throat, while Luk stroked the beautiful fuzz on his scalp, until Luk almost passed out from coming so hard.

Chapter Nineteen

Maddie and Jack's pool was still wearing its winter coat of algae, thick and green, when Jude pushed the side gate open. The long winter grass had taken over the paving, and no one had beaten it flat yet.

The door to the studio was propped open, letting in the sunshine and spring warmth of the September day, and Jude could hear Luk playing, something hot and electric. Of course, it could be Maddie or Jack playing...

Jude put his guitar case down on the couch inside the studio door, and grinned. Luk was playing a red Fender Jazz, wailing away on the guitar through the amp and speaker stack, with Jack hunched over the sound board beside him, headphones on, concentrating on the readouts.

If it wasn't the Fender Jazz that had been stolen from Rick's van, it was an identical model.

Luk stopped playing, and Jack said, "That's good, Lucien, I've got the feedback sorted now."

Jude touched the guitar, lifting an eyebrow, then kissed

Luk, while Jack said, "Whoops, folks. Gotta give an old man some warning."

"Sorry, Jack," Luk said, turning his head, and Jude kissed his neck instead.

"Hi," Jude said, stepping back and looking at the guitar again.

"It's back!" Luk said. "Scratched and scraped, but definitely Maddie's Jazz. The mahogany Maton was being fenced by the same person, but has gone off to be rebuilt before it comes home."

Jack stood up, taking his headphones off. "Hi, there, Jude. Good to see you. If you two have finished being disgusting, set yourselves up, and we'll check the levels and get moving."

Jude ran his hand over Luk's hair, ruffling the tufty growth where his last buzzcut was going woolly, and Luk grinned at him. Jude wasn't much better, only he was growing a beard, too.

"What are we playing?" Jude asked Luk. "And which guitar do you want me to use?"

Luk lifted the strap of the Fender Jazz over his neck and propped the guitar on a stand. "Wanna start acoustic? Then switch to the electrics? That work for you, Jack?"

"It all works for me, kids," Jack said. "Let me just buzz the missus, so I can shut the door."

Jude picked up Luk's six string and sat down on a practice chair, while Luk connected the pickups to the base of the guitar.

Jack pressed the intercom and said, "Hurry up, woman," into the mike, then grinned at Luk and Jude. "That'll annoy her and make her move. Give us some chords, Jude."

Jude strummed the Ovation, while Luk slid a headset and mike over Jude's ears, then kissed the tip of his nose.

Maddie appeared in the doorway, hobbling with her

walking stick, her breathing labored, while Luk was settling himself with her gorgeous handmade acoustic bass guitar.

"Hurry, hurry," she muttered to herself, but she pulled the door closed and locked it from the inside so the recording session wouldn't be disturbed, then sat down on the couch.

A quick voice check, then Luk counted them in, tapping on the body of the acoustic bass with his fingernails.

The opening run of chords was simple, for Jude, through the introduction, while Luk put some depth into the sound with the bass. They'd record the track again with Luk playing the Ovation, putting a melody line over the top, and hope it fleshed the track out.

That was all someone else's worry. Jude's job was not to muck anything up with the chords, and to sing the song Luk had written when he'd come to find Jude on retreat.

"The law of sunshine states
That the world is hued in colors.
Like a rainbow in a film, like a song that's sung in tune,
Like the grass that's always greener, a forgiven misdemeanor,
Like a sky that aches with blue, and the love I feel for you."

The bridge was muted, in this version, just solid chords, all sounding sweet through the headset, at least to Jude's inexpert ears.

Luk nodded, two bars from the end of the bridge, and Jude grinned at him.

"When we're apart, I know by heart,
The skies are holding back the sun,
Holding back the sunshine, holding back the sunshine.
When you're not near, the facts are clear,
The skies are holding back the sun,

Holding back the sunshine, holding back the sunshine."

When Jude glanced at Maddie, she had her eyes closed, her face creased with concentration, but her fingers were tapping the head of her walking stick.

"The law of sunshine states
That our days are full of promise.
Like a game that's half-way through, like a wish we know comes true,
Like a favorite scent in summer, an old friend that calls our number,
Like a heat that warms us through, and the love I feel for you."

Jude finished, right on target, the faint hum of the two sets of pickups mixing with the breath sounds from the pair of them, until Jack shut the mikes off.

Jude slid his headphones off, just as Jack said, "What do you think?"

"And Luk's doing his thing on the next round?" Maddie asked, opening her eyes.

Jack nodded.

"Then let's hear that, and you can do a quick mix."

Half an hour later, the four of them sat, listening to Jack's quick-and-dirty mix. It sounded good to Jude, but not at all like them.

Luk, Jack and Maddie seemed less impressed. "I dunno," Maddie said, on the second listen. "I listen to that, and I'm hearing a church group, not The Tockleys. Give us a hand up, Jacko."

Jack helped Maddie to her feet, and she shuffled over to her wall of guitars and pulled down a pretty steel twelve-string.

"Bloody thing is out of tune," she grumped, settling herself in the practice chair Jude had been using. She tweaked the tuning, making minute changes, then said, "Well? What are you bastards waiting for? Hook me up,

Jack. And you two, get over here. If we're doing another recording, I'm not playing solo."

Jude and Luk exchanged a glance, then Luk grabbed the Ovation. If those two were playing, Jude didn't want to be trying to keep up with them.

"Where's that chord list Jude was using?" Maddie asked, while Jack crawled around on the floor between her feet, dragging pickup cable. "I'm too old to play that lot from memory, not while I'm sober. Jackie, stop groping me, you dirty old man."

"Force of habit," Jack said cheerfully. "You're hooked up, Maddie. Let's have a level check from you."

Maddie played a few chords, and Luk and Jack both said, "You're out of tune."

"It's the second A string," Luk said helpfully.

Maddie shrugged and tightened the string a little, while Jude said, "Sounded fine to me."

"That's why you're not in charge," Luk said. "Just sing, don't mess anything up."

Jude put his headphones and mike back on, and Jack made a sympathetic face at Jude.

"Again," Jack said, and Luk tapped his fingernails against the bass guitar, counting them in.

Maddie wasn't gentle with the twelve string. She pounded the strings, her gaze jumping between the chords and lyrics Luk had stuck to a music stand for her, and what Luk was doing with his hands on his Ovation.

At the end of the song, when Jack turned the mikes off, Maddie pulled her headphones off and said, "Fucking brilliant. Get me a beer, Jackie, before I die of thirst. So? What are we recording next?"

Luk threw his hands up in the air. "Anything you want, Maddie."

"Beer, then a playback," Jack said. "Before you all rush ahead."

Maddie sat, one foot up on a footrest, her arms draped around the twelve string, beer in her hand, while Jack played back the recording. Maddie and Luk, playing together, sounded stunning to Jude, the guitars wonderfully complex and intertwined, and his own voice, over the top, sat well.

"Give me a moment," Jack said. "Let me toss the two recordings together... It's going to be rough, without any mixing done."

The four of them sat, Maddie with a spreading smile of pleasure, listening to the rough version. It sounded like they had a room full of guitars, all being played by Luk. Jude's voice, double-recorded, wasn't perfectly synched, giving some odd harmonies, but the four guitars...

"It's still thin," Jack said. "Can Luk put some electric bass into it?"

Maddie nodded. "You put that track down. I need to go back to the house, and I'm not going to make it unless Jude gives me a hand."

"Are you alright?" Jack asked, his voice worried. "Do you need a hand getting up?"

"Knee's seized up," Maddie said. "Nothing major. Jude can make sure I don't pitch face first into the pool."

Outside the sound studio, the door closed, Maddie shrugged off Jude's hand on her elbow. "Nothing wrong with me that a new knee wouldn't fix, and I've already tried that. I just wanted to talk to you in private. Let's put the kettle on."

In Maddie's kitchen, Jude filled the kettle and put it on the stove while Maddie wheezed her way through a cigarette. "Are you in touch with Lori still?" Maddie asked, between gasps.

Jude nodded, leaning across the marble counter to where Maddie sat at the kitchen table. "We write most weeks. She's at her mum's house still, in Albany."

"How's she going?" Maddie asked.

"She's still got an external frame on one leg, and seven pins in it, and needs crutches. She says she's going mad with boredom, and is tired of daytime television. I think she's better, in herself."

Maddie nodded. "Reckon she'd like to come back to the city for the recording sessions? She could stay here. There're no drugs on the premises, we're clean-living people these days. And she doesn't need to be able to walk to record, long as she can still bash a pedal with one leg."

Jude grinned. "I think Lori would love that, Maddie."

"Ring her up, then," Maddie said, waving her cigarette stub at the phone on the kitchen wall. "Ask her. Let's make it a surprise for Luk, hey?"

Jude knocked on John Lennon's chest, and Luk called out, "Go away, Penny."

"It's me," Jude said.

The door opened, and Luk pulled Jude into the room, banging the door shut. "You're early," Luk said, balancing his guitar on the desk chair, then the pair of them fell onto the bed. "Early on a Sunday? How'd you manage that?"

"Got the first bus," Jude said, his mouth against Luk's neck. "You sure you wanna be doing that?"

Luk slid his hand inside Jude's fly. "You want me to stop?"

"I could lie and say yes, but you'd be able to tell. Thing is, I'm sure I noticed other people in the kitchen when I came in. I could swear your mother and sister were both home."

"We could be quiet," Luk said.

Jude propped himself on one elbow, lifting his weight off Luk and reaching down to extract Luk's hand from his crotch and do his jeans back up. "As if."

Luk flopped back on the bed. "Damn. Take me home with you?"

"You're always welcome in my bed," Jude said. "You know that."

Luk kissed him, which did nothing to strengthen Jude's resolve to not fuck right then, then clambered over Jude and off the bed. "I'm going to shower. Back in a bit."

The acoustic guitar was within reach, so Jude picked it up and shuffled up the bed, getting comfortable. They were supposed to be recording 'Possession' first that day, then 'Fall Back, Retreat,' and even if Jude was only singing on those tracks, it wouldn't hurt him to revisit the chords.

Luk came back in, still damp from the shower and wearing just a towel, but he didn't get dressed. He sat, on the foot of the bed, listening to Jude, water dripping from the clumps of his hair and streaking down his back while Jude finished 'Possession.'

It was one of those raw moments when Jude felt stripped bare, nothing between him and the world, between him and Luk. It was possible Luk felt it too, shivering in just a towel, the last of the song heavy in the silence.

Then Luk reached out and touched Jude's knee, a moment of contact. "I can't wait to record that," he said. "I just wish Lori could be here, to play counter-beat percussion on a guitar back for us. She's all that's missing."

Jude nodded. "She is."

They scrambled across the garden bed to Maddie's house, vegemite sandwiches in their hands, Luk carrying his guitar. Jack was in the sound studio already, tinkering with the sound board.

"Maddie said she'll be here in a bit," Jack said. "Shall we get the levels right, then some work done, before she comes back and interferes?"

Luk handed Jude the Ovation and busied himself checking the tuning on the acoustic bass guitar of Maddie's. Jude raised an eyebrow at Jack over the back of Luk's bent-forward head, and Jack nodded his head fractionally.

Maddie had gone to collect Lori from the city bus station.

They were doing the second recording of 'Possession,' with Jude beating hand percussion on the back of what Jack assured him was Maddie's cheapest guitar, and Luk working his own acoustic, when someone banged on the studio door.

"Shit!" Luk said, and Jude could hear he was deeply annoyed at the recording session being interrupted.

Jack switched the mikes off, and Jude put the guitar he was holding down.

"Hang on," Jack said, and he unlocked the door and held it open.

Maddie hobbled through, then Lori swung through after her on crutches.

Luk shouted, "Yes! Lori!" and Jude found himself blinking back tears while the three of them hugged, Jude and Luk having to hold Lori up when her crutches clattered to the ground.

Jack and Jude helped Lori onto the couch, and she lifted her leg up onto the coffee table, the external frame still bolted to it, scary and heavy. Lori looked different in ways other than having scaffolding on her leg, too. Her hair was short and dyed black, tied back in two tufty ponytails, and she'd put on weight, rounding out her body.

"Don't look at me like that, Jude," Lori said. "I've

turned into a bogan, in trackies and no make-up."

"You're gorgeous," Jude said. "And you know it, Your Highness."

Lori wrinkled her nose at Jude and held her hand out to Luk, who was hovering beside the couch. "Surprised?"

"Blown away," Luk said. "Did the others know?"

Lori nodded. "Don't hate Jude for not telling you. I didn't know if I'd be allowed to come up to the city until Friday, when my doctor finally gave me the all clear. I had to sign a contract saying I wouldn't go to any venues, or hang out with any of Rick's friends, before I could come here."

Jack came back into the studio, carrying a battered electronic drum kit. "This might be yours," he said. "It wasn't well enough labeled for the police to be able to seize it, so I went and had a word with the fence in person, and he was kind enough to return it. I figured if it wasn't yours, it was a close enough match."

Maddie chuckled richly. "Yeah, he took one of the blokes who used to roadie for us, back in the day."

"Oh... Oh, that's my kit," Lori said, her voice thick. "I can't believe you got it back again."

Luk and Jude glanced at each other, and Jude was sure Luk was remembering the roadie they'd run into at the Railway Hotel. Someone might decide Jack was too old and slow to be a threat, but that man had been a monster. Any sensible fence would have just handed over their entire stock.

Lori wiped her eyes, still in the careful way that she'd always had when she'd worn heavy mascara. "Oh, fuck," she said. "I can't cope with this emotional stuff. Can we just play?"

Luk and Jude had to drag a chair from Maddie's kitchen into the studio for Lori to sit on, and find a crate for her to wedge her leg scaffolding on, before she could sit behind her drum kit.

"I don't think I remember how," she said, looking up at Jude and Luk, who were standing over her.

"Course you do," Luk said. "It's not fucking rocket science. Hit those pad things with the sticks, preferably in time."

Jack brought a set of headphones and a mike over to Lori. She pulled the phones on over her ponytails and flipped two fingers at Luk, then settled the mike in front of her mouth.

"Two bar lead," she said. "On my count, for 'Not the Only One.' You bastards had better not have broken my song."

The three of them ate pizza in the middle of the afternoon, sitting on the overgrown paving around Maddie's pool. Luk leaned forward, holding his pizza out of the way, and peered at Lori's leg where the pins went into the flesh. "How long will it be like this?" Luk asked.

"Couple more months," Lori said. "There wasn't enough bone left, so I had to have grafts put in. It all takes time."

"What will you do then?" Jude asked, handing Lori another piece of pizza.

Lori picked a piece of pineapple off the top of the pizza and flicked it into the weeds. "Dunno," she said. "I could come back to the city, get a job in a shop again. Jude lives a clean and responsible life, so I know it's possible."

"Jude's not clean and responsible," Luk said, sitting back up and reaching for the last piece of pizza. "It's a fucking show. He's a hedonist, actually. He just doesn't drink or do drugs."

"You worked this out at the retreat?" Jude asked, stealing a piece of olive off Luk's pizza.

"Too right," Luk said. "And, hey, didn't you just break

a precept by taking some of my pizza?"

"You gave it to me freely," Jude said. "That's not stealing."

Lori lay back on the weeds, laughing in the sunshine. "I've missed you both so much."

"Missed you, too," Jude said.

The back door to Maddie's house slid open, and Jack walked over, camera in his hands. "Smile everyone, for the CD cover," he said, but they already were.

Chapter Twenty

The Green Room at Big Day Out, between the two main Orange and Blue Stage complexes, wasn't actually a room. It was a huge tent, with a barricade of security guards at the entrance and a tantalizing glimpse of the Promised Land beyond.

The security guard looked at Jude's pass, checked it against Jude's driver's license, then against his clipboard. "Right, gotcha," he finally said. "The Tockleys. You're on the Green Stage at six."

Lori handed over her pass and driver's license, grinning over her shoulder at Luk.

Luk grinned back at her.

The Green Room wasn't just any tent. It was a super-heated, overcrowded circus tent, full of managers and musicians and hangers-on, shouting and sleeping and crying and fighting and drinking. The tent flaps on the other side opened onto a bank of portaloos and showers, and the modified shipping containers and caravans belonging to the headline acts.

The three of them walked through the chaos, moving

slowly so Lori could keep up. Catering caravans dispensed food and drink, and an open bar consisting of a couple of beer kegs and an endless supply of plastic cups provided the booze.

"That's..." Lori said, her voice failing, as an instantly recognizable musician pushed past them, muttering into his mobile phone.

Luk tightened his hold on her waist, keeping her steady on the rough grass underfoot. "Sure is. What do you want to do? Get something to eat? Find somewhere to sit down?"

"It's the beer garden at the Railway," Jude said, from the other side of Lori. "Just much, much larger. We get somewhere to sit, and we try and stop Lori from clobbering anyone with her walking stick. Is there anyone here you've got a vendetta against, Lori?"

"Fuck you, Jude, and go find us a table," Lori said cheerfully. "Luk, did you bring the vodka?"

"What happened to clean living?" Luk asked, helping Lori past a table of well known Australian rockers who were stuffing themselves with hamburgers and beer, to where Jude had dived through the crowd to claim a garden table and some folding chairs.

"Fuck clean living. This is Big Day Out, and we're playing the Green Stage. I need a drink," Lori said. "There's sobriety, and then there's taking it too fucking far."

Luk looked around. The band at the table beside him had a bottle of tequila, propped amongst their hamburgers and cups of beer.

"Hey," he said, leaning across. "Mind if we have a swig?"

The bloke who turned to look at Luk wasn't much older than him, and he looked tired and drunk already.

"Sure," the bloke said, handing the bottle of tequila

over. "Who are you?"

"The Tockleys. I'm Luk, this is Jude and Lori."

"Hey, you're on ahead of us. You must be some locals. We're Transit, and I'm Mick. Rip the crowd up for us, okay?"

Luk nodded at Mick and handed the bottle of tequila to Lori, who unscrewed the cap and took a drink.

"That's vile," Lori said, handing the bottle back to Luk. "I'd forgotten how bad tequila is."

Luk took a swig, then wiped the top of the bottle on his T-shirt and put the cap back on, before passing the bottle back.

Mick lifted the bottle in a silent salute, his gaze riveted on Lori.

Lori narrowed her eyes at the stranger, then grabbed the front of Luk's T-shirt and pulled him across so she could plant her lips on his.

"Thanks," Lori said, when she let go of Luk.

Luk smoothed the front of his T-shirt down and cleared his throat. "No problems, Lori."

Jude crossed his arms. "Not me?"

"Like anyone would believe you kissed girls," Lori said.

"I might," Jude said.

Lori and Luk looked at Jude, who'd shaved his head, but not his beard, and both of them started laughing.

"Nah," Lori said. "Someone hit you with the gay stick today."

"Want something to eat?" Jude asked, standing up. "Or is it too hot?"

It was hot, a stinking summer's day, the kind where the sea breeze didn't even bother coming in. Too hot to eat.

"Burger," Lori said. "And electrolyte replacement fluid. If someone wants me to drum in this weather, I'd better fluid-load."

Jude pushed behind Lori's chair, pausing to bend over and kiss the top of her head, then he kissed Luk on the mouth on the way past.

Mick, at the next table, turned around and said, "Funky."

"Yeah, well, we're all good friends," Luk said, taking hold of Lori's hand where it rested on the table.

Lori was grinning when Luk turned back to her. "I love you," she said.

Jude came back with a tray of food. "Burgers, for you meat-eaters," he said, putting the tray down, then sitting down. "Chips, for all of us, and they'd better not be cooked in the same fat as the meat. And several bottles of electrolyte replacement fluid. No beer. You can get your own beer."

"Beer later," Lori said, reaching for a burger. "I'm probably a complete lightweight these days anyway, and shouldn't drink too much."

"Wombats!" someone shrieked, above the noise in the tent. "My favorite non-arboreal marsupials!"

"Robbo?" Lori asked, looking around.

"Has to be," Jude said. "There he is."

Robbo pushed his way through the tables toward them, accidentally whacking one of the headline acts in the head with his ukulele.

"Lori, pretty girl," Robbo said, when he'd clambered over Mick's legs to get to their table. "Kisses for everyone. Mwah, mwah, mwah. How are you, Lori? I barely recognized you."

Lori lifted her leg up, so Robbo could see there was no scaffolding on it. "All pieced together, thank you. Still walking with a stick, but apparently all the best rock chicks use walking sticks."

Robbo blinked. "Okay. Congratulations on the airplay you're getting. I keep hearing some band that sounds like The Beatles on speed, and it turns out to be The Tockleys."

"We try," Jude said. "Congrats to Delicate John. You're off touring, aren't you?"

"Newcastle, Wollongong, Dubbo and Bathurst, and every other town in the East that is foolish enough to have us. Bet they only invite us once," Robbo said.

"How's Rick?" Lori asked, reaching out to hold Luk's hand, her own greasy with burger.

Robbo shrugged. "It's not good," he said. "He's spiraling down. Don't go near him."

"I won't," Lori said. "I just, you know, wondered."

"I'm glad you're doing well, darling," Robbo said. "I feel bad that I shared a house with you, but still didn't have a clue."

Lori shook her head, and Luk could see she was close to crying. "Don't, Robbo. I wanted to hide it all."

"I'll come and watch you kids play," Robbo said. "We're on later, so I'll be able to."

He turned to go, and Lori said, "Wait! Rick's not here, is he?"

Robbo shook his head. "He couldn't afford a ticket." He looked at Jude. "Dave is, though. He's working the Green Stage, where we're all performing."

Jude shrugged, looking completely calm. "Good," Jude said. "He can hear the song I wrote about him, then."

"Ouch," Robbo said, grinning. "You're a bitch, Jude. Catch you all later, wombats!"

The band ahead of them on the Green Stage was a mid-list touring band, and when Luk peered out from backstage, it looked like there were a few hundred people out there in the late afternoon sun, thrashing around on the grass in front of the stage.

Jude slid his arms around Luk, hugging him from behind. "Wow," Jude said. "I can't believe this is happening. Are you going to be alright?"

Luk squeezed Jude's hands. "I'm scared shitless, but I'm kind of hoping that once we're out there, the music makes it okay."

Jude chuckled, against Luk's neck. "I actually meant, 'Are you not too horny?' I remember promising you a headjob before each time we went on stage, and we missed out this time."

Thinking about Jude sucking him made Luk's belly warm. "Don't care," Luk said. "Really don't care. I'll be hard the whole time from the adrenaline, and when we get off stage we can lock ourselves in one of the Green Room loos and do some screaming."

The band onstage finished, and Luk took a deep breath. The Green Stage wasn't like the Orange and Blue main stages, where the two stages were run in tandem, one in use while the other was being set up. With this one, the stage techs would bump this band out and The Tockleys in as fast as possible, and everyone would help.

The bass guitarist from the other band paused as he carried his amp past them. "They're a good crowd," the guitarist said.

Luk and Jude hung back, waiting for the techs to give them the go ahead to start moving their equipment. Jude said, "See that bloke? The one with the roll of gaffer tape that's crawling around at the front of the stage?"

"Yeah, I can."

"That's Dave."

Luk watched Dave stand up and unroll a length of cable. "The poisonous Dave?" Luk asked.

Jude chuckled. "Sammie? Or Alison?"

"Can't remember which," Luk said. "One of them."

Dave was older than Jude, and was kind of cute in an older guy way, with glasses sliding down his nose and a bandana around his head.

"He's bald, isn't he?" Luk said.

"Yeah," Jude said.

Luk grinned to himself.

"You're good. Just watch out for the stand-up comic," the stage manager said, and Luk picked up one end of the amp they'd hired, and Jude grabbed the other.

The stand-up comedian ducked and weaved around them, only sometimes being in the way, while Jude and Luk helped the stage techs haul speaker stacks off the hired truck that was backed up to the rear of the stage. The comic might have been funny, but Luk couldn't tell, he was working too hard himself to be either amused or scared.

Lori couldn't help them set up, so Luk went and retrieved her from the armchair she'd been left in when it was time for sound checks.

"Do I look alright?" Lori asked, holding onto Luk's arm with one hand and her walking stick with the other.

Luk looked down at Lori. "Your nipple is showing, Baroness," Luk said. "Right side. You look gorgeous. I do like the black-and-purple hair, it looks really hot on you. And that necklace thing is really pretty."

Lori let Luk settle her on a chair, behind her drum kit, while she pushed her breast back inside her bra. "Thanks, hon." She looked up at Luk, her hand on the string of beads around her neck, and he kissed her forehead. Then a stage tech handed her a headset and mike.

They sound-checked quickly and efficiently, and Luk made himself look out across the blocks of footlights to where a terrifying number of people were sprawled on the grass or sitting near the barricade, waiting for them to start. Sammie and Alison would be out there, and his mum and Penny. Maddie and Jack were VIPs at Big Day Out, rumbling around the venue on a golf cart and being babysat by a security guard, and he could just make out the shape of the cart at the back of the amphitheatre. The Tockleys would play 'Jackrabbit' at the end of the set, for Maddie and Jack.

A sound tech handed Luk a beer, and he drank half the stubby down, then put the bottle beside his amp. Jude hitched the strap of the repaired Maton up a bit higher, then bounded across the stage to bump against Luk.

Luk grabbed Jude, stopping him from leaping away again, and they kissed for a brief moment, then Jude was off across the stage, and Luk could hear wolf-whistles from the crowd.

The stage tech waved, and when Luk glanced at the sound box, Jude's ex was bent forward over the mixing board, headphones on.

Lori tapped the edge of her snare drum. Her voice came through the huge speaker stacks behind them as she said, "We're The Tockleys, and this is my fucking song," and counted them into 'Not the Only One.'

END

The Tockleys

Printed in the United States
131737LV00004B/82-99/P

9 781603 705394